Unintended Consequence

A Novel

G.A. Chamberlin

Titles by
G.A.Chamberlin

The Handmaiden Legacy

Cultural Attache

Rare Earth Element

Outbound

Somma

Unintended Consequence

The Particle

The Kneeling Woman

At Auction

~

Kathleen The War Years

Unintended Consequence
Printed in the United States
ISBN 978-0-9904027-5-6

Crown Eagle Publishing

Distribution by Ingram

Cover Design by Jennifer Chamberlin

Rare Earth Element

climate, culture, commerce...Too important to ignore, too well written to overlook. And too technically suspenseful not to wonder about...

* * *

The Handmaiden Legacy

The Handmaiden Legacy is a contemporary thriller full of corporate interests, beautiful seas and ancient legacies...

---*G.A. Chamberlin is an International Thriller Writer!*

"International Thriller Writers ...that will surprise "
--Agent, Thriller Fest, New York City

* * *

Cultural Attache

"...Amanda Wells is lecturing on the historical integrity of medieval works at the University when she is informed that the original manuscript of a major work...has been stolen from the vault.

Unintended Consequence...

An International Thriller

"...Amanda looked over the balustrade from the top floor. She could see all the way down to the entrance of the historic building of Washington DC where a checkered parterre could easily host two Medieval court jesters. Grand marble steps appointed with red runner carpeting coiled exquisitely up Regency brass railing to surround a cut-crystal chandelier. From above, a hand on the rail was often visible as staffers on her research team ascended to the upper offices of the four story Beaux Arts Building. A lovely place to work, they all told her.

But as she was about to ask the receptionist if Barbara had arrived yet, her eyes suddenly narrowed.

"Janice..." she asked into her cell phone earpiece "What is that package at the bottom of the steps...?"

Unintended Consequence

A Novel

G.A. Chamberlin

Chapter One

The rigging tinkled softly. Safely at anchor for the night, the yacht listed gently to portside.

In the darkness they lay together on the bunk of the Forward cabin. His hand smoothed up the sheet beneath her, then down her spin. She arched her back, lost to his kisses on her lips.

His breath was warm on her face. "The cabin is...so *hot*"

"Umm...Who is...?" she sighed

A calm bay and warm night air brought moonlight through the porthole. He leaned against her, and she breathed in his ear.

From its mooring, the boat commenced its natural swing to starboard side, and they fell asleep, their boat a hammock.

Less than ten miles up the coast, a sea state of calm lay beneath a sheen of black water, the moon playing on its surface with the face of a jester. A small dome arose from the sheen, then burped like an air bubble. Another broke the surface. Soundless, darkly.

A light breeze stirred with a hollow wheezing that silenced even the dancing reflection of the moon.

Less than five minutes later, at one tenth of a degree below latitude, another bubble dome rose to the surface. Like a breathing assailant, the effect was travelling south at a gradual descent of five nautical miles per hour.

The last thing that Trevor felt like doing was to get up and check the boat: It had bumped twice already, and was coming around for a third swing on its moored tetherline. The tide was receding from the cove and the keel of the boat, drawing nine feet of depth beneath the hull, was clearly bumping off the bottom with some regularity.

"*Uhm*" murmured Amanda folding over, too sleepy to help.

"Stay. I'll get it..." he whispered, sliding off the bunk and pulling on his trunks and deckshoes. He unlocked the cabin door, tiptoed passed Gwynie's cabin - the child was fast asleep - and moved quickly aft to the companionway of general quarters.

The boat appeared to be in good shape. Trevor moved across the forward deck to check the anchor bowline. He paused, breathing in the night air. Then faced astern and made a decision. Tapping the roof of the Forward cabin from topside, he turned to the aftlines. He would need Amanda's help. They had to move the boat.

Amanda appeared topside and there was little need for explanation. The tide had moved out so fast that the soggy shoreline was filling the night air with the smell of exposed seaweed and tidal fouling. That meant they had to move before getting themselves stranded. Never mind the logic of why their Marine Nautical chart failed to signal shallows. At sea, you never argued with the weather. You did what you had to do first. Then you argued.

Trevor made his way around the deck hauling in mooring bumpers and uncleating sheetlines to the mast. Amanda went below to prep for engine ignition. She flung wide the doors to the engine room, turned on the cabin lights above the generators and started flipping switches to divert power from the batteries in the Housing Unit. Two massive 8.50 Hp diesel engines prepared to ignite. It would take a few minutes. She examined the length of the battery cables to check on their secure leads - no moving boat could ever be too sure. Grabbing two life vests she reappeared topside, nodding to Trevor. He needed help pulling the anchor chain out of sticky mud.

She coughed, her throat raw and bitter, and looked around them. The sea was calm. The yacht had not settled on the bottom, it was still afloat.

Now below decks Trevor flipped on the Ignition switch to the Engine. It failed to start.

Topside, Amanda moved aft to the steering helm of the sailboat, opening lockers for stainless steel winches that might be used on furling barrels. She jammed them into their sockets and locked them into their wells. They might use sail. But as she noticed, there was little air for any kind of wind.

Trevor tried again. Amanda caught her breath, the odor of the bay getting a little nauseous, and she wished he would get going.

A third time Trevor forced the Ignition switch, grinding longer than he should.

The diesels coughed, then began their rhythmic chugging. In an empty cove on a dark night, the sound was almost deafening, but it was so isolated they could be the tree that fell in a forest and no one would know...

Amanda looked out at the blackness around them. It was strangely disorienting. No bearings. No shoreline to see. No channel-markers ... not even a buoy's night reflectors.

Beep.. Beep. The boat's depth-sounder Alarm went off.

She was running out of time. Shallow draft beneath the hull.

She had maybe one chance to get to the deeper Channel and out to sea before the tide left the entire vessel stranded in the Bay. Nor should the keel find mud. Steering in the central trough was critical. She looked around. *Where was the channel entrance in all this blackness?*

One shot. That's all she'd get. One shot to get through the narrow channel, no room for deviation...*Where were the channel-markers?* She must power up for Forward Speed.

Trevor was below.

She tapped the deck-hull for warning, he would hear it: His hands should be clear from any moving parts - In fact, he should be out of the engine room, the doors sealed. He was still at the bilge pumps...

Beep. Beep. Beep. She tapped the deck again. "Now." she called out.

Trevor came up and sealed off the cabin doors to adjust for night vision at the helm. Amanda heaved on the ship's wheel, plowing her props through the soft churn beneath the keel from their anchorage into the deeper channel.

She handed the helm to Trevor.

Beep. Beep. Beep.

She could see nothing. She peered, listening with all her instincts at a horizon for any bearing...She pointed. He threw the wide steering wheel over and the boat chugged forward.

Amanda knew the drill. When underway at night, an entirely new skill-set came to bear. Nautical charts, compass, flashlights and radio channels were critical elements to nighttime navigation. But without orientation, she had to rely on her own depth of experience in seamanship.

She spotted a green flashing-light sequence and from its position on the chart, she plotted a compass course bearing for Trevor to steer to.

"Whatever you see out there...Hold fast to the bearing..."

The depth-sounder alarm switched off, satisfied at the sea depth beneath the hull.

Within half an hour, the next green-lighted buoy indicated an entrance to a marked harbor. Then she saw the red-flashing channel markers. Counting the seconds between the flashing, they would be guided through the darkness.

Before long, they actually could see the buoys that housed the lights. To starboard, red lights appeared, and with that, they knew they were entering the channel of the sea Inlet.

Here they would re-anchor and find safe mooring for a few hours.

Beep. Beep. Again too shallow...

"Jesus." They reversed their engines, and managed to turn the vessel around before running aground.

They travelled down the coast, able to see shore but unable to approach....*It was as if the sea had rolled out.*

They had motored straight for three and half hours before discovering their final destination. It was the entrance to a major river.

Gwynie had slept through it all. Still, as relieved as they were to fasten to the docks, fatigue and distress were visible on their faces.

This was the last day of their vacation. The boat was heading home, regardless.

Once off-loaded, the vessel would be docked for the season. She would doubtless need repairs and all her systems checked.

Between them, it had been decided that Amanda was to go to Toronto to attend the Annual Stockholder's meeting. Trevor was to fly to London. His mother was ill.

The month ahead of them would be a short one; business priorities would soon be settled.

Amanda sighed. It had ended too soon.

* *

Gwynie blinked from a face painted in red, white and blue. They were all going to the Game at the Verizon Center. The Washington Caps were playing Boston.

Sandra had swarmed the house with friends up for the weekend from college. And Jacob, Barbara's assistant presently in Washington doing errands for the Firm, had shown up at the house with a large delivery box in his arms, declaring himself the official party expert on Ice Hockey. Why? Because his father had been a Russian hockey playing professional for the Boston Ice Hockey Teams twenty years ago.

He set down the box, had them lined up to face him, and presented each with an oversized Caps Team Shirt. "For the Game." he declared.

"Jacob." yelled the girls, thrilled and appalled.

"*So* cool…" said the guys. "I'll take Number 48…"

"I'll take 49."

"Guys." yelled Sandra "the game requires…self-control."

"Anyone for snacks before you go?" asked Amanda over the noise.

"*Yeah.*"

The front room readied for the great excursion.

They put on their shirts over clothing, a ritual *de rigueur* by Washington fans converging on the Game from every Metro stop Downtown.

Jacob wasn't finished. "Hush." he admonished, his finger to his lips "I have something more here...."

He leaned over into the box and looked straight at Gwynie, shyly standing off. "Come here, young Lady"

Sandra brought her forward. Gwynie peered up at him, her finger firmly stuck in her cheek, unsure of things.

"And this is for *you*." he said, pulling out a team jersey to fit a child.

Gwynie grinned.

"Awe...." chorused all the girls.

"Time to go." bellowed the guys "Let's go."

They poured out of the house, a rag-tag team of fans themselves.

Sandra, who was charged with the care of Gwynie for the game, dashed back and pecked her mother on the cheek at the door "Loveyu Mom. Don't worry. I won't take my eyes off her. She has a full army here watching for her. She'll have fun."

"We'll spoil her." yelled Lucy, waving from the crowd.

"Enjoy." said Amanda. "There'll be food waiting when you come back. So save your pennies guys."

Amanda closed the door. Tomorrow, she knew, they were all returning to school. Most of them came from too far away to fly home for the Fall weekend. This was Sandra's hospitality to them since their college campus was only 75 miles south of Washington DC.

* *

My darling,

It was Trevor's favorite way to begin his letters...

"I miss you terribly. And there is little I can say that will explain my absence, mainly for security reasons.

As a member of the Admiralty, you know that it is my duty to protect and defend my country. It's not just the Northern Isles that I seek to protect, but the rest...

I wish not to alarm you, but we may be looking at an incident, if not a global disaster. I must give this my best efforts, but the dangers are real.

You know what to do. Be wise...

In the meantime, if you have anything urgent that needs attention, go to Arguetta. He can be trusted.

Remember, I have loved you from the first day you made landfall - wet as a bilge rat and idiotically mistaken...It was your pureness of heart that I fell for.

And I love you still...

Amanda read the letter only once.

She didn't need to read it again. But she kept it close, every sentiment etched on her heart. Trevor had been a diplomat when she first met him. They were in Beirut together, and yes – it was over a false alarm incident. But diplomats did not use their words lightly. This she knew.

Her actions from this point forward were propelled by the presence of his letter, and it stayed with her, folded neatly at the bottom of her bag where she might well have touched it a dozen times a day, beneath it all. Beneath the make-up; the keys, the purse, the daily chores of living...

Trevor's words surfaced only occasionally and intermittently. Usually when she had the greatest need for his comfort. But mostly when events on the ground warranted his warning. His note was clear.

"Be wise... as serpents, and be harmless as doves" was the admonition he gave her. Words from his favorite Gospel, she knew.

And she was to take his place in a world of finance and international threat.

* *

Toronto.

The limousine turned the corner of York and King Streets and parked at the front of the building. From the rear door held open, a slim woman emerged.

Wearing a dark suit exquisitely tailored, she stood to survey the pavement and put on her dark glasses, her shoulder-length auburn hair barely tussling in a sharp inner-city breeze that roiled the street.

Two limousines followed to disembark passengers, mostly men unloading document carts, gear, electronic devices and briefcases - some with hiking mountain wear and ski racks, for later.

Bankers were gathering from all over the world. For three days, the Annual Stockholders' Meetings would take place in this hotel. Security agents were posted everywhere, and the Press had limited access to CEOs and invitees. Today, they represented some of the largest sectors of global economies. In monetized terms, they signified stability for the Western world.

Across the street cable antenna were setting up for the Media event to broadcast.

The Toronto-Dominion Center was home to the Toronto Stock Exchange. Seventh largest Exchange, it was owned as a subsidiary of the TMX Group, rating senior equities across the boards of Canada; United States, Europe and other resource-rich nations. As an Exchange, it stood alone as the leader of mining; oil and gas sector listings, even as it listed various other exchange-traded funds; split share corporations, income trusts and investment funds.

Remodeled from the original Art Deco building, the central lobby showcased its beginnings - the original stock exchange floor from over a century ago. Conceived by twenty four men in 1852, it merged with its key competitor the Standard Stock and Mining Exchange in 1934.

An ultra-modern brass, chrome and glass design exhibited state of the art upgrades of modern architecture. TSX had become a world player in an entirely electronic virtual trading environment, appointing for itself a major figure as its Chief Executive Officer.

Soon after, it streamlined investment and stock functions to contain the Bourse de Montreal; the Vancouver Stock Exchange; the Alberta Stock Exchange Canadian Venture Exchange, all merging finally to create the CDNX.

Known as the TSX "for-profit" entity within the British Commonwealth, the London Stock Exchange had recently announced its intention to merge with the TMX Group, expecting to bring a market capitalization of almost six trillion Sterling, thereby making it the second largest Exchange Board in the world.

But in a surprise move, resistance to the London merger came from the Canadian Government, citing too much foreign control vested in its Canadian natural resources and financial Clearing Systems. A hostile rival bid was entered by a Canadian-led group which brought forward sufficient cash to silence the debate.

Today, the morning weather was cold and crisp. Amanda's trip to the stock exchange brought her directly from the Airport, and she popped out of the Limousine with an easy bound and a cheerful smile.

"Wow." she said, looking up.

The Exchange Tower itself was thirty six stories, containing over one million square feet of office quarters. It filled a block fed by the Toronto underground system. As a unique landmark, the structure was designed to complement the grand architecture of Brookfield's *First Canadian Place*.

Amanda's luggage was carried in by the Porter, and it was delivered to the suite registered for her in the Hotel. That is, after her purse fell and burst open on the ground, sending jelly beans all over the curb and her lipstick rolling under the limo and down the street drain.

"Oh, my jelly beans." she said, looking at the scattered colors that Gwynie had given her when they parted.

The Doorman smiled, and he called out a busboy.

Inside, the mood was different. "Mrs. MacDonnell. Welcome." said the Concierge, coming forward to greet her.

The Sterling Bank, owned and operated for two centuries by the MacDonnel family of Scotland, was here being represented by Amanda Wells.

 Trevor MacDonnel, Chief Executive Office and Charter board member chose to represent himself every year at the Annual Stockholder's meeting. Only this year, he was in demand elsewhere, and as the Press Release said, had volunteered his wife to take his place. Amanda was to meet first with the CFO on Trevor's behalf, and then take a tour of the premises.

> *"...Carry on with your work, my darling. Represent me and my interest to the best of your abilities: I have advised my lawyers to give you full agency in these matters. You are*

deserving, and perfectly capable of doing so as a thinking and caring professional..."

Amanda paused to look around.

The building offered food courts, multi-tenanted floor lobbies; large spaces of the old exchange; a glamorous business center with banking and finance displaying Canada's biggest banks including the CIBC; Bank of Montreal; Bank of Nova Scotia; Royal Bank of Canada and Toronto Dominion Bank.

Amanda walked down glossy floors of the second tier where a procession of energy industries lit the pavilion with Logo icons. There was the Cameco Corporation, Canadian Natural Resources Ltd., Canadian Oil Sands Trust, EnCana Corporation, Huskey Energy Inc, Imperial Oil Ltd, and Nexen Inc. Many of them were supporting ventures displaying marquees for insurers and underwriters, she observed. She felt like she was at a Fairgrounds - large enterprise drilling; offshore platforms; pipelines, tankers, storage, systems engineering companies and shipping carrier companies in a spectacular display of companies that hired thousands of people... and capitalized venture and investment monies for so much of the world's energy production.

Amanda lifted her i-phone and took a picture of the dazzling exhibit. She was impressed. Easily an investor could immerse himself here for three months before needing air, she decided. Here was an Emporium of energy-rich producers working to fuel, finance and facilitate a post modern world.

"Mrs MacDonnell." called a woman coming down the concourse.

"I'm Rebecca Meinheim. So pleased to meet you." she said, shaking hands in spirited warmth. "Trevor told me to find you...Did you have a pleasant journey?"

"'*Amanda*,' please. Thank you, yes..."

"How do you like the Corporate exhibit?"

"It's a fantastic array...of the industry..." said Amanda.

"It is indeed. So glad you approve. Energy production is quite a wonder of science, I think" said Rebecca, a touch of realism framing her face.

"I agree" said Amanda, adding "And...I can only imagine how much hard work went into preparing this program, yes?"

Rebecca beamed.

They walked and, finding a quiet café at the end of the pavilion, sat at a side table, coffee and biscotti ordered. Amanda took a deep breath.

If it weren't for the warm reception given her by the CFO of Trevor's company, Rebecca Meinheim - a woman, Amanda could have felt overwhelmed.

 "We're a little outnumbered here, aren't we?" said Amanda at the swarm of executives in sharp-cut suits filling the building.

"Nonsense." laughed Rebecca Meinheim. "We women belong here."

They bantered, and before long Rebecca's laughter had its effect. Amanda relaxed.

Later in the day they spent an hour together at a quiet Conference table where Rebecca Meinheim made her presentation of the Bank's Executive Summary to brief Amanda. Most were summary documents for review that needed further scrutiny, she said. But mostly, they represented solid figures and a sound balance sheet.

"I don't mean to wear you out with these documents all at once...We can continue later, if you'd prefer?" asked Rebecca.

Amanda had the distinct feeling that Rebecca felt uncertain about Amanda's retention, or even interest. Engaging with business colleagues was one thing, but discussing business with the wife of the CEO was quite another. She might have been totally disinterested.

Amanda surprised her. "How do we rank in terms of performance, overall?"

Rebecca looked at her. "Actually, we rank very well indeed. Most of our subsidiaries are doing well...Here, It's been a great year."

"And we are up to date with all compliance requirements?" asked Amanda.

"Absolutely."

"Wasn't there a claim outstanding...or something?"

"Yes. There was. But that was cleaned up last month by our legal team with a satisfactory settlement once all the facts came out. The claim was dismissed. We are clear and without cloud on that one..."

Amanda smiled, a look of appreciation on her face that told Rebecca she understood all that must have gone into those long hours at an office working for her husband's company. "Well done." she said simply. "You've done a great job. Thank you."

Gradually, Rebecca loosened up with the facts, figures and critical path items that needed attention. Finally she looked up and said "Trevor was right. You *are* fully capable of representing him."

"Thanks. Do please carry on..." said Amanda, glad to focus on matters that Trevor would be interested in. She listened attentively and took notes on small tasks of enquiry as the issues developed.

Finally Rebecca sat back. "Come on, you need a break. I've monopolized you long enough..."

Rebecca led Amanda to elevators that would take Amanda to the upper levels of the building, the higher Hotel suits where she was accommodated. It was a convenience arranged by Rebecca.

The Annual Meeting was to take place the following morning, and it would be televised for news and business information.

For tonight, suggested Rebecca, they could dine downstairs in the Concourse. There was a Restaurant. Amanda agreed, if wanting an early night. No city lights for entertainment, thank you.

During the meal, Rebecca briefed Amanda about other attendees and what to expect at the Annual Meeting, and the evening passed quickly. They laughed about what to wear, and what time to rendezvous.

"...Only *one* woman to watch out for...Her public Motions are *venomous* to the voting body" she said, the elevator doors opening. Suddenly Rebecca's breath seemed to catch in her throat...

A woman stepped out, accompanied by three men at her side, one who then remained inside the elevator. The woman recognized Rebecca, nodding barely, and proceeded with the men at her side.

"Mr Hightower..." said Rebecca, stepping in.

"Ms Meinheim." he responded with a nod.

"May I introduce Mrs. MacDonnell, attending the meeting." said Rebecca.

"Very pleased to meet you Mrs. MacDonnell..." he said. "Please enjoy." he added, stepping out the elevator that pinged to a halt one floor up.

"Your husband's bank is not without recognition" said Rebecca.

"...But he was surprised to see me here?"

"Yes, he was. As was Lauren Papendopolus." said Rebecca. "Leader of the Atlantian Tribe of Cannibals on the Energy Investment Front."

"Oh dear..." said Amanda, her confidence wilting as the wife who defends husbands' interests.

"Don't let them patronize you." admonished Rebecca, adding "You're terrific Amanda. Come up to Canada more often and have lunch with us from time to time. *That* woman scares the hell out of me...Actually, she scares the hell out of *everybody* here."

"Oh?"

"Yes. I was about to warn you. It's a power-play. They're evidently having a pre-powwow gathering in their corporate offices before 'presiding' over the Shareholder's Annual Meeting. She's on the platform."

"What role does she play?"

"Who *knows?*" shrugged Rebecca. "The man to her left was the CEO of a major venture firm that was indicted for misrepresenting debt in company offerings; the other is a lawyer, Laurence Hightower."

Rebecca was tired, clearly. Yet she smiled with relief to find a friend in Amanda, and was letting her hair down, at least for now, on the eve of an annual event. "Tomorrow is a big day" she sighed. "No telling how things will go..."

Amanda found her way to the upper levels of the hotel, relieved to find solitude in the quiet comfort of her hotel room.

 A bouquet of flowers and note was there from Trevor; a bar full of drinks, snacks and water was at her disposal. Her baggage, delivered, was resting on a luggage trellis, and the bed was turned down with a white bath-gown at hand. She took in a long and deep breath.

It had been a long day in travel - to say nothing of farewells and arrangements to leave the children behind... Then logistics and corporate briefings with Rebecca.

She looked down at her purse. She'd come a long way from jelly beans. She fell back onto the bed, exhausted. She lay there for 10 minutes then got up.

In the Guest walk-in closet was an assortment of towels, linens, deck-gowns and outerwear for anything from swimming in heated pools to skiing.

She took her shower, then found a desk for her computer. On her laptop was a long list of items to work on. She wrote her report and observations for the matters at hand.

 "Hello my darling..." said Trevor softly over the phone.

They talked. Amanda worried that she was out of her depth in representing his interests on a corporate board.

"I trust you" he said "And you're one of the smartest people I know. You'll do us proud." he added cheerfully.

She knew that it was to show the flag, mostly. Their Bank name was well known, as was that of the CEO. Now...his wife. Of course he'd have an Administrator on hand, plus a couple of legal agents for the Meeting. But it was the notion of being seen as an interested party amongst stockholders that Trevor valued most, she knew. Even for the Gala events of the following evening. "Besides…" he had said on the phone "you always look stunning…with or without me there."

Meanwhile, all arrangements had been made. For the time spent up here in Canada, Amanda knew she had an entire complex of luxury shopping; living quarters, entertainment, services and communications. At least she felt safe.

Further, while up here, she would need to make several calls. Especially to family.

Amanda had other commitments as well. Particularly those requiring professional attention. She had a business of her own.

Her Washington DC Research Firm had performed services for critical legislation coming up on Capitol Hill. Work was stacking up, and there was much to be done, as she told her staff. She had brought some paperwork with her…

That's what you hire great staff for, she could hear Trevor say.

And she had. Barbara, her senior Researcher was in New York; Janice, her office Administrator in Washington DC manned the office. Likely, they could carry on with the Firm's business well without her. They worked as a team. That was the secret to their success.

And success it was, the Firm had turned away contracts and commissions for work in order to maintain quality control.

Still, for now, the priority was the matter that brought her to Canada in the place of her husband. Trevor was the love of her life. Representing his interest could come first…

She read most of what Rebecca had given her. It was almost midnight before she closed her laptop, and she was surprised at the hour.

She thought of Gwynie as she closed her eyes in exhaustion.

* *

The first day was a blur. Mainly, it was a day of introductions, opening speeches and corporate annual reports to set the stage for the following day, the Annual Stockholder's Meeting.

The Press was in full sway interviewing as many personnel as they could snag. All in all, it was a festive day, cultivating a sense of excitement and expectation as leaders mingled. There was much talk about updates, reform, innovation and new opportunities for the industry...

Rebecca was relentless in her introductions. Amanda was shaking hands with one senior executive after another; taking cards, remembering names, and even making notes on the side for all who asked to network with Trevor's interests. He was, she discovered, a favorite banker in the industry. His interest in Research and Development was keenly known, especially as a brand name with high standards for safety, health and social responsibility.

"You know...sustaining high standards may be a tad more expensive for the energy industry, but it's the way most investors would rather have it..." said one Senior Account manager.

"...You can't imagine how the word gets around: Your husband's company has a reputation. It is the one everyone wants to be a part of..." said another.

For Amanda, it was a long day, yet it was a fruitful, and she felt pleased with herself "How did I do?..." she asked.

"Boy oh boy. You sure were a hit today. I could hardly keep them in line, all of them wanting to meet you." said Rebecca. "You're an asset to have around..." They laughed.

Glancing down at her watch, Rebecca added "There's a Cocktail Party at 6 pm, followed by dinner in the Banquet Hall for all guests and attendees.."

Amanda, her hair softly loose around her face, came to the Cocktail Party for just an hour, and as she stood in a short-length black crinoline dress and necklace of top-tier cut diamonds given her by Trevor, she looked elegant. She was warmly welcomed by several of the visiting wives who had accompanied their husbands for the event.

"Well, you can look stunning..." said Rebecca, eyeing another round of introductions approaching, "but I understand completely if you want to be excused from the dinner. Oh, that's absolutely alright. You've done duty enough for one day."

Later that evening, Amanda stepped out onto the Veranda of her room for some fresh air. The scenery took her breath away. A sky-full of stars illuminated snow draped mountains standing astride city valleys and highways, night lights of deep hues and purple sparkles showing the way...

Tonight, with a light meal ordered, she would watch some Canadian news and turn in early with just a little preparation for the Shareholders Annual Meeting tomorrow.

 She sent off a few messages.

Morning came soon enough, and Amanda was easily ready. She turned to her cell phone and dialed the first Contact number.

She spoke to Clara first, then Gwynie. They were about to take off to school. "Mommy will be home in a few days, Sweetie. OK?" said Amanda.

"OK" said a tiny voice.

"Kiss. Kiss. I love you."

A giggle. "Byeeee..."

Amanda checked her messages. She had a list of reports to read and a ton of priority items come up for immediate review. More calls for later in the day...

Finally, she turned to her own appearance and her gear.

Satisfied with what she saw in the mirror, Amanda tucked in her silk blouse, put on her suit jacket, gathered her bag, briefcase and materials and walked to the elevator. She was wearing a Givenchy white tailored suite with black pearl earrings.

The Breakfast Room of the hotel Restaurant was filling up with Investors still arriving for the Annual Meeting. Waiters served hot foots of every variety from five continents.

One woman, thin and whitewashed with sand colored hair, sat alone across from Amanda. She tugged at chunks of a croissant to pop into her mouth which she swallow whole with coffee. No breakfast meats, fruits or juices. Just a bread dish. She looked up, her brief smile icy.

Amanda looked down to read the newspaper. The article had Trevor's face on page two. The Wall Street Journal's feature about her husband's company absorbed Amanda:

Poised to explore drilling and mining operations in regions too cold to survive in, he was noted for his prospects for expansion and development.

The company was highly recommended by ratings companies and financial sectors, especially for its business as an underwriter of energy operations.

Trevor's face was etched in grainy lines - something the newspapers did for icons of some recognition, his eyes able to transmit a gentleness of spirit and of course, his good looks. To the financial world, Trevor MacDonnell was a winner. Amanda smiled.

The woman at the next table got up abruptly and left.

Clearly, it was time. Amanda checked her cell phone once more before turning it off, and she entered the great auditorium packed with stockholders. She wore a name tag, and a seat was marked with her name on it at the second row. Rebecca would be arriving later.

On stage, corporate leaders took their place near a podium that allowed for recitals of Annual Report presentations. Overhead were electronic screens; prompts and background effects of high gloss celebrity billing.

The Conference was quickly under way with business biographies on screens - leaders of industries, luminaries and legends of the corporate world.

Behind her, to her surprise, sat the same woman who had occupied a nearby breakfast table this morning. She smiled.

Twice, the woman gripped the back of Amanda's seat and seemed to jostle it momentarily.

Gradually, as charts lit up on the overhead screens and speakers took to the podium, the audience became deeply engrossed.

Amanda could hear the rustling behind her. She turned, and found the woman clutching her stomach. She smiled weakly.

Years of travel with her children had prepared Amanda to always carry water, even now for sipping. Amanda dug into her deep Cesare Paciotti bag, and passed back a small bottle of Perrigrin.

"Thanks…" the voice husked.

At the podium Lauren Papendopolus was speaking about a new fuel revolution with "enticing new drilling possibilities in a rapidly melting Arctic region - likely to produce new sources of energy…"

She pointed to the charts and as she spoke, Amanda noticed a clear discomfort by some people seated at her side, as if averse to such an idea.

… "Further, the convergence of new technologies and source extraction techniques promise cheaper and more efficient fuels. Already, we have seen interest by the Russians, although they have unlimited supplies of energy to sell…"

One man, seated on the stage, brought his hand down on his lap with a thump, perhaps in surprise at the political turn of her tone in a public address. She faced him down.

…"But let's face it" she ploughed on, "we have a 60 million barrel a day requirement to fill our needs in North America alone."

"*Shush.*" sighed someone behind Amanda.

"We will need 47 million barrels a day in the next 20 years just to compensate for the wells that are drying up." Lauren was smiling as she turned to sip water.

"Ladies and Gentlemen, imagine where that will put *us* when governments, world-over, come to *us* asking…"

The room of investors shifted around. Had she promised candy or… was it a Call to Arms, wondered Amanda.

Papendopolous was smiling victoriously.

A lead CEO leaped on his feet and came forward with a resounding "Wow. What a picture for us to dream about…*Thank you Ms. Papendopolus.*"

The stage lights brightened and the mood lifted.

Several in the room were getting up to leave just as Amanda heard the voice behind her *"Oh No."*

The woman behind her leaned forward and spoke into her ear "Please help me. I feel ill…"

It came as instinct perhaps, that moment when you react without thinking. Or perhaps it was years of experience with children…

Amanda turned quickly, and moving the vacant chair aside, stepped back and helped the woman stand up and pass down the row of members.

The auditorium house lights were just coming on as they raced for the door, the woman doubled over and heaving convulsively. They barely made it to the Bathrooms where Amanda kicked open a stall door and the woman threw up violently.

"Thanks…Thank you" she managed to say, standing unsteadily.

"where are you staying?" asked Amanda.

More vomiting.
"I…err…I came straight from the Airport to the building. I planned to fly back out tonight."

More dry heave.

"Where are you ...from?"

"Denmark." said the woman.

Vomit.

"Can I call for medical help?"

"No. No need. Just something I...ate."

"Look...I have a hotel suite upstairs..." said Amanda. "I check out tomorrow after the dinner. Would you care to lie down on a bed for an hour or two?"

More dry heaves, and they both realized there was no option. Lying down was necessary.

Once in her room, the woman stretched out on the bed. Amanda gave her fresh drink; brought her a towel, and placed the phone close by with the Hotel directory... Was there anything else that she might need?

 "No. Thank you so much. Please carry on...I'll be back downstairs shortly. No need to stay with me, really."

Amanda went to the dressing room and changed out of her Givenchy suit. It had been splattered with vomit. She refreshing herself in the Bathroom, and dabbed a light touch of *Je T'aime* perfume from a golden-leafed bottle that Trevor had sent her from Paris, and she returned to the bedroom.

Her room guest was stretched out on the bed. A soft groan came from the woman, her eyes closed.

"Look. I think it best if someone come up, alright?"

The woman nodded vaguely.

Amanda phoned down to the Concierge and asked if a Nurse could be sent to the room.

The woman clearly wanted to be left in peace. Amanda gave scant thought to her personal belongings. There was little here of any value, other than travel toiletries...

"I'll go down to the Concierge and be sure they come up with help, alright?"

Amanda rejoined the Annual Meeting on the ground floors. This time, Rebecca was waiting for her.

The morning's agenda went smoothly. At one point, Amanda was introduced by a speaker at the Podium

"Mr. MacDonnell's most beautiful wife...is with us today representing the Firm...*Please*?" he asked. She stood up briefly to acknowledge some short applause, and the proceedings resumed.

Amanda whispered to Rebecca, asking her to forward a copy of the supporting data cited in the Chair's presentation.

 "Minus...err...*Russia?*" added Amanda, referring to Papadopolous' address.

Rebecca nodded.

Amanda looked at her watch. She sent off a short text message.

> *"Delay by one hour?"*

> *"OK"* came the response.

The Annual Meeting adjourned for lunch. Rebecca understood that Amanda had a Conference-Call coming in from Washington. The Conference-Call was coordinated with her own Firm: A new client wanted to discuss particular elements of a case which they had commissioned for some research.

Rebecca shifted seats with Amanda and was preparing briefs for the next round of proceedings.

"...Oh, and I have a woman in my room upstairs..." said Amanda. "She's ill, I talked to the Concierge..."

"Shall I go check?..." asked Rebecca, her phone now buzzing.

Amanda nodded and Rebecca understood. "Hello?.."

Amanda went up to a gallery cubicle of the auditorium behind glass panels. There, she could plug in her electronic device and conduct business with her Conference-Call on her laptop...

But with all the distraction, she realized she had left her laptop upstairs in her briefcase. She raced through the Concourse of the Hotel Lobby, examining her cell messages all the way up to her room.

She unlocked the door to her room and stopped dead. The woman was gone.

Amanda checked her message from the Nurse who reported that she found the room empty.

She looked around. Everything seemed untouched. Except for a small indent on the bed covers, she had disappeared without a trace. No Note. No message of any sort.

Amanda thought it strange, if not entirely out of context... Still, she was rushed and would follow up later.

Amanda returned just in time to receive her call, and she was soon back in her seat next to Rebecca for the afternoon.

The day turned out to be exhausting. She was piling up with an assortment of queries; documents, and a dozen calls to make. She looked at her watch.

Soon the Meetings would be concluded - the Awards and Citations Banquet to include final remarks and recognition for a conference well produced; a brief Press Conference with photo opportunities for the attendees, and then she could get home.

Just one more day to go...

"Are you flying out tonight?" asked Rebecca at breakfast, fresh and impeccably dressed, if a little fatigued.

"Yes" asserted Amanda. No question.

"But..." began Rebecca. Amanda had been selected to sit at the top table of the Banquet, so she would have to stay to the end. It would be a night flight.

"So, is there anything else I can add to your package?" asked Rebecca.

All day yesterday something had been puzzling Amanda. So strident were the acquisitions and commitments made by CEO Lauren Papenpodulus that there was little she could recall that didn't sound tinged with foreboding... Then again, maybe she just imagined it.

"Oh, no thank you Rebecca." she said.

Amanda felt as if there was unfinished business. Perhaps it had something to do with the unexplained absence – *Sans un mot* of the mystery woman.

What happened to her? Was she still around? Amanda felt responsible somehow, even a little annoyed.

Neither had Rebecca found her. Rebecca became concerned too. "Shall we file a report?"

"No" said Amanda. "She was leaving anyway. She was just taken ill, I guess..."

"Did you see her tag, or anything?" asked Rebecca.

Only once had Amanda glanced at a loose card in the woman's clutch bag, it had been flung on the counter of the Ladies' Bathroom. Little time to think of much else other than the emergency at hand. But the card was richly embellished with a gold embossed stamp at the center, like a small bouquet design. And again it fell out at the bedside table when the woman took out a pill from her purse.

"Una" said Amanda. That's all she saw.

No address.

No company.

Rebecca promised Amanda she would follow up with more questions at the Hotel. They should be able to determine her identity.

Amanda told Rebecca that she would write up a quick report for Trevor on the flight home. Good professional training really, to complete task-reports while things remained fresh in her mind.

More than anything she wanted to assure Trevor that they had paid his respects to his investors attending the Annual Meeting here in Toronto... Rebecca had given her Lists and compilations of all the latest financial data on the Bank, and Amanda had met with them in small gatherings.

They wanted to network, they all said. Chiefly, they would support his decisions as the CEO. Rebecca helped with a lot of questions, but Amanda wanted to cite them in her report to Trevor.

There was more to discuss.

"And these issues... " said Rebecca, her red hair piled up like Rita Hayward for the day "are of special interest.

They represent items and values of risk exposure that we insure. Some need thinning, some need extinguishing. Some are worrisome, such as this company: Here we may discover financial failures of the corporate kind, poor compliance history, I'm advised...*Be wary of this claim.* Especially if they get caught up with U.S. operations of law."

Amanda looked up. "Got it." Her phone buzzed. It was Washington again. This was not a world she drank with her morning coffee.

She returned to Rebecca. "Can't we examine their malfunction and negotiate a deal with the creditors?"

"No chance. They have been drained of cash."

"How come?"

"I dunno. One investment firm pulled out suddenly and a filed a suit of protest for failure to perform, leaving the creditors to all come calling to us."

"*Who* would do that?"

Rebecca sat back and took a deep breath. "LaMaas. A man Lauren Papendopolous cavorts with..."

"Can't you talk to her?"

Rebecca paused. "Sorry. The climate for successful business is foul. Nor should we holding the hand of the malfeasant, I'm advised. Besides, most of them have lost interest in their business. So, I've made notes on each case...Have Trevor take a look?"

Amanda nodded. Her phone buzzed. It was Gwynie. "*Hold on?*" whispered Amanda to Rebecca.

"Hi Sweetie." she said.

Rebecca smiled and waited.

"And finally..." said Rebecca, the day having come to an end. "*Please* come up and visit us again Amanda. Bring Gwynie. We girls could have a great time for the weekend..."

They laughed.

 "Besides, it would do wonders for my credibility in this town if I were seen with you. You've been a *huge* success."

Amanda smiled. If it pleased Trevor, she thought, then she'd been a success. "Thank you." she said simply.

But as she studied Rebecca's face, she realized there was more. Her invitation to come up was an appeal for help. Amanda realized that Rebecca lived in a banker's world of fast-paced finance experts; voracious appetites for money, and an increasingly dangerous business scene. Gone were the days of regional pride and small enclave business ventures.

Neither had the economy been doing well for many sectors, nor had soaring inflation helped. There was stress everywhere, thought Amanda.

Environmentalism as political doctrine, she knew, had taken on a fierce bent of public intimidation. It had pulled out of whack all sense of balance and reason, striking dark cords and veiled threats for Activism, as if taking hostage the commercial world. Obstructionism prevailed. Everything was slowing down to a crawl with claims, litigation or unsanctioned demands. Saving one's skin was the order of the day for most corporate lawyers, Rebecca had said.

Definitely. Rebecca lived in a rapacious man's world, and she was a pretty remarkable women herself. But she was alone.

"Don't worry, Rebecca. You're 'family' as far as Trevor is concerned. Stand firm. You're doing a fine job up here. And remember, our door is *always* open. Do fly down routinely, for any weekend - our house will be your place. There's a guest apartment, here's the key. Bring your fishing rod." she added.

Rebecca was visibly moved. "Really?"

"Yes. Really. I mean it. I shall also be happy to come visit you. We'll make it a quarterly event: A weekend of fierce shopping together? Plan on it, ok?"

They laughed.

Rebecca held out her hand, then gave Amanda a big hug. They walked out to the elevators together.

"Let me know how things go. And if there is anything I can do...anything at all. Trevor's Bank is significant, and does make a difference up here. We go where others don't. Our Company is a godsend for those still operating in the field. We do believe in good business practices and solid fundamentals. That...I'm very proud to be a part of. Tell him."

"I will." said Amanda with a final hug before stepping into the Limousine.

The Airport was surprisingly busy, filled with world-travelers crossing time zones and continents with impunity, and she observed a few familiar faces also leaving town from the Annual Meeting.

In the Waiting Lounge Amanda opened her laptop, and began her work. She looked up and thought about the conference. It had been lively, even spirited with many attending from cross-industries. No wonder the Media had a full slate of celebrities and icons to interview.

She had made notes from the meetings, mainly lists of things to mention: Speeches – their chief message, tone and implications. Especially those Financial Statements attached, citing long range projections and growth charts.

Profits had been good. Consistency was registered and stockholders should expect an increase of dividends, even corporate buybacks were in the mix.

But a few radical blips needed to be mentioned, too.

She added the list of Attendees from the corporate host page; confirmed her own passwords and sent off a note of thanks to Rebecca. She also asked for the *Advanced Membership List,* updated, with a complete bio of all who attended.

Time to go. The Flight was announced. She closed her messages and inhaled deeply. *Mission Accomplished.*

Amanda collected her bags, coat, scarves and her reading material. She proceeded to the Gate, and prepared to show her Boarding pass, being amongst the first in line.

She had almost moved beyond the waiting area when she looked up at a TV monitor and caught a glimpse of a face on a Special News Broadcast. She paused, allowing fellow passengers to proceed in the queue.

Hightower, the man who had stepped into the elevator with Lauren Papenpodulus was on the screen. He had spoken to them from the podium - of course he was recognizable. Hightower had introduced himself as the CEO of the company who represented an Exchange. He had informed Stockholders about opening new fields of business venture - capitalization of large sums...

The Chief of Police came on at the scene of the crime. "He was last seen at the Toronto-Dominion Center attending a formal event..."

Amanda gasped. He had been found dead just hours ago, last seen leaving the building. "If anyone knew anything..."

Amanda called Rebecca, her phone reception was already blocked out of reception range...No answer. She decided to leave a message.

Last Call for the Flight.

Amanda quickened her pace. "Rebecca..."

What should she ask? Was there any connection to the Annual Meeting? Was there anything she might do? Mainly, she was concerned for Rebecca...*How was she managing the news...*

"Call me when you can..."

"Your Boarding Pass, please?"

Amanda checked in and the moment was quickly gone, the news now well behind her.

"Welcome aboard, Ladies and Gentlemen..."

Amanda shut her eyes. She thought about the events of the day, the night, the News...It was an hour of subdued and soft lighting on the plane, but turmoil of the past three days still swirled in her head.

Rebecca - her eyes full of concern for company interests, and all the work that dogged her. Added to the experiences of a total stranger who threw up and mysteriously disappeared from the hotel. Then calls to and from Washington; calls to Trevor; corporate speeches and legal issues that sounded like potential disasters, or triumphs or mild threats – Amanda wasn't quite sure which.

Plus a steady stream of formal business introductions; business connections; investment chatter and a Gala Banquet to beat the band with new names, faces, remarks...

Still, Amanda was glad that she had arranged to leave that night nonetheless - Finally, with a soft seat beneath her, and the drone of a wide-bodied aircraft carrying her home at 35,000 feet, she succumbed to sleep.

The Steward was taking orders. She had not realized how fatigued she was. Yes. Coffee and a full meal, please.

It wasn't until she was well into the flight that something occurred to Amanda about the CNN News broadcast.

What did he Police Chief say? What did he mean *If anyone knew anything...?* Surely he wasn't implying foul play?

The man who was murdered, she had met him. They had chatted briefly. He was last seen at the Toronto Dominion Banquet.

So, then she might well have talked with... who? His *Killer?*

Surely not.

She looked out the porthole. The plane had already begun its descent. She was glad to be flying home. They were on the approach to Reagan Airport.

As cities go, Washington DC was a beautiful capital, and she could see the Potomac River flanked by green trees, its radial streets and parks...white granite monuments.

 She would call Trevor. Then Barbara. She would check on Carla's schedule with Gwyn coming home from school. Janice too, and the others, all with calls waiting to be returned...

* *

The call Amanda received from Barbara in New York came as a complete surprise.

"What happened?" said Amanda, gripping the receiver of her desk phone, waving off Mark who stood at the door of her office.

"I don't know what happened..." whined Barbara "The New York Police called the Grandmother and asked if there was someone in the house who could identify his body..."

"My God. I'm sorry. What a terrible loss. Anything to explain how that could have happened?"
"I don't know..." sighed Barbara.

Amanda waited. Barbara was clearly still coming to terms with the report. "I just can't believe it."

"Sandra said she thought she saw him talking to someone they didn't recognize " said Amanda. "Maybe he was approached earlier. Maybe someone said something...?" She paused. "How's his family doing...?"

"They are coping. I have talked to them..." said Barbara. "I'll talk to them...I must do something..."

"Barbara. It's a terrible shock. Just be careful. Take it easy. One step at a time. OK?"

"Who.. *Who* would have thought?" continued Barbara inconsolably.

"Barbara..."

Barbara was wailing.

Amanda gave her time. Then she said "Let's see what the Medical Examiner says. And the official Police Report. There's likely going to be an Investigation.

Someone must have *seen* something. Especially since he worked for us as an Intern... "

"Yes. I'm sure they will be." insisted Barbara.

"So. Gwynie? Sandra? How are they doing...?"asked Barbara.

"They're fine... Barbara I'm so sorry. He was a good kid."

"Thanks. He was. I'll be talking to his grandmother." She paused. "How are you doing? How was Toronto?"

"I'm back. It was a marathon up there. Otherwise, we're on track. Sandra came up when she heard the news. They all liked him... She'll be going back to St. Mary's Monday. Gwynie can go back to school then too, I'll see. I'm coming up to New York in a couple of weeks myself... "

"That's great... A few days rest at the beach will do wonders. I can come down to see you there?"

"Ok" said Amanda. "Tell you what, let's call Mr. Roblier and ask him to stand-by for legal support if we are asked any questions by the authorities. Especially regarding any work-related questions. Roblier should be with us as we answer questions about the Firm. Just tell them what you know, and leave all the other enquiries to him..."

"OK" repeated Barbara "I'll call him tonight. He may have questions for us up here in New York. We hired the boy up here remember, then we sent him down to DC."

"Yes."

"Roblier will want to check on our paperwork regarding compliance, insurance, bookkeeping etc. So I'll have our staff prepare for him."

"So, you're ok?" asked Amanda again.

"I am. Not that we were doing anything out of the ordinary. Like, what *were* we doing? The kid was collecting field samples for a Survey report. What's that?...*Jesus.*"

"Take it easy Barbara..."

"No. And I want *them* to explain what happened out there... That's what I want to hear from the police...He was *my* hire Amanda. His grandmother trusted *me.*"

"It's not your fault Barbara. Don't feel overwhelmed...Nobody could have known."

Amanda waited, then said. "Please offer the family our condolences. Can you ask about Funeral arrangements?"

"Sure."

"Take it one day at a time Barbara, OK?"

Barbara was a strong woman. Amanda could sense that she was gradually collecting herself.

"OK"

The boy died while working for the Firm. He was doing a field survey for a coastal development site needing an environmental study and a research report. He had been hired as a Summer Intern.

When Amanda came home, she found Gwynie wearing the Caps T-shirt that Jacob had bought her...

* *

Brian Endavoris was an old hand from way back. As a teenager in Texas with Mexican roots, he was hired by a drilling company for dirty jobs at site work. That is, long before Immigration laws much rated any political bent, he just worked hard and advanced like any other Texan.

Over the years, his expertise expanded, and his proclivity for absorbing local problems made him a Foreman.

With a modest ranch, and some professional standing, he became well liked, and he frequently accepted work on offshore rigs. His fortune grew, and he paid taxes without complaint. He even owned a small land claim and operated a couple of recycled oil rigs.

But he was getting older and increasingly out of work. Not that he needed the employment, being amply invested. But he cared for his business, his sons and family.

He knew the oil spigot had shut off since the BP disaster. Of course he knew how it happened. Why and how it occurred could easily have been solved. Those in the industry were getting fat and lazy with sloppy standards, recycled technology and complacent expectations by senior management for profits.

When he was on a rig, there was real quality control; state of the art technologies, and then more quality controls by innovative and trained engineers.

Still, he got a call not long ago. It was an offer for some work offshore. At his age, the job was as good as it got.

That is, if he wanted to keep his family benefits package updated. So he signed on.

Plus... out of nowhere came a bonus he could not refuse. "For his good work" they said.

He was offered the commission on a Jack-Up placement in the North Atlantic.

Not much had changed in the thirty years of offshore drilling technology. Most drilling units enjoyed the euphemism of being offshore "Exploration and Development" rigs.

He saw them as Jack-up platforms stationed all over the world, drilling and operating in every environment, in every sea, and for every enterprise that could haul oil out of the ground to make money. The short and the long of it was that they brought energy to a modern world.

He knew the drill. This, he had no objection to. What he disliked were the politics that devised ways to use these fortune-building workhorses as targets for political capital. A Jack-up platform was dangerous work.

For this job, they could not have picked a better man. True, he was Latino - descendant of Castilian ancestry, and he could have passed as a Swedish Caucasian with his square faced features and blond hair. He could clean up nice, he wife often told him. But the rest of the time, he was purposefully unseen as a crewmember on a rig smeared in crud and wearing splattered overalls and an oil-stained face.

The bottom-supported mobile offshore drilling unit had been slow towing. Onboard the ship in the accommodations quarters, the Command was occupied with paperwork and sea state conditions as the rig was towed from zone to zone. As they entered cold weather conditions up north, the seas began thrashing with gale force winds.

Nor could there be any delays: This was a corporate race for positioning the rig against increasing resistance from a growing political sector of environmentalism. Ever since the furor arose about the melting ice cap that pitted eight nations and 250 scientists against drilling in the Arctic National Wild Refuge, all seas were open for Activist obstructionism. The Atlantic Ocean was no exception, and it was a potential threat against any industry oil rig.

One surprise did come, and from quarters unexpected, given the political climate. The Teamsters Unionists had embraced the energy sector. And while ANWAR was half a world away, they liked the idea of highly paid construction and industry jobs that came from such ventures.

Too bad they were fading away, thought Brian as the weeks turned into months of rig placement. One thing was right. When the Teamster spokesman said that they'd have to prepare their guys to spend months, even years working on the open water, he was not far from the truth: This kind of work left merchant marine boys on land.

The rig meant business. This jack-up rig was going to have to stand still on the sea floor and rest upon four legs - even before being "jacked up" above the wave action.

That meant serious long term risk. Perhaps his bonus... Something he had thought about all the way there.

The longer he was on board, the more he thought about it's potential. This rig was no ordinary rig he'd ever worked on. No Sir. Not only did this sucker have a set of open-truss legs made of the highest grade steel, but columnar legs. Evidently, there were big plans here for a fierce sea. He surveyed the plans.

Stabilization schematics showed mats and spud cans for this oil rig. So the sea floor was soft here, he noted.

He knew that the mat they would be laying on the seafloor was designed to support the legs and keep them from sinking into the bottom in a way as to distribute the weight of the rig.

It was "A" shaped, connecting each of the legs. But something new had been added. Perhaps due to the BP disaster, but here was an additional requirement to double up on the sea-floor pad, as if it were unstable. They wanted Spud cans also attached to the bottom of each, so that if the spikes driven through the mat fatigued, they could rest on the mat by default. That is, if...if... the ocean floor was steady.

Clearly, there were concerns...

Anyway, all he was interested in was the *post* stabilizing operations. The elevating devices that would need weeks of work once the Jack-up was on location. The part, as his family called it, when the whole rig and drilling platform had to be elevated beyond the reach of the sea, as if were Poseidon himself.

But that was his expertise - the elevating devices that used hydraulic cylinders. These things could extend and retract to climb up and down the legs. Well, that's what he was trained on.

However, here they used other elevating devices to lift the platform. Rack and two pinion gears moved the legs up or down. It was delicate business. You could easily capsize a rig out here.

He had his plans. All he had to do was wait his day. He knew what to do, and how to place his charge. It would have to be at just the right elevation - when the rig was most vulnerable.

Was it worth the bonus? His life too, perhaps?

Damned right it was.

Theodore LaMaas set up a legacy fund for his family, besides.

* *

Chapter Two

New London, Connecticut

The *SSV Cherokee* pulled away from her docks and made down the Long Island Straight. She was yellow, a recycled towing vessel that had propelled many missions out to sea, her ship's crew were old hands at routine sorties. Some, Polish born and merchant marine-trained, but all certified by the US Coast Guard to conduct sea traffic operations.

Furthermore, below the waterline, she had full salvage capabilities and icebreaking hull-strength.

In the Pilot House Captain Sorrenson, a Swedish mariner with a long career related to underwater exploration, saw the wire hydraulic pressure gauge toss up and down. His payload was invisible - slow to respond and causing resistance tension on the towing apparatus. On the surface, she was towing nothing.

NR-2 sent up her message to release the tow lines, and the submarine stood off, purring under steam from her own nuclear power plant.

She was one of the strongest and ablest vessels in the submarine fleet.

"Reporting for coordinates, Sir" saluted the young Midshipman.

The Captain turned to the Political Advisor at his side. They stood at the Command and Control platform of the vessel.

Trevor smiled at them both. "We coordinate with the Soviet ship *Sunrise* at these coordinates, please." he handed the document to the Captain.

The Captain's face showed no outward sign of emotion, but it drained of color. He registered the Orders to his clipboard.

"The *Sunrise* Sir?" repeated the Midshipman to his Captain.

"Deliver these coordinates if you please Midshipman Hawkins." he said, handing over the clipboard.

The Captain relinquished his station to his Executive Officer. "Proceed as follows. Take us out to the main; plot a course for the said coordinates, advise on best approach... Con is yours." he said.

"Aye Sir"

Trevor took a step backward and subtly gestured.

The Captain said nothing. He moved to the rear section of the command center beyond the aft consoles, and eyed him.

 "Don't worry, she's a harmless science research vessel... And our friend." said Trevor.

The Captain looked back to his Second Officer who watched for a nod of confirmation from his Commander.

They were disciplined officers of the United States Navy. Trained, experienced and at the peak of their performance; able to methodically execute orders without the slightest hesitation.

Yet these coordinates were set for the most climate-averse and perilous conditions of underwater sailing known on earth. The North Pole. The polar cap.

"Make ready to enter the continental shelf at these depths 078.3225; bearing NNE at 22 knots speed only."

"Aye Sir"

"Ship to 078.3225 Depth. NNE at 22 knots speed."

The crew responded to the coordinates for the ship's new course bearings.

Captain Pete Robinson of the *NR-2* returned to the navigation station and looked down at the chart as the coordinates took shape. He let out a long breath.

His face said it all. This was not what he had expected. First to be towed out before light and without detection by a dockside Submarine Support Vessel. Now this?

What was up?

The Soviet submarine *Sunrise* was a renamed November-class attack submarine. Older perhaps than most, she had been built during the early cold war years as the newest in technological advances of the Soviet arsenal, owning superior weapons capability.

As far as they knew, she had never seen action. But her threat alone commanded respect. Now she was used chiefly by the Soviets for training purposes.

"... a harmless science research vessel?"

Trevor read his thoughts and approached with a second document.

"This will be her hailing message at these coordinates. And together we travel to the Gakkel Ridge."

"The Gakkel Ridge?" repeated the Captain, if a little too hastily.

Trevor smiled. "...Told you we'd need to wear our Longjohns for this mission."

The crew was within earshot.

"Captain..." added Trevor disarmingly "Please let's get a cup of coffee now that we're under way, I do get sea sick you know..."

At that retort, the crew relaxed.

The lights in the command center turned green, and the routine procedures of a submarine cruise was underway with all hands performing as trained.

Below, in the Captains quarters, it was a different story.

"The Gakkel Ridge is dangerous as hell...What are you doing putting us down there?" Pete asked.

"The mission is this. We are rendezvousing with the Soviets, and in a joint venture of cooperation, removing some seabed implants..." said Trevor.

"*Seabed implants?* What the hell does that mean?"

"Don't be naive Captain. The Soviets *and* us... have been positioning submerged weapons for years. We are each arrayed one against the other. While we still can, we are disarming; removing and retrieving as many of them as possible..."

"Vestiges of a cold war, eh?"

"Well yes *and* no. These days, it's harder to define our friends from our enemies. The Soviets have the same problem. We want to take NO chances."

Trevor found a spot in the cramped quarters to sit, and he took his time to explain.

"The world has advanced strategically and technologically in ways beyond our play. It's time to secure our arsenal from the reach of potential third party marauders...We've agreed to make it a cooperative mission. It's now or never..."

"How long will it take?"

"About seven days, I imagine."

"*Seven days*?" Captain Pete Robinson took a step. "How many of these *seabed implants*...exactly, are you thinking of retrieving?"

Trevor unfolded the Arctic map and laid it on the table.

"All of them. Here. Here and Here..."

"So how does *that* work?" said Pete looking fiercely at Trevor. "We hand our nuclear war heads buried in the sea floor to a November-class Soviet Attack submarine?"
"Actually, it's the other way around. *You* will be hauling off *their* warheads..."

"Now you're joking. We don't have the capacity to storing an arsenal..."

"No. But the *Cherokee* does."

" *What*...that damned rust-bucket on the surface?"

"She's certified by the USCG as seaworthy, isn't she? She is an icebreaker, right...?"

"That's what surprises me." sneered Robinson.

"Don't worry. By the time these things reach the surface, they will all be disarmed. I have the Soviet's word on it."

"The captain's *word*? Oh really?"
"Yes."

"Well, let me tell you something Trevor. What you're asking me to do is to *undo* everything I have ever been trained to do...." he rolled his head towards the upper deck crews on board the submarine.

Trevor took a step back and waited.

"So…" said Robinson, recovered. "You want us to unearth our own missiles - *and theirs*, and then float them to the surface and dump them on the decks of that wreck like we were all diving for oysters or something…"

Trevor was shaking his head. "Not quite…"

"What. There's more?"

"Yes. The Soviets want to help. And they want to give you their own onboard weapons cargo."

"Now you're really joking right?"

"As I said before, it was a cooperative agreement reached in London between all three governments. Yours, theirs, and mine."

Pete said nothing.

"So, we have work to do."

"I'll say. It's the god-damnedest Orders I've heard yet. These aren't toys you know - the potency of one of those things detonating is… devastating."

"Let alone *several* detonations at one time…?" finished Trevor "Highly catastrophic globally."

"How do you mean?"

Trevor leaned over the map. "Here. The Gekkar Ridge…" said Trevor tapping the spot.

"That's one of the most unstable sea beds on earth now with Arctic melting. Earthquakes." said Robinson, suddenly stiffening.

"Precisely."

"Jesus."

"Right."

"We don't exactly have the best retrieval capabilities...We are assigned as a Research Vessel with limited scope..."

"That's fine. They have scientists on board - as worried as we are by the way... And they have a few tools. They have teeth..."

"I'll say they do. .."

"Come on up. I'm getting seasick. I need some air." said Trevor.

"Jesus." spluttered the Captain, by way of release. "What a wimps-ass. We aren't even rocking yet..."

"No. But we will be over the Ridge. Interesting geological features there... Those earthquakes are opening up daily..."

"One more thing..." said Robinson "You do have a map plan for retrieval, right?"

Trevor hesitated. "There are sonar signatures on the bottom of the ocean. We find them; verified their locations, and up they come."

"How?"

"You said yourself that you're a Research Vessel. Since we have the ability to get right down and look at them, we get to inspect them at the sea bed. We find their sonar beacon. We visually identified them, take pictures, and bring them up?"

"I don't like the sound of this. It's close work."

"That it is. We'll use the submarine's side-looking sonars. You have three viewports on the underside of the submarine?..."

"We do." said the Captain, leading the way up to the mess.

His lieutenant appeared.

"Send me Missoni, Smith, Swartz and Menendez, please." said the Captain.

"Aye Sir."

He turned to Trevor. "If this an underwater salvage, they are the best Navy salvage operation trainees on board."

Trevor nodded.

* *

The flashing cameras came to a halt, and the gavel came down to silenced the chamber within the United States Congress.

Sarah Hennesy took the Oath to speak the truth. She sat down.

"You may proceed" proclaimed the Chair of the Senate Committee.

Amanda looked at the text, Sarah's voice reading...

"Mr. Chairmen and Member of the Senate Committee on Trade, Climate and International Energy Commissions.

My name is Sarah Delaney. I am an attorney. I live in Washington and hold the position of Counsel to the Vice President of the Association of Manufacturers and Energy Consumers.

This Association, as the Committee already knows, represents all of the classes of trade and commerce using energy sources across the country. I am the spokeswoman by special authorization of the Association, although I strongly suspect that the opinions I am here expressing represent the views of secondary users, related.

I am here to assert that there is extreme prejudice against the energy industry. Such prejudice damages our ability to function in a normal fashion. We consider it of such concern as to appeal for protection under Fair Trade, and to ask for shelter from threats that might ultimately damage the United States. .."

It was a long day. A day that began with weeks of preparation in sessions of paperwork or... blood, sweat and tears as Barbara put it.

Including yesterday. Amanda was at home at her laptop when her cell buzzed. She was adding the final touches to her client's Statement before Congress...

"Hi. I'm downtown. Sweating like hell, sitting at a coffee shop and my head is spinning. Any suggestions?" said Sarah.

Amanda laughed. "What's up…?"

"I'm down to three choices: A white ensemble by Banana Republic; a zany-stylish but dignified pant-suit by Valentino, or a dark set by Ralf Lauren. What do you think?"

"Well…which do *you* feel good in..?" said Amanda. "Remember, it's a Media-fest…"

"Right. The dark set by Lauren."

"Good choice. Anything might happen out there…Better to be subdued."

"So. It's a silk-grey shirt; black pant-suit trimmed with black-pinned satin."

"Sounds classy." said Amanda.

"Yes. And expensive. I'm concerned it might be like… too *uneventful* - So, add a glamorous necklace of glitzy diamonds?"

"Err…" hummed Amanda.

"Black is black in style again, huh?"

"Just keep it simple. You won't regret it. A somber appeal with classic assurance, that's all."

"Maybe add a string of crystal, or pearl earrings?"

"Earrings are fine. You'll be fine… I promise."

"Got it." said Sarah with a sigh of resignation. "Better a sincere witch than a dancing fool, right? "

"You nervous?"

"Yep. Nervous as hell. So, I'll wrap up here and get back to work by...three at your office, ok?"

"See you there." said Amanda, and hung up.

Amanda returned to the page. The speech might be too long - she should trim it by at least a thousand words.

"In view of the observations made by Activists, I should recognize that this group is well within its rights to exert its opinions and concerns. However, due to stunning new revelations that have recently come to light... and having exhausted efforts to protect ourselves, we feel it imperative that Congress be informed of the matters that adversely affect our ability to conduct business...."

Well, if reading the words to herself was good, what mattered was the day that *Sarah* would have to utter them out loud in public where they would be officially recorded for the *Congressional Quarterly*.

Should she lower the tenor, she wondered?

Amanda was concerned. Sarah Delaney had much to deliver before the Congressional Senate Hearing. It was a controversial subject before a particularly contentious panel of Senators. But even lawyers needed brevity, strong as her petition was, and difficult as the topic might be.

She struck out the last two paragraphs. Then looked at the text again.

If the truth be known, this was the battle most fought between Amanda and her client. Sarah Delaney was the one who had to deliver the speech. Amanda Wells who had to write the speech.

"Too many words" they would laugh, both having seen the rendition of Emperor Frederick telling Mozart that his musical composition of *Figaro* had just *"too many notes."*

More than anything, Amanda wanted Sarah to be heard with distinction, clarity and credibility. She was.

"The Association was organized in 1934 and represents a consolidation of several previously existing semi-independent organizations and groups. These groups have variously been at the forefront of technological advances; new markets and innovative thinking both for themselves, and, as history has shown, for the greater good. They deserve their hearing."

 --All the hard work was now paying off in a splendid delivery, thought Amanda. The points of the topic had long ago been passed around at the law firm of her client.

Amanda was given a general consensus of what was in the interest of her client to deliver. But at the end of the day, it was Amanda Wells' research group – many of them lawyers themselves – who could be relied upon to deliver the goods, as one of them said.

Amanda looked up as Sarah continued her Statement.

"More importantly, they deal with patent matters of interest to the nation's commerce, and I speak here for the industry in particular – for the safety of all the men and women who work for those companies; for the Executives behind the corporate decisions, and for the interests of risk-exposure by stakeholders. It is therefore highly desirable that there should be a uniformity of policy and method in dealing with many of these challenges. It is for this reason, that I am before you today..."

Congress, on any given day in Washington DC had a bell-weather system of its own. If the media across the land had been dull and without event, then that was a *good* day:

But if, for example, some event had overtaken the Press, then everyone had to register their comment. Even before an empty chamber - their words must be recorded to assure their constituents back home that elected representatives were on the job doing duty on their behalf.

If a scandal had hit the nation, then it was only party-spokesmen who put forward a Press interview.

If however, the country was waiting on a Congressional decision, then it was a full-scale media event with a group of key congressmen gathered to represent their political interests.

Otherwise, it was business as usual for Congress.

Rarely did a public demonstration alter the temperature within the halls of Congress. Lobbyists were far too productive to allow dissidents to be disruptive. As the saying went: *If there was a real cause for redress, there was a lobbying firm.*

This Hearing was scheduled on a good day. Congress was out, actually, in Recess for the summer. With the exception of a few committees and hearings that went on quietly, regardless, little gripped the nation's attention.

Perhaps it had been scheduled that way on purpose. Still, this speech was one that had to be delivered, even if for the record, Amanda knew.

Now moment was upon them. Their day had arrived.

"You look lovely." whispered Amanda as they took their seats.

Sarah sat at the front table, microphone and water jug to her left, minor media at the foot of the Senator's bench, mainly for taping purposes only.

Beside her sat Mark Weston, their attorney, able to advise her throughout if she needed him. Especially when the questioning began. But now, it was her moment to deliver her Statement for the Record.

Amanda, seated behind her with two assistants, had handed over to the Clerk of the Chamber a copy of Sarah Delaney's statement for the record. It was entered as S. 1045, June 22-23 of the year.

"...It is with much pride that we point to the revenues in taxes that our industries contributes to the nation's wealth, especially in the jobs we create. We are amongst the most responsive to government compliance and safety regulation.

"...However, we are now at an impasse. One - that we cannot achieve by ourselves. It calls for emergency operations. For that, we appeal to the American people and their Senators for clear guidance and help.

Should we fail, the nation will come to a halt. The information is alarming. Allow me to share with you the latest revelations that concern us..."

Sarah reached for a drink. Amanda touched the back of her chair as a vote of assurance. She was doing a fine job. But judging from the movement at the panel, the Senators were already restless and moving about; penciling in their questions; talking to their Aides; rising for another purpose to attend to, and passing notes down the line to the Chair.

Amanda knew they were in for a long session. This was tough business - hardly a favorite topic. Yet Sarah had to be kept going. She had a lot of ground to cover before they shut her down. .

* *

Chapter Three

Russia, 1701

It was October, his mother had to remind him.

He put on a homespun head sock that left openings for his eyes and mouth, and over it, a bearskin head cover that shielded his ears and neck. He sank his toes into red hide fur boots, lodging them firmly into the thong weaved snow-shoes that gave his legs traction in soft white snowdrifts. This would conserve his energy when traversing distance.

A large sack of gear was pulled down over his clothing, making him appear to be three times his size. He saved his ungloved hands for accepting a package from his mother - if only to make her happy, a package of banded bread and cheese. He stepped out and rammed it quickly into his sack then gloved his hands for protection against the ice cold air. In these temperatures, a man could be subdued in a matter of minutes.

Sadusk emerged from scrub woods surrounding his village plateau, he turned toward the ravine. He was too excited to think much, although he knew full well that any house-sortie could kill a man if he was caught unprepared for survival in the Russian tundra.

All he knew was that his work in the barns with hops and grain was complete; his skin coated with bear grease, and his sack was full of charcoal sticks, paper, paint and woolen gloves with open fingers...

He had carved his own pencil box to contain the delicate charcoal dowels which he had bound in strips of thin linen for stiffness. On the sliding sheath of the pencil box he had painted the iconography of Christ from paintings he saw in the Byzantine Church. He was young when they took him to the city, but he remembered. Funeral of a Tsar, they said... To pay a tribute as feudal payment, his old uncle told him at the time.

 In subarctic Russia where he lived, the weather could drop to reduce the landscape to barren wilderness, especially in the long dark winter where the days were short. If the wind did not blow, as today, then if felt bearable and could be endured.

He reached the peninsula, a low lying basin without permafrost because of a surrounding maritime sea. With only a few weeks of weather remaining, he had just enough daylight to capture the event of the migratory bird flights.

He quickly unpacked his carry bag, and pulled out his utensils of charcoal. He used hand motions to waif; feather and sketch conifers and broadleaved trees on a parchment. Discernable, but shaded by snow gathered upon ornaments. This year, the climate had been remarkable, he knew. From Scandinavia through most of Siberia it had been different... He would capture its effects in the sketching.

What he saw here...It was unheard of. This was his mission, he decided. Then he heard it.

The soft rolling *preep*. Soon followed by the anxious *wheet*. Again. "*Preep –wheet.*"

It came from a small creature with a spatulate bill that popped out of nowhere, as if nothing in the world could harm its tiny form. It was an adult, with red-brown head; neck and breast, and dark brown streaks.

He sketched fast. Its under-parts were blackish with buff and pale rufous fringing - if with some reddish coloration. It must not be frightened off...

He fumbled feverishly for the items in his pencil box. Its upperparts brownish-grey, with whitish fringing to the wing coverts. This he must record. Quickly. *Quickly.*

"Preep –wheet."

The breath from his mouth was a short fog. But he persisted with as little motion as humanly possible.

It was rare, and would have a name. Someday. His charcoal pencil moved swiftly, capturing its outline, then with oils he combined for quick coloration. The bird approached. He threw out some bread...

He held his breath. The neck was red. It allowed him to peer closely. There was *less* white on the forehead, and less fringed rufous at the brick red fringes by its scapulars...

He and his friends had talked about it.

He would barely breath, the warmth emanating from his lungs filled the air around his lips with pale vapor, and it might alarm the bird.

This was too exquisite. Against the snow it made a stunning contrast. This creature of magic had migrated from summer polar weather and come to breed in the Chukatosk peninsula on its way to Eastern Russia.

Someone had told him that their eggs, when laid in the warmer climate zones finally, were spotted by local egg harvesters in Pacific rim countries like India, or the Bay of Martaban. As a result, and within his century, his father had told him, the bird would no longer be. And *nobody* would know about them. Except he...

This was his calling. That he should paint them whenever he could, and though they laughed at him in the village where he lived, his paintings became a matter of pride for all but the hardiest in his community. His sketch was pinned to the wall above his bunk, in the two-room house they inhabited as laborers.

Within two months, it was covered, like many others by more recent painting or sketch. More animated and colored than the earlier, each would be pinned over by the latest, such by the next summer, his mother paid for supplies from a caravan of Romanian gypsy merchants selling earlier editions of his work - including the bird.

Sadusk was angry with her, but soon realized he was providing her with a currency. With his paintings, she was bartering for goods, such as the fabric she now wore, and he smiled to himself as he thought about what he was achieving.

 As the evenings wore on, he would lay on his bunk and wonder about the attention that his work might fetch further down the line of traders... Would they be found pleasing in the larger markets of the big traders? Perhaps they would like the birds? Perhaps he should paint more conifer trees, at dusk, when the snow was soft and the sun of summer barely there...

The question that lingered with him the longest however, was whether or not he had fully drawn the redness and contrasting feathering around the speckled body of the bird. He wondered if he had done right to leave it as a subdued fused coloring. That's because it was deceptive. A luminescent agate of the natural environment, yes, yet in catching the silky sunlight, it could fairly glisten when blurred by flight.

Would anybody else see that? Had he done enough to demonstrate it? That thought comforted him.

* *

Amanda decided to work at home today. She was writing up a final report due Downtown by noon the next day.

She had received an email from Rebecca in Toronto.

> *"There is a stir about competitors for the rights to drill... I see that we are making a bid. That's terrific. Further, I see it earmarked for investment overseas... Hope we win the bid."*

> *As ever, good business strategy.*

> *Tell Trevor I'm very proud to be part of this. I'll send him a schedule of oil distributors and shipping companies. Perhaps even those companies which we insure.*

> *Lauren Papendopolous is breathing hard. God knows what she's up to...*

> *See you soon.*

> *Best, Rebecca."*

* *

1774, Colony of Maryland

October, as summer leaves turned from languid pale to yellow, the brigantine *Peggy Steward* entered the Chesapeake Bay. She approached the entrance to the deep harbor at Annapolis, and sailed across the mouth of the Severn River to head into the wind before slacking her topmost canvas.

With only a missen staysail to guide her in, her bow heaved to the lee of the harbor. She dropped anchor and swung-to on the slack tide. There she would remain fast to her mooring.

Even as an older vessel her cargo was sound. Below decks in the hold were two thousand pounds of tea for the colonies.

From waterside, the *Peggy Steward* was a stunning sight. Her three masts swayed gently, her rigging testimony to transatlantic voyaging. A setting sun splayed across tranquil waters and illuminated the ship with a golden aura of grandness. Seagulls screeched as seamen set to coiling her feathering ropes for stowage. Somewhere would be the Master of the Ship, said those perambulating the docks of the colony.

By tomorrow, they knew, repairs would be underway with fresh hemp and tar and pitch to caulk any open seams. Later, with the Master's permission, seamen could come ashore to the Taverns to partake in traditional rounds of ale at the Purser's expense. Those listening would hear of spellbinding tales of trans-Atlantic storms. Local youths relished London's sailor stories.

Strong, well manned and fully laden, this vessel was center of the mercantile world, if not imperial society. Here the *Peggy Steward* carried wares and goods from London agents for local merchants in the colonies.

Her ownership was the wealth of a privileged man. The *Peggy Steward* belonged to an Annapolis sea merchant named J. Stewart, Esquire.

In the Tavern, as wealthy merchants and landlords sat smoking, others were freshly returned from Philadelphia.

Those representing the interests of Maryland to the Continental Congress were known by all. Charles Carroll of Carrolton, a tobacco planter, Samuel Chase, a lawyer whose practice often defended debtors; Thomas Johnson, a lawyer; William Paca – schooled with Chase, a landowner; Matthew Tilghman and John Goldsborough tobacco planters, if on the Eastern parts of the Bay. They came routinely to Annapolis, even as they represented their region as delegates.

They felt secure, these gentlemen. As colonists, they lived off interest from monies given out in loans to reliable customers and they comported themselves with assumptions of "patronage." Their reward came from the enjoyment of deference within an hierarchy akin to their London bankers. For these men, and for all who revolved around them, the mercantilist trappings of their world was as essential to their identity as their ideology: Their merchandize dressed and fed the colonial society that paid its debts; built its houses and delivered its taxes for protections and security...

In Annapolis, they engendered the intellectual, economic, political and moral leadership of the community, many of them having economic ties to the central finance region of merchants and bankers in Philadelphia.

But there was conflict. Especially in Philadelphia where a dispute with the English King of colonial America was agitating.

Maryland had been engaged in commercial enterprise since 1740s flourished through the 1760s. The influence of the ship-building city of Baltimore, combined with the interests of the plantations on the Chesapeake Bay, gave this territory one distinction that no other colony possessed, even as a Proprietary colony, that of a new and emerging colonial American character, independent agency.

Moreover, the recent French and Indian war had spurred demand from the British Empire for Chesapeake products. This drew talented newcomers to town; German merchants and craftsmen came from Frederick County; Irish born and Scots-Irish came from Pennsylvania and Delaware.

Ships of Baltimore registry, and clearing through the customs houses of Annapolis also engaged in coastal trading with Virginia, North Carolina, Boston and Newfoundland. They carried tobacco, iron, and wood to British ports; then onward to deliver grains to Spain and Portugal. On their return voyage, they provisioned equally. From England they imported dry goods, hardware, servants, or convicts. From southern Europe they brought wine.

Such trade laid a firm foundation for moneymaking. Credit arrangements enabled them to act as wholesalers for British import goods. They became more sophisticated in their manufactures: They developed heavy shipping; built larger furnaces and produced pig iron for England. Others distilled rum as trade for the Royal Navy. And as shipbuilding increased, so did the shopkeepers, sailors, servants, carpenters, caulkers, tailors, millers, bricklayers and office clerks. The result was that Baltimore of the Chesapeake became a profit center.

However, investors often obligated themselves heavily. Indebtedness inched higher every year from 1759 such that in just four years, Marylanders were importing more than they produced, purchasing more than their crops could pay for. And it worried the landlords and merchants who sat in the Taverns of Annapolis. They wanted news.

The Royal taxes were getting higher, and the colonists were disputing them.

In New York, where tension between the colonies and Britain first emerged, a controversy had erupted over the American Revenue Act and Sugar Act.

The legal practices of the likes of John Jay were fully engaged in the recovering of commercial debts for British merchants. It was said that by 1773, Mr. John Jay had more than one hundred cases pending the Supreme Court; another hundred pending in New York, and more than three hundred in the Mayor's Court of New York City.

In Maryland, Crown agents began collecting moneys owed the Crown. A tax on all tea.

The *Peggy Steward,* owned by a local colonial merchant named Stewart, had a hold full of tea.

* *

Amanda and Barbara were having a drink at Pussers Dockside.

They giggled their way through colorful punches and a waterside band playing on tin drums and marachas. The Restaurant at the Marriott Hotel on the waterside of Annapolis harbor offered a clear vista across the harbor.

They especially liked watching overwrought yachtsmen maneuvering oversized boats. Or was it the kids in dingy-sized Optimus Prams zipping across the water between the bows of multi-million dollar yachts - all of them trying to dock in a congested harbor of tin drums, tourists and colonial Annapolis T-shirts.

Beyond the harbor were stark stone jetties defining the perimeter of the US Naval Academy. Students jogged around a playing field to the tall Crown Sailing Center. Heavily guarded Gates sheltered the academy compound. Here in training were Midshipmen preparing to take command of the world's most fearsome arsenals at sea.

For Amanda and Barbara, the occasion was less than festive. As the day wore on, they retreated to a quiet waterside café for an early sunset dinner, both reflecting upon a matter than left them with a heaviness of heart. The death of Jacob, the young Intern in their employ.

"How he would have loved all this..." said Barbara.

A copy of the coroner's report was in Barbara's hand. She looked up, still in disbelief.

Amanda reread the report. "Cause of death *Methane poisoning*?"

"The conclusion is based on the finding that the body was dehydrated. What does that mean exactly? Didn't he have a cooler onboard for drinks and snacks...?" said Amanda.

"Of course he did. The trouble is that when the body is exposed to high levels of methane gas, it depletes the oxygen level in the body, causing it to show signs of dehydration"

"But dehydration doesn't kill you..." said Amanda.

"No. But the police report said there were signs of 'inattentiveness' on board. Like the aspirin bottle was empty. He had thrown up repeatedly. He had knocked over stuff, and when the accident occurred, he was not wearing a Life-vest. He seemed to show signs of his motor-skills impairment. In fact, it's entirely possible he passed out altogether..."

They paused, taking in the mesmerizing haze and heat across the harbor. The waiter came and offered them another coffee.

"What confirmed it for the Coroner," said Barbara "was this... 'Evidence of heart palpitations'"

"He had the boat radio button switched ON, but no transmission was sent out?" asked Amanda.

"Yes. But this was hardly a kid who didn't know his way around boats, remember. He fairly begged us to put him on the marine waterfront survey project." Barbara looked away. "I had to speak to his grandmother the other day. She told me he wanted to be in the Navy."

Amanda reached over and placed her hand on Barbara's arm. "I'm sorry. I know you have family attachments"

"No. I'm glad you hired him for work. He was very proud of *that* Amanda. Thank you." She paused. "Just another boat accident reported by the Coast Guard to investigate a drifting vessel. That's how they found him. He was unconscious when they recovered the boat.."

It did them both good to talk. Somehow, reciting the incident left them calmer. They were reconciled to what had happened. If only they'd disallowed him to board a small outboard to image the coastal waterfront of the proposed development.

What happened? He was within sight of the beach.

* *

School had closed early. Gwynie had been delivered home by Carla, and the child she was set to chasing dogs all day.

Amanda was in the library working. Around and around the house Gwynie ran, interrupting Amanda's concentration.

"Carla..?" called Amanda, asking for help, a phone to her ear.

Worse, the phone rang often. Twice they called from the office. Once it was Barbara. Two calls from insurance agents asking about items on a police report. Then Janice, Administrator from the office. Could the staff all add a day to their leave for the 4th of July since it fell mid-week?

At one point, Amanda found Gwen standing in the doorway. "I want to speak to Daddy." she demanded imperiously.

"Sweetie. That was not Daddy on the phone. He's a long way away, and will be coming home soon"

Gwen left.

Back to work, until the next phone call.

"Daddy?" came Gwynie again.

"No. Not Daddy."

The child was clearly upset, Amanda could tell. She was driving the dogs wild, and delivering loud crashing sounds wherever she could to get attention.

Finally Amanda swiveled on her desk chair, picked her up and plunked her on her lap. She squirmed unhappily, the dog panting beside them like a loud Boeing 747.

Gwynie smudged the desk papers with her wet fingers and hit the send button on an item that Amanda was working on, incomplete.

"Gwen?..." began her mother in her admonishment tone when the phone rang. It was Sarah.

The child frowned - dirty deed done, and squirmed off Amanda's lap, the dog in full chase again.

Only later after dinner did Amanda understand. Gwynie was missing her father. Today at school they had asked what her Daddy did. Her finger in her mouth, Gwynie said she didn't know where he was. She didn't know how to answer them.

Amanda gathered the child on her lap and consoled her. He was... a captain of his industry... she tried to explain.

"Like as ship?"

"Like a ship.." repeated Amanda, hugging the child. "And he will be back soon. He thinks of you all the time."

Gwynie smiled, all resolved.

Later that night, after book-reading and prayers, Amanda tucked Gwynie into bed softly with a kiss.

"I love you Mommie." said the child, eyes closing.

Trevor's absence was beginning to frustrate the household, thought Amanda.

It had been too long.

* *

Sarah paused.

"In an effort to show societal responsibility, we do not shirk from the data facing our nation. Rather, we engage with it directly in order to bring about suitable change and competitive venues that allow us to function properly...

"...But just as we cannot be responsible for this dilemma by ourselves, nor can we solve this dilemma by ourselves."

"In the first instance, while we understand the general argument of global warming, we do respectfully submit that from a commercial competitive perspective, the laws have been stacked against the United States as contributors to total global carbon emission. For example, in the baseline assumptions ascribed to the United States by the International body - NO surface carbon-absorption data - including oxygen-producing trees are ascribed to the United States. Trees of course have mitigating value: We are shown as having no such mitigating value. That surely distorts the data, and shows the divergence between fairness and prejudice against developed nations."

The Chamber was somewhat surprised by this statement if not shocked. A few heads turned to each other muttering. "I have trees." said one Senator. "Huh?.."

"Sure" said another "My State had millions of acres in parklands and timber forests."

"Moreover, whereas the world-wide environmental movement has continued to focus on human-generated emission of global warming gases, I am here to tell you that they have failed to grasp the accelerated catastrophe of the storehouse of natural carbon sitting

beneath the Arctic. Or the subsea emission of volcanic eruptions in the last five years.

Our planet is changing. Our climate is changing. Our populations are growing. But humans are but a small part of this change. And certainly, our Energy industry is being unfairly singled out for political reasons using flawed science and social fear...

Sarah was doing a great job of articulating the needs and concerns of her industry to the Senate Committee.

However, Amanda noticed a growing political discomfort.

* *

That night, Amanda started to breath easier.

For the first time in weeks, she felt some tension falling away. Relieved perhaps, if in small measure, from all the pressure that had been piling up in her life, and it felt good to have her room to herself for a little quiet time.

In fact, there was something she wanted to do - images she wanted to review. Rather, computer digital images that had probably sat on half a dozen disks, and needed printing up...

She found them. They populated her laptop with laughter, color and excitement – illuminating the room like a live rewind of moments together. Here was a complete collection of family photos, and she determined that she would fill the house with them. Especially for Gwynie...

That summer had been glorious. Boating, fishing and their annual two-week family cruise on their boat off the coast of Maine. That is, Trevor, Amanda and Gwen because Sandra went to Europe.

Here, an image of the yellow plastic ladle - the ladle that Gwynie pulled out of the galley drawer with a matching red plastic salad spoon to bash against cooking pans. It was laughable. Of course the green salad mixing bowl was not far behind... and with all the colors arrayed around her, Gwynie was off and away with the band in her world of imagination as the boat pitched and rolled upon the gentle waves of the water.

Amanda smiled. For Gwyneth Ann MacDonnell, the boat was her second home: No silly crate; cot or Fischer Price baby-crib was necessary either. Just the bunk for her bed, like any other crew - below decks and forward of the dinning suite, held in place by safety netting to make a soft cradle where she slept, the very boat her rocker.

But then she started climbing on their next cruise: Up onto the chart table. Under the dining table. Standing at the portholes. Turning on the galley faucets and once, she even appeared topside with the toilet brush in her hand from the Forward Cabin? Trevor was *not pleased...* true. Amanda cleared her throat at the memory of that one.

"Better the Terrible–Twos on board than running wild in the house" observed Trevor, his own forehead the target of some overhead boat beams...

Amanda had to laugh. His head must have bruised well. This 'sailing' was ill-suited to a man raised on hunting and riding. But their marriage had found ways to compromise. Over the years, it worked well as their family had grown. Trevor-Reginald was at St Andrews in Scotland, and Sandra here at St. Mary's College of Maryland, just south of Washington DC, on the banks of the Chesapeake Bay.

The Maine cruise was still their favorite vacations, even if the boat was showing its age. Perhaps it was the music that night, she remembered from the photos - piping in over their deck speakers from radio Canada, and those early languid ballads. Or perhaps it was the brightly starlit heavens that filled the dark skies of Maine.

How could she forget those nights with the boat gently at anchor in a quiet cove when Trevor held her, reaching under her heavy sweated to feel up her back and pull her close to him under a magic sky that could easily buckle Amanda's knees.

Of course, that was before this last trip. Before he left for London.

That he should be leaving for London was not something unusual. It was a business trip. Gwynie, would stay at home with Amanda while Trevor divided his time between Washington and London. It was the nature of their professional world together, and never apart for very long...

But she remembered that night not only for its tender lovemaking, but for the recollection of two other events.

The first, a long description about an event in London that had stirred some alarm in Trevor. He was concerned. Too much risk-taking by money managers to whom his bank had some exposure.

She remembered it well.

"But isn't risk at the heart of banking, from the very beginning?" asked Amanda, thinking historically that it was his Scottish bank, since the 17th century to support the Bank of England with finances for early colonial venture to the Americas, and later, to develop a monetary currency as a Central Bank.

"Well Yes" he said "If you consider all the wild schemes and plans made over time...But this is different. This is a world of high-tech software and hardware, making permutations, trades and assessments with dizzying speed and large sums of money."

"Oh, so it's the amount of money moving about?" "Yes and no. It's more like the *principle* behind it all, taking with it so much *trust* by so many others that worries me... "

He had looked out at a darkened sea, as if corralling his thoughts "For example, there is this one group, out of New York that made a transaction nine months before going public to pay its owners $398.5 million as a tax-deferred dividend..."

"...Leaving the stock buyers of the IPO to carry the debt?" said Amanda.

"Exactly. And 'knowingly' -that's what the Justice Department had to prove."

"How did it make its money?"

"Well. That's the point. Few of these groups make money the fundamental way we do with products and services, or good management and a profit as return. No. What they did was to borrow $500 million from an overseas development company, saying it would be used to expand investment products..."

"And?"

He turned to her somberly. "80% of it went directly to its owners and founders. That's what the regulatory filings found. Then, separately, the group negotiated bank credit from its favorite client – *another* questionable arrangement – with the option to distribute *an additional* $400 million just prior to its initial public offering in the Lending Agreements."

"*Wow.*"

"*Wow* is right. But it makes the rest of us look bad with conventional ways.

"It's a private equity firm, isn't it?" "Umm. Used to be. I can understand what's roiling European sovereign banks: These solid name banks have drifted into investing like private equity firms. They are now playing with sovereign moneys, like gambling chips..."

"But you, my sweet…" said Amanda raising her lips to his face "are still sailing in wooden vessels, right?" He laughed. "Right."

Yes, Amanda remembered that conversation. She touched the image of their boat…

The second event of that night came just before dawn, when he peeled away from the main cabin's bunk and popped open his laptop. A message had come in from Eunice, the Household Secretary of his estate in Scotland.

"I am afraid it's almost time. You must come quickly. She may be fading fast"

Amanda saw the email, and raised her hand to her lips. "I'm sorry my darling…"

"She knew we needed to have our cruise…" he said, "and she wouldn't let me join her. But I won't let her slip away at the hands of her Nurse. I can't…"

"Of course not." insisted Amanda, springing out of bed. "Bring her here to the States. Immediately. She can be with us till the end if necessary…Oh Trevor. I'm so sorry…The Lady Dowager is so precious."

"She's had a full and wonderful life. Let's celebrate that." he said firmly.

"Of course we must."

It was his mother's health that had taken a turn for the worse. Trevor did not want her to succumb to the British Health System that administered euthanasia to the terminally ill.

He would bring her to the United States if he had to. Not that the care was any less efficient. Just the end of life treatment was somehow gentler in America than Europe.

On this point he and Amanda were firmly in agreement.

Unfortunately for Trevor, his mother died the next night - peacefully in her sleep two days after he arrived, and he was at her side. In a way, he later said, it was exactly how his mother wanted it.

 Amanda had not seen Trevor since then. The vacation had wrapped up so suddenly, that there was not going over chance to console him.

Then his letter....

Somehow, after he completed all his mother's arrangements in Scotland, he had to go to London where he kept a town house for business. Reggie was frequently with him, that she knew.

* *

By the turn of the year, the bird picture painted in the Urals by Sadusk had found its way to Austria through Hungary.

The wagons from Romania arrived. They had crossed the landscapes of Europe since the 14th century. They were Gypsies, finding some measure of wealth in their travels as merchants. Without ownership of land, danger came to them from the politics of the states they travelled through. Many locals viewed them as harmless; others as foe, and they were treated like vagabonds. Especially if there was wealth to be plundered in their wagons...

It behooved the travelling gypsies therefore, to economize on their space. Rolled parchments or art fit easily into their cargo without calling attention to vandals. Like the drawing of Sadusk. Otherwise, their most prevalent asset was their troupe-skills of entertainment while transporting mercantile wares. They always drew visitors to market.

Many were of Armenian descent, some Christian, most of Jewish ancestry. They crossed boundaries and territories, adhering to trade routes with seasonal reliability, bringing goods, novelty and news to regions in passage on a regular basis.

Once camped, they had license to muster in the outskirts and suburban parts of town, though never allowed entry within the walls of the city state. They carried their wealth on their backs, often in gold trinkets and jewels or vestments, or precious pieces of decorative art.

Over time, they offered social connectivity from city to city, freely transmitting knowledge and information from one population to another, including news, geographic lore, stories and narrative.

Storytelling, a function of singular dissemination in the middle ages crossed rural landscapes, offering a measure of immunity from danger for Gypsies, - if not safe passage across hostile armed camps.

Few left a footprint, bringing rather goods to regions as distance-merchant, and some did accrue wealth. But as the renown theologian Martin Luther observed, they were vagrants.

One wagon procured a work of art that was quickly absorbed within the city walls. From there it travelled to Paris with a party of Musicians, as part of a gift to an aristocratic cousin. But the party was waylaid at a hostelry, and their horse in need of a shoe. The Foundry was paid with the Sadusk painting.

By the early eighteenth century, at the iron foundry, the painting was picked up by the stable-hand of a Lord who sought entry to his circle of landowners. The landowner who bought the painting resided in the city, his post was provisioner of the Royal Household Princes in attendance to the King of France.

But the painting failed to find its way into a gilt frame. It rested, all this while, rolled up as a parchment scroll, along with maps and charts and navigational material that held the keys to overseas trade, merchants and navigators.

Later in the century, and only by accident, the painting unraveled from a large pile, falling to the middle of a stone floor. It lay there - resilient, the stunning expression of a bird against a snow field, oils and a sketch, its cry still audible. The painting came to the attention of a man who knew the role of high baroque fashion.

It was exquisite, he said. Perhaps a painting of such vibrant; raw and foreign nature would pique the fancy of the Ladies in their highly emerging Salons?

Unsigned, its origins and descriptions were unknown however. It was taken to a potter to be made into a decorative artwork of porcelain. Paint was applied by hand in extenuation of the painting, and it was declared an item of beauty. But it was never delivered.

Several years later, the porcelain was accepted as payment, in lieu of coin, for services-rendered. Then it entered the workshop of a porcelain collector, and jeweler.

There, as the industrial revolution changed agrarian fields into steam and iron for new technological developments, a decision of design was made for an Imperial Account. The ceramic was viewed, and sketches made: Inspired, the bird from the painting was to be rendered in a new medium, silver, and should resemble the porcelain. Further, a small mechanism was to be placed inside the body, such that when it opened, a small rotating platform of spring blossom would turn to the tune of a songbird.

Further, being an Imperial account, tiny jewels were placed in colors closely represented by the original painting. The result was a complex figurine sculpture of paint, jewel and detail. The body was to hold the agate coloring of the Ural mountain stone; but be carved yet from crystal. The opalescence would be captured with soft metals of gold, silver and platinum.

When the finished product was presented in Court, it was put on display for viewing. The bird, said to be carved from rock crystal in the fashion of the Medici workshop of Florence, was a sensational success.

The prize became gift as the carriage that carried the bird in a cherry embossed box ran well-sprung and smooth across the landscape, its polished mahogany inlaid with an Imperial coat of arms.

Its destination was not entirely known, except that it travelled some great distance. First by sea, then by land, according to the shipping manifests of the chronicler of household accounts. It was intended to cross an ocean to the American colonies, as a deposit for a large purchase of land and mineral wealth...

But as Revolution and war spread across the Empires of Europe, gold was used for other purchases of value.

By the middle of the eighteenth century, the beautiful bird had found its ways into several boudoirs in France.

At one place in particular, it was roughly snatched by the strong arm of a gambling man who lost it that night at his gaming table. The recipient, son of a wealthy landowner, was happy enough to receive it, and considered the debt paid in full.

But these were changing times, and doting women could be just as easily impressed by innovations and new developments as by baroque décor. His winnings would service such ideas.

The new owner's father, a Burgundian who provisioned the courts with wine by Royal License, would approve. No longer a singing bird, it contained under its secret mantle a timepiece.

That night, in a lighter transport bearing the coat of arms of his household, he visited the premises of one particular paramour to whom he made promises: Together they crossed the city. Just before dawn, he got out of the carriage, his black cloak in a swirl. He knocked on the door of a merchant with his silver-headed cane. A candle taper appeared at the door.

They talked. He would be back in three days, he said. Then he re-entered the carriage - a happy laugh receiving him. That, and the heavy scent of a powdered wig of the Royal Court.

Before the three days expired, disturbances hit the city with violence. Reprisals were promised, people moved about surreptitiously as the French Revolution spread.

The young man's father, the Burgundian trader arrived in town from the Provinces, as scheduled. Together, he and his father were to ride to the Royal Accounting House in their carriage under full-armed escort to receive payment in gold for three months supply of Burgundy wine.

Not only did the Accounting House fail to pay in full, but the carriage itself was attacked along the highway. All were killed, including the Footmen and horsewhip. The young man's father was left up a tree astride a bough, his body pinned to the trunk with a dagger through his heart.

News of the robbery travelled fast throughout the city. What alarmed the son was neither the event itself, nor even the horrific death of his father, but the mobs of Paris. They did not decry the dastardly act. Rather, they celebrated the death of a man of wealth.

The young man made a decision. His father's household business arrangements had a ship fully laden with Bordeaux wine preparing to set sail at noon. He had a plan.

As an afterthought and for normal assurances, he returned to the home of the goldsmith and ascribing the payment of it to his father's business account against the Court Supply Books, took possession of the crafted work. It was procured in its box, wrapped with burlap and straw, then tied with course metal banding. The ship sailed for London.

Within a week the ship's cargo was reloaded onto another vessel moored at the docks of London destined for the colonies with items of trade goods; wares and supplies. The box and container was itemized on the Bill of Lading as *Tresor de Henry de Burgundy*.

In the cargo of the vessel was also tea, heavily banded, and all properly stamped to Crown agents as tax and custom duties, destined for the port of Annapolis in the colonies of America.

The Peggy Stewart.

* *

Chapter Four

The ship's tremors were unnerving.

Earth movement dissipating through ocean water held captive the vessel. For a Captain accustomed to the resonance of his ship at sea, this was as uncertain and unpredictable as any motion on land. There was no mitigating its impact, nor masking it. Every man on board the submarine felt the tremor as it shuddered and vibrated like a Tramway crossing. This was not something from the sea.

Trevor looked at the Captain. Things had not gone well. The sea around them consisted of air bubbles and agitated suspended sediments. Visibility was nil.

Time for a distraction.

For two days now, both the Engineer Officer and the Executive Officer had lain prone in forward quarters of the research submarine. There, crew could crawl to stand a six-hour watch of duty. There, from three small portholes, they had visibility outside the vessel.

They could see anything that might present a hazard to the submarine, especially if Sonar had not picked up any hazard signal on the side scanners.

For two days, they had reported little.

Worse, the covert rendezvous with the *Sunrise* had failed to materialize.

"Alright Gentlemen. This is the Captain" announced Robinson looking at Trevor. "Now for some entertainment. We have a main show in the Mess, and on your monitors for observation. All are free to watch and sit back. We aren't in the tropics by any means, but maybe we can learn something from it. Enjoy."

The clip was engaging. Especially when told by a pretty scientist. It began with a swim in a luscious tropical ocean reef teeming with fish and algae.

A few audible *ooohs* and *aahhs* wafted up around the ship's crews. But they were soon hushed into silence.

"Recent research, since 2013, shows that preserving more than 10% of coral reefs worldwide would require limited warming to below +1.5°C if using general ocean circulation models AOGCMs. Obviously at less than 10%, that's hardly leaving a reef system world-wide.

"In fact, the global area of reef systems have already been reduced by half. Bradbury, in his discussion called Zombie Reefs as Harbinger for Catastrophic Future" shows that the reefs which are nurseries to fish stocks and other life forms have become zombie ecosystems - neither dead nor truly alive in any functional sense, and on a trajectory to collapse within a human generation..."

The Captain received a buzz from his electronic device. It was the First Officer. "Sir, We have a visual report from the Forward section."

Robinson and Trevor advanced the length of the Submarine, and Trevor waited as the Captain crawled into the viewing station beside the Engineer Officer.

In very poor visibility, with disturbances lifting debris off the bottom and floating upward, Robinson saw a large dark apparition that appeared to have three eyes.

"What depth are we ranging in?"
"At about 125 – to 150 meters Sir…"

"Did it *ever* get clearer?"

"No Sir. But it's definitely moving. Sonar picked up fragmented signals…"

"Is it biological?"

"No Sir. "

"Does it seem threatening or adverse?"

"No sir. It appears to be…well…just as blinded down here as we are."

"It's *them.* Switch on three lights. Nudge to face it, nose to nose, and watch for any response or movement."

"Aye Sir."

Three of the four 1000-watt thallium iodide lights were switched on at the exterior bow of the submarine. The action, above decks at the sonar station, solicited a large signature.

"Dip the bow 10° *only*" Robinson ordered.

"Can you hear me Sweeny?"

"Yes Sir. Ten degrees bow only."

"Tell me what she does…"

The movie was still playing and the rest of the vessel's crew carried on without awareness of the motion change.

They waited.

"It's just sitting there." came the transmission. Robinson backed out and turned to Trevor.

"If that's the *Sunrise,* I'm nervous as hell. Why can't she hail us as she is supposed to?"

"She's vulnerable. We're already seeing methane plumes rising from the Ridge. She could have seen some trauma. Besides..." said Trevor "She may not want to risk much more transmission signaling. She's already fooling around with experimental ranges..." he added.

"Please explain?" asked Robinson

"She might fear overlaying electronic signals to which her systems and cargo might be sensitive. She's emitting a whole new signature-set, as in, experimental signals Captain, but for a *different* mission..." "...different *mission*?"

"Yes" said Trevor. "It's called Solar Radiation Management..."

"Why?"

Trevor faced him. "It's not yet approved, exactly. But it's entirely viable."

"I'm a research vessel. I should know this..."

"Ok" said Trevor "The US and Russia are developing a net of powerful radio-beam-frequency transmission stations around the Arctic. They are using the critical 13.56 MHZ-beat frequency to break down the methane in the stratosphere and troposphere to encourage nanodiamonds and hydrogen..."

The sweat was now visible on the faces of both men. The temperatures at this section of the ship was higher than normal, the spaces confined. The Captain's face remained puzzled.

Trevor continued. "...in case you haven't noticed, were swimming through methane bubbles released from sub-seafloor gas pockets. As we're witnessing a massive loss of Arctic sea ice, it's dissolving the cover of a vast storehouse of frozen methane..."

The Captain understood.

"Plus, we're in shallow seas that allows such gas to reach the surface: Once released into the atmosphere, global warming accelerates at an *exponential* rate."

"Of course." said the Captain

Trevor continued. "**Solar Radiation Management is an attempt** to eliminate high global warming potential methane: The nanodiamonds may form seeds for light-reflecting noctilucent clouds in the stratosphere. They become a light colored energy-reflecting layer when brought down to the Earth by snow and rain. That keeps the planet cooler."

They were walking aft. "Why watch a video on coral reef extinction when we have you Mr. MacDonald?" said Robinson. "Explain more - why don't you later, when we have time. Right now I'd like to know what this behemoth is doing 100 feet off my bow."

"We don't have a lot of time, actually..." pressed Trevor. "If they have commenced HAARP transmission systems, then they are able to electronically vibrate the strong ionospheric electric current that feed down into the polar areas in *least*-evasive methods..."

"meaning, what?" asked the Captain.

Trevor took him aside for some confidentiality. "They're trying to directly eliminate the buildup of methane in those critical regions: But there's a problem..."

"Sir." yelled out Sweeny. "She nodded too Sir... She recognizes us by 10°."

"Ok. That's her." affirmed Robinson.

He turned to Trevor. "Care to have coffee with me in my quarters and explain a few things to me now? What's the problem...?"

"If they are probing with transmission signals..." said Trevor "Then *they've* already started a countdown."

Robinson's face went pale.

* *

Washington DC

"So what I want you to ask yourselves…" said Amanda pacing the full width of the classroom with chalk in hand "Is there cause for civil disobedience here, or just Revolutionary War? Was this patriotism, pure and simple… Or more? And if so, why? For what purpose? How do you define the differences of persuasion?"

One hand shot up. "Professor Wells, where does it say that the African race was present on this scene, and why were slaves given their freedom by Cornwallis?"

Amanda put down her chalk and patted off the dust. "At Yorktown - and that would be a few years on, the notion of stealing the enemy's means of resupply and productivity was a venerated Roman tactical strategy of war: Take out the labor base, and you have your enemy confounded. Take out their provisions and supplies, and you have your enemy immobilized. Stem the food and water of a city besieged, and you starved out your enemy."

She smiled, then continued "… The African slave contributed to the early American story, if not in high manner, then in countless ways of selfless labor and support. Willingly or not, their efforts propelled the new world to early economic success following the Revolution. And even before. So to say that the early American history had no contribution made by the black race is in error. However, it also important to remember that until the middle of the 17th century, *all* of white Europe was still a slave society by default -

unless inherited. Individuals' liberation came gradually, throughout history, and at great cost..."

The African American student grinned, and her white neighbor poked at her shoulder for a tease.

Amanda was teaching a course at St. Mary's College of Maryland, a university campus set on the oldest historical site of early colonial settlement.

Here a museum had flourished, as had ship construction of early vessels. They moored at the dock and turned their sails to the Chesapeake Bay for tourists. A tri-centennial anniversary had celebrated the beginnings of colonial British America.

Located on the tidal shores of Southern Maryland this small, liberal education college held a reputation for excellence. Amanda's daughter Sandra, was enrolled in the Economics Degree program, had chosen it as her preferred college. She then joined the sailing team.

The two events were mutually exclusive.

Amanda's reluctance to impinge on Sandra's independence at college was the reason she declined the invitation to teach there, in fact. However, Sandra persuaded her, citing the need for good Faculty on campus. They came to an agreement. Amanda conceded to accept the post of lecturing professor for evening classes for one semester only. So she drove from Washington DC to St. Mary's campus on Thursday nights.

Sandra had quarters on campus. When her mother came down as Faculty, she agree to babysit Gwyneth for a couple of hours while Amanda taught class.

Truth was, Sandra loved seeing Gwynie. The excuse was fine at first. That is, until half Sandra's class took a shine to the child and stayed with Sandra while she did so: Gwynie, evidently became everybody's 'home-life' visitor.

In winter weeks, they took over a small student lounge with Sandra, playing a Disney movie on the TV for Gwynie as she drew her pretty pictures under their influence to emulate modern art in charcoal; or medieval imagery in crayon - depending on which scholar was in the room.

As the dogwood blooms appeared in Spring and Bay heated up, the campus was vibrant with interesting flower beds; trees and lawns, such that they went outdoors and settled on the gentle green slopes that rolled down to the sandy and shallow beach where boating events and waterside sports occurred at the boathouse and pier.

For Amanda and Gwynie, driving down to the college was always a cheerful excursion, if a long drive away. So Amanda would prepare to leave earlier in the day with stops planned.

 A quick visit to the Homestead Gardens for plants, flowers or gifts to take home. Then a stop at the Rosewood Horse Stables where Lilly, Amanda's friend, kept a barn of horses either in training or readying for travel to exhibition events – something which Gwyn really liked to see. A stop for a bite to eat followed, usually at a delightful Amish Restaurant of Southern Maryland where homemade jams, fruits and vegetables could be added to their pantry.

They knew when they were getting close to their destination as they drove down along the Chesapeake Bay to Southern Maryland, passing Calvert Cliffs and its massive Nuclear Power Plant; then Patuxent River Naval Air Station where fast incoming jets and military vehicles swirled with activity, and finally, Technology

Park, home to some of the advanced defense research corporations in the world. But that's where the roads suddenly dwindled into rural lanes for quaint hamlet-like tidal inlets where first landed the early settlers of America, perhaps wondering if this were viable ground to plant...

Chesapeake evenings could cast lengthening shadows of blue and green hues along narrow roads. But for crickets and summer frogs across extended house lawns, night could follow easily in these parts.

 Gwyneth, having been rocked asleep in the rear, would sit up and now eagerly passing her hands along the front seat's head-rest in anticipation of jumping out for Sandra.

Evidently, they kept secrets.

Sandra had told Gwynie that she was a 'water-baby' and could be taken out on the coaches' boat for the Thursday evening practices of the sailing team. Dubbed 'the gorgeous gang of fearless college sailors' the sailing team comprised of Sandra's friends.

The team had provided several alumina for rankings in World Games, Olympics, National College Competitions and World competition standing. Both the Women's and the Men's teams populated every class boat.

Thursday nights were sometimes varied. Arriving earlier than usual, Amanda and Gwyn often sat on the lawns of the docks and waited for Sandra to finish. The setting sun could spread a path of diamonds across the water, softly scented by tidewater marsh grass, and be punctuated only by songbird.

Contemplating history, Amanda saw why colonists fought so hard for the right to settle here. And no wonder the Imperial Crown defended this territory in revolution: Surrounded by endless fields of tobacco and rich crops, here was the crucible of early colonial trade overseas for the Empire. Here, everything was dreamy.

Amanda was preparing to teach a class.

* *

Captain Robinson had two Russian officers on board the *NR-2* as guests. They were dinning together in his quarters, Trevor seated to his right, his Exec Officer to his left.

The two submarines had been operated in tandem for four days: In shallow seas, transport from one submersible ship to another was not uncommon. Both were Research Vessels and designed for contingencies, including extravehicular salvage and rescue.

Further, a surface ship was hovering not far from hailing distance, USS *Cherokee* - her most recent message sent by radio transmission just patched through to Captain Robinson.

He stood up and looked at Trevor, the message easily bothering him for a thousand different reasons. He said "The *Cherokee* had sprung a leak and requests mission-ET remaining for return to harbor."

Robinson turned to his guests, one a scientist, another a senior office of the Soviet Navy. "How long do we have to complete the job down here gentlemen?"

"Three days..." started the one Russian Commander.

Robinson relayed the message up. The response was immediate: "I have two days left up here *maximum*."

"Stand by..."

It didn't need to be said, but they all knew it was the added weight she was taking onboard. The *Cherokee* was hardly a new ship.

"Can we do this *two* days?" Robinson asked quietly.

The Russian Officer had his mouth full of baked beans and ham. When he stopped chewing he said "Two, then...If we work hard."

Robinson returned the message to the *Cherokee*. "Remain engaged as long as you can Captain. Inform of your status every six..."

The situation was quickly unfolding with some alarm, the dinner cleared away and weather charts spread out before them.

Finally Robinson's Exec Officer spoke up. "The weather is getting bad up there: Their point of critical mass may jeopardize the mission, and very suddenly."

Robinson eyed him with the look of men who liked the comfort of round tables and advisors. This was, by definition, a research and reconnaissance mission. But at sea it was the job of the Executive Officer by default to immediately outline the worst-case scenarios for possible decisions.

Robinson understood. They were at sea. This research mission had now become a defense mission, and would need Washington's attention for an upgrade and update of status.

"The conditions are not good down here, either." said the Alex Ulsie, the scientist. "I need to start *my* work." he said.

"Not until our primary mission is completed, I'm sorry Alex..." said Robinson.

"No. No..." he smiled politely. "I understand completely. It's just that *time* is not on our side..."

As they vacated, Robinson turned to his Russian guests "May I have a word with you privately, please?"

Later, Alex took Trevor aside. "It's worse than we thought."

Trevor invited him to his cabin.

"The Ridge is opening up."

"The tremors...?"

"It's not the tremors that are a problem. It's the methane release. It's as bad as the Siberian Shelf. We need to engage in geoengineering of SRM on scale not before anticipated."

"I informed the Captain that you might have begun your SRM. It's not yet fully sanctioned, you know..."

"The Arctic is warming rapidly. Much faster than global warming. The sea ice volume is dropping off a cliff..."

"What are you saying?"

"I'm saying that we may have a collapse in sea ice within twelve months..."

Trevor looked at him for a long time. He knew the facts. He took out his notepad and listened carefully. "What is the sequence of events following, Alex?"

"Once the sea ice collapses, we breakdown the shelters for important marine food chain; that creates immediate climate disruption and weather extremes in the Northern Hemisphere." He paused.

"Go on." admonished Trevor.

"...Then we see loss of reflective capacity from sea ice and the Greenland ice-sheet melts. Permafrost covering most of the Northern Hermisphere including permafrost under the Arctic Ocean also melts...." He took a breath.

"...Once we've accelerated the release of methane, weather goes into "global weirding." Natural disasters, mudslides, unsustainable vegetation, widespread crop failures, food shortages"

"...Then social and human systems start to collapse..."

"How long?'

"Less than five years, start-to-finish" he said.

Trevor looked at him.

Alex continued. "Yes. You can talk to the politicians. But once the sea ice collapses, it's the beginning of the end..."

"Wait... There's more?"

"I just heard from the Max Planck Institute for Meteorology in Hamburg, Germany. The oceans are already becoming more acidic – absorbing increasing volumes of carbon dioxide from the atmosphere to form carbonic acid.

"Sulphur?"

"Yes. But beyond the earth's radiation budget..."

"Did you inform the Captain?"

The Scientist looked down. "He has a enough on his mind...He doesn't need our issues."

"I see. How much time do you need, now?" said Trevor.

There was a knock on the door. Robinson. "Everything ok?" he asked.

"Yes. We're putting together a time frame" said Trevor.

"I'm re-doubling the schedule. We'll use the manipulator arm and each send out a team of EVA divers...That should speed things up." said Robinson. "Will that help?"

"Is it safe?"
"Not really..." He looked at them both "I don't exactly have a choice. Mercifully, we are not a great depths here on this shelf."

He looked back at them. "Let's hope the *Cherokee* holds up."

Trevor turned to Alex. "Get your gear. Start tonight. Work on the seafloor immediately with the others and plant your research probes swiftly. Possible?"

"Yes. I have two helpers..."

"Fine. I'll inform the Captain. Stay of their way with their task." said Trevor.

* *

1774, Colony of Maryland

The ship stood off, freshly voyaged from London.

The harbor could shoal up easily. Especially in the Fall. The wind could rise from the Northwest and send every anchorage to swing on her tether.

The *Peggy Stewart* was leaking water at her seams. Increasingly, yards of heavy cordage soaked in tar sat coiled on her ageing decks. Overboard, the vessel seeped, her timbers soaken. From her hull, she developed a growing dark puddle of tar oil, her waterline low in the water. Tomorrow she would approach the dock and be unburdened of her cargo.

All day in the town, as usual, there were those who passed by in their covered wagons, including Masters, Pursers, Merchants, Bankers, Lawyers, Agents and Tavern maids. Especially pretty ladies wearing cloaks and gowns who knew that onboard the *Peggy Stewart* were boxes of china, finery, ribbon and silk and sugar and tea.

The situation was getting worse abroad. Inside the Taverns there was much to say. London traders were dunning Maryland debtors with high interest charges. Worse, London retired paper bills issued in the 1750s. There were no metal coin to be had in circulation.

The planters of Maryland saw depressed prices of grain. Glasgow trading houses - all of them falling into failure, one after the other due to London bankers, were now indebted to Dutch bankers who provided the prevailing uppermost credit. The Dutch demanded of the London currency houses payment in cash, calling in their Financial Notes of Credit.

It roiled the markets of trade, shipping and export across the Empires. It caused taxes the rise. Bankers, merchants, families and factories of labor were falling into ruin daily. The wars, the wars of Europe costly with soldiers left in the field to forage and fight at the same time...The colonies were uprising.

The lampooning and pamphleteers recording such demise could be hilarity itself where it not that Europe was sinking into a Depression; disease and plague no longer dormant in the shadows...

These were bad times in London, all sailors said.

As for the rest of the party in the Tavern, they complained of Boston, New York, and Philadelphia: They played at Landlordism, 'tenantry of the colonial countryside.' Emulating traditions of British agrarian territorial patrons, all of them.

 Upper and lower classes in the local colonial newspapers confronted each other with rancor: Wealthy merchants were still making their fortunes on trans-Atlantic commerce - a ruling elite dominating Colonial General Assemblies and embracing a plantation culture.

"And Oy, what about all 'em religion palavering?" added Tavern maids: "Bringin' all them immigrants, 'filtratin' them ranks with religious dissenters calling it a *Great Awakening*."

 "Aye like the great *awakening* you give me ... in the middle of the night?" offered one as she wailed off with her jug."

They sensed tension in the air. It was still warm for October, inside the Tavern even hotter.

But it was true. Religious diversity roiled the colonists. Lutherans, Calvinists, Mennonites, Moravians and some Catholics and Jews joined Anglicans, Congregationalists, Presbyterians, Baptists and Quakers, all of them shaping colonial character and vying for the hearts and minds of new thinkers to *"bring light out of darkness."*

...As if the *Peggy Stewart* in the background held some sway in their new world. They ignored her.

But some in the corner of the Tavern listened. They did not laugh. They did not have to. They had done their deed: They were the smaller planters, like John Hall and Matthias and Rezin Hammond - longtime members of the Country Party in the General Assembly with homes in Annapolis and plantations in Anne Arundel County.

More than others, they were struggling to pay their debts; adorn their women with luxury items and bedeck themselves with outward signs entitling them to 'patronage,' the demonstrable class gift of assured credit.

They had distributed Handbills. They would gather that night for a Meeting.

They consulted together before the meeting. There was a plan. They would take the town by surprise. In the face of increasing pressure from London creditors, they pledged to issue a charter document the *"Annapolis Resolves"*...

The plan was this. If they *ALL* abstained from paying their dues to Crown Agents... then as a collective they could coerce their creditors...

Not like the *Peggy Stewart* here, for example. As a carrier of taxable tea cargo, it continued to enrich its owners with goods imported because it had paid it's full tax dues to the Crown before leaving London.

"Non-importation and Non-exportation" they called the plan.   This amounted to no-collections.   Not by debtors. Not by the Crown. Not by any party.

-Nor any owner merchants of ships.

Today, they had decided to take action. Here was the *Peggy Steward* with 2,000 pounds of tea aboard.

 The sight of the *Peggy Steward* offended them because the owner of the ship, Anthony Steward, believed that no debts should be denunciated. He did not embrace the plan.

If he had already paid the detested duties on every pound of tea in the ship's hull, it was *only* because he was fully able to pay his debts when the ship was unloaded.

Hall and Hammond held their public meeting October 19th. 1774.

The crowd gathered. Hammond, Charles Ridgley, two young Anne Arundel physicians, Charles Warfield and Ephraim Howard incited the crowd with speeches.

They became fervent, abusive. They would tar and feather people like Stewart, even burn his vessel...

The crowd roared in protest and growing anger. They marched towards the house where Stewart and his family slept, their intentions yet uncertain. It was still arid and tinder hot that day from a lingering summer.

 They roused Stewart from his home and escorted him angrily towards his ship.

Chase and Charles Carroll, leadership of the General Assembly as large landholding planters, were alerted. There was trouble in the streets...

They ran out to address the crowd. The crowd was out of control. Charles Carroll stood up to appealed to the crowd. Chase also.

It was no good. They were being overwhelmed...

In that case, said the two leaders... at the very least, they pleaded, "Gentlemen...I beg you...a *lesser* punishment ...*For the name of God.*"

Whose God?

The mob flashed into violence.

Stewart, now terrorized, begged for his life and agreed to their terms. He agreed to set afire his own ship, the *Peggy Stewart.*

The tar and coiled ropes took to the fire...

The flames took to the timbers and filled the harbor. Fire plumes of dark oakum leapt into the sky and covered the town with smoke with such ferocity that it struck fear into the hearts of all, its implications clear. Then the tar-caulked timbers became the incendiary and burned, blistering long into the night and well into the next day...

"*If this is Liberty, If this is Justice*" wrote John Galloway to his father in his nightshirt and pen under the lighted taper of his attic window, "*it ... makes all men of property reflect with horror on the present situation: to have their lives and properties at the disposal and mercy of a Mob is Shocking indeed.*"

The *Peggy Stewart* and her cargo sank to the bottom of the harbor. Little was known of the amounts of the cargo and its damage.

A Revolution against the King, they explained. Perhaps.

But a Revolution against the elite of their own: A quiet *civil* revolution fomented into a national agenda against the greatest patron of all - the King of England.

A civil revolution incited by mobs overtaken by debt, greed and jealousy.

* *

Amanda popped two pieces of toast in the toaster, and reached for the morning newspaper.

Today was a big day. The final day of the Sub-Committee Hearing. Sarah was to deliver her conclusion. The investigation in the Hill had been partially presented, then adjourned for other more pressing matters, evidently.

Today the meeting was reconvened, and would wrap up the questioning for her client, they promised her. Amanda's Research Firm had worked tirelessly to prepare their client for the Hearing, and now finally it would be over.

She would take a break, she decided. Enjoy the weekend, perhaps. She looked at herself in the mirror before leaving: One more day of work, then a weekend away.

Thank God for the house that she and Trevor shared since his tour of duty as Ambassador in Washington DC... It was a godsend. Especially now that work had brought her back to this side of the Atlantic for a few months.

In addition, there was the weekend retreat on the Chesapeake Bay. A farm on the Eastern Shore where they had shared years of happiness fishing, eating, and gathering as family.

She paused. She missed him.

Trevor was gone so much of the time, it was her work load in Washington that kept her busy. That, and a desire to offer stability for the children in a lifestyle that included shuttling between two continents as a matter of norm. The children, who had both completed elementary school in America, were attending boarding schools in Great Britain. Adam was soon to sit for his A level exams, and on his way to University near London.

Only Gwynie was with her, now attending kindergarten. Something Trevor wanted, now that he was retired. *Supposedly.*

Amanda had received a visit from Matthias, the Firm's Attorney earlier in the week. Their research work was now becoming demanding: The case for the defense lay spread all over Amanda's desk on Massachusetts and 24th Street.

Amanda would dedicate herself entirely to helping – just as soon as she was done with Sarah's Haring before the Senate Sub-Committee.

Matthias agreed to wait. But he did explain it in brief.

The suit was brought their client by a developer who cited possible hazard to his beachfront should there be an oil spill. It was property located along what had been known as an environmentally sensitive area on the Northeastern Coast of New England.

Moreover, the community objected. It was a frivolous suit, since nothing had occurred. But it was filed as a Brief to the Environmental Agencies involved - something clearly induced by Lauren for Papendopolous to undermine the credibility of the Sterling Group, one of Trevor's enterprises affiliated with his bank.

"Why target *me*?" Amanda said later to Rebecca on the phone.

"She's had it in for our bank for a long time. Once you showed up at the Annual Meeting, she figured you were a force to contend with. Anything to damage your credibility would be good for someone like her…" explained Rebecca.

 "She doesn't know us. Nor does she know what we do here at my Research Firm."

"She knows. Trust me. That's what barracudas do…"

"I'll alert Matthias."

"Yes. That's what Trevor would want you to do…"

The matter was worrisome.

The young Intern Jacob had been working on that project when he died. That was the last thing that Papendopolous needed to know about.

Not only was it necessary as a project for work, but the boy had died while on a field examination in that area while doing preliminary research.

* *

Amanda received a call from her office.

Matthias was asking for her about a task that would normally have been Trevor's to take on.

"I'm sorry to burden you with this" he said.

He asked Amanda to find an answer to critical information. The legal case had taken a turn. She had to speak to an Admiral Argueta. There were questions related to Trevor's bank that needed answers.

"Enquiries in the matter of environmental compliances..." he said "about Trevor's activities?"

What was all that about?

* *

Admiral Argueta disliked entering the gates of the Whitehouse.

They recognized him at the guard station. Security had long ago learned that duplicity was amongst the many tricks mastered by an enemy.

Argueta smiled barely.

Come to think of it, nobody at the Pentagon particularly liked being called to the White House for meetings. It suited careerists little - politics fleeting and the public fickle. Especially after the last Administration which had turned everything on its head as if were an alien occupation force. It would take a generation to get over a betrayal of conventions that the Pentagon held sacred.

 Worse though, stemming from bad policy, were oppressive taxes that had induced depressed economies and damaged working Americans.

While it was the job of the State Department to identify trouble spots, it was the new job of the Pentagon to strategize counter-measures: Counter-measures that met with the new tools of warfare, like software rather than hardware. Or, individual intelligence over Armies. Or public dissemination over secret acts.

But Arguetta was neither deluded nor distracted for a minutes. Politics or policy notwithstanding, American defense was designed for one thing, the free flow of free market capitalism.

He understood that any small device - with terrorizing destructive force, could cause serious damage to global economies, especially in a world showing signs of little sympathy or support for Allies and Friends.

Truth was, issues had become too costly; unmanageable, and unsalable. Compliance was the new norm.

One instrument of alienation that besieged them the most however, increasingly, was the one thing that this White House was tampering with, and this worried him.

"Morning Sir."

"Good Morning"

...was the economy.

...Half the country seemed out of work; the Government out of funds; and the markets out of customers. Intelligence was already showing the tears in social fabric that followed.

... Sure, there was *political* capital. Venture capital even. But little that the population could embrace as new vision and new industry. He was worried. For the first time in history, this problem was beyond the Americans to solve.

For the first time, this meant a national defense that knew not the face of its enemy.

"This way Sir, if you will..." offered the staffer

His mind would not stop roving. It was the national debt owed to foreign governments that was worrying, the White House was too free with their overtures, he thought.

He took his place at the conference table after a solid round of salutations. Everyone else in the room knew it.

Except for one, evidently. The same man who came into office on the staff of the President following a political campaign that many thought had been manipulated. His name was Bill Baxter.

He walked in and offered on the overhead screen a presentation of the event that just occurred.

The Chief of Staff walked in. "Hello Arguetta. I'm glad to see you... We want you to be in on this matter. There may be some connections to other issues..." He took his place. "Please carry on." he said, nodding to Baxter.

"So far, the Jack-Up Rig that blew up can be said to have had little damage to the sea..." He clicked the next few satellite charts.

"In this image, we see her approaching this quadrant...But judging from the conflagration that is associated with the explosion, we must suppose that all was not related to the incendiary device itself. Here, I introduce Dr. Hensen for more information..."

"Yes...Err, hello. " said a white haired Government Contractor standing up.

 "What we seem to have here is a greater spread of damage that looks as if an oil spill were catching on fire. But as we know, this Rig was not yet pumping. In fact, there is no oil around it all. If anything, it was a dry rig that was blown up for no reason at all other than to call attention to the concept embraced by the rig.

"A political statement, then?" said Baxter.

"Possibly" said Henson politely "God knows we have enough enemies thinking up ways to embarrass us using key and vital industries..." He paused, looking at the image.

"What we don't need is another offshore drilling debacle..." interceded someone else.

"But look at this..." Henson's thoughts and eyes were focused on something no one else the room could see.

 "In *this* image you have an explosion on the rig. In the next image you have what we see here. But if you time the sequence, the fall-out of the explosion is rapid. *Too rapid...*" he said, lost to his thought as if formulating a conclusion.

"So what are you saying?"

"We'd need to look at this more carefully. It's as if something were *already* in place for half a mile beneath it, something that could easily have triggered the explosion..."

"Or...become triggered by the explosion?"

"Something that we clearly don't see. It isn't oil. It isn't...Well, I'm hesitant to speculate without further examination... It's invisible to the naked eye."

"Surely you have some idea - even if you amend, please give us the benefit of your thoughts Dr. Henson" insisted Baxter.

Henson took off his glasses. He turned to the table. "Honestly, if I didn't know better...then I'd say would be a highly flammable methane gas."

"Meth...What does *that* mean?"

"It means the sea is seeping high quantities of methane gas..."

"So, if it wasn't sabotage..." questioned Baxter.

"I wouldn't rule that out..." said Aquetta.

"No. Perhaps not. But it would only take a spark to set alight a zone of concentrated methane gas. Let alone kill everyone around it."

"So, what are you implying then, if not sabotage? Bad management by another oil company...?" began Baxter, rehearsed in the way of these things.

Henson just stared at him, and the room was quiet. No one said anything.

"Global warming?" said Argueta.

"Yes." said Henson. "But hardly in the way we are accustomed to using that terminology...."

The words just popped out of his mouth, and he regretted them instantly.

It was politely done, of course. But the implications couldn't be louder than if someone rang a church bell. The situation, as they put it, had now become a crisis. Not just your political pabulum about energy policy that saved the planet. No. This was America's worse fear: The Arctic was melting too rapidly. Moreover, the sea was delivering toxic amounts of methane gas. The two posed a danger.

True, a warning, as explained by Henson. But something else lay just beneath the thinking: Something that exposed the imponderable. The frozen Arctic - as those familiar with strategic defense understood, defended America's northern border.

What lay ahead would have terrifying implications, and if the White House could render moot the Pentagon's mission to defend her Nation.

Argueta stopped. He looked up. He was met with silence. In the silence it could heard loud and clear what everyone was thinking: What hampered the White House, regardless, was *indebtedness.*

Indebtedness of a Nation that could be challenged with serious and devastating threats of annihilation. Forget the Constitution, the flag or elements of obligation that Argueta could dedicate his life to serve.

Arguette made his way out the building.

America was a continent rich in natural and essential resources. Some considered this plunder. This President was not interested in tainting his political reputation in exploiting resources. This condition was not conducive to his kind of thinking. This man, decided Argueta, was dangerous as hell, and stubbornly political.

'Hardly in the way we are accustomed to using that terminology' – my Ass.

How about, rather: *Pre-emptive strikes by parties interested in our national resources.*

* *

Chapter Five

They missed him.

Jacob was not down with Barbara. He had been found dead. He had been on an errand of some importance to the Firm in New York, in earnest conducting a task of employment. The job was related to an Environmental Impact Statement required for a Federal Mining Permit: The corporation applying to the Federal Government Mineral Mining Services was a British oil exploration company funded and insured by Sterling Bank, Trevor's company.

The inquest had been held. There was no malfeasance. But no one could understand the cause of death.

It had been seven months now. Barbara was preparing to come down to DC alone.

The Beaux Arts building was located just off Massachusetts Avenue on 18th and 24th Street. Built in the 1920s, it was considered a Washington gem. Some called it a townhouse just off Embassy Row on Massachusetts Avenue with the height and stature of a formal brick city residence. But it was more. It had the feel of an independent work of art with space and rooms that articulated Washington as the Nation's Capital.

Many told Amanda Wells how it inspired them to work for her. Mostly they told her how much they loved working for the Firm.

The floors separated the office functions: On the third level were spaces where municipal and institutional contracts required a professional staff of three. They shared four vast rooms between them off the landing.

On the second floor where a small atrium, kitchen and bathrooms had been designed as private quarters, two formal parlor rooms and two rear working rooms served as office space for tasks related to clients overseas, many of them holding the Firm as retainer only.

At the ground level, where a baroque ballroom once filled the building with guests and events, the Firm kept Office Reception quarters for meetings, conferences and consultation with visiting clients. For that, all who entered met with Janice, the Receptionist, who ran the place like a well-orchestrated military outpost: No budgets, no access. No excuses. Thank you.

Beneath them were garden quarters for kitchens, pantries, bathrooms and general rest areas - a favorite place for all things informal, restful and unofficial. A rear door led through the garden and porches to their garages – opposite those of another Embassy which fronted the next street.

Amanda Wells had the topmost floor to herself and could look down the stairwell of the Beaux Arts structure to tell who was in which office working on what: Her Research Firm had multiple contracts going at the same time, and it was all they could do to meet demand. It was how Amanda Wells occupied her time these days as the senior partner of her firm in Washington DC.

Amanda peered over the banister of the top floor of the Beaux Arts townhouse and could see all the way to the foyer, four levels below. Between her two offices – the one to work privately, and the other a conference room, she had to across a small landing.

Normally, since a few of her government projects required security clearance, only her chief personnel had access to that floor. But the Conference room was used for weekly staff meetings. For that, the room was cleared of papers and she invited them all up.

They loved it. Especially since a small side pantry for drinks and coffee came in handy. It made for a close relationship of trust amongst her staff.

Not that Amanda had intended to make her research firm a place for high-level classified material, although they were qualified. But in a city needing quality work and integrity, it was her reputation that brought in more work that she needed.

The building served her well. It was necessary to be close to the center of government, and convenient for her satellite offices in New York. And Barbara.

Barbara was her first and oldest employee. She would remain in New York, and, if necessary holding down the Fort, as she liked to remind Amanda. Barbara and her assistant Jacob managed affairs in two offices, representing the Firm's interests, if sending down work down to Washington to be executed.

Jacob had been their Intern. Jacob, the grandson of one of Barbara's family friends was promised the job, not that he was particularly qualified. But being a student, he could be an Intern.

Son of a Russian ice hockey player, he had enrolled himself in college. And that was good enough for

Barbara. She had used him in her office as an Intern when business was slow.

Above all, she liked to speak Russian with him, a language that she and her family still shared at gatherings. Plus, another advantage to having Jacob, was that he loved to drive. Especially on errands as a courier; and driving down the New Jersey turnpike to Washington with documents that needed same-day deliveries at the Firm. It was most convenient.

When Amanda was on travel with Trevor. She left the run of the Firm to Barbara who would pack an overnight suitcase, and head for Washington to take over.

Barbara, when she came down to Washington to work, seemed to regard the city as a place for quasi recreation. It would include office hours from dawn to lunch; early afternoon excursions downtown for museums, concerts, dinner and evenings out, followed by a meal of some complexity down in the kitchen quarters. Yet the staff barely knew the difference when Amanda was gone, such was the smooth transition of workflow.

It was only when Jacob had started to come down that things got out of hand. He quartered down in the basement. And he loved sports events.

He drove them all crazy - wandering from office to office chewing peanuts and candy wearing jeans and his T-shirt. He switched on every electronic device he could find to view a game, and he talked to his Russian friends in New York on the phone...

They sent him on errands. All day, all over the city as a Courier on errands the small staff of professionals used Jacob as Postman.

He was frequently lost in traffic. On his bike, his helmet strapped on, he gradually got to know the city. Capital Hill. K Street. Georgetown. Foggy Bottom. He even went to Arlington occasionally – a distance that required crossing Memorial bridge and back to the Parkway. Yet no matter whether he cycled to the same offices three times in one day, or wherever they sent him, he always came back grinning.

Pretty soon, they realized he was having a blast.

Jacob, torn between a love for the Capitals Hockey ice-hockey game and the New Yorkers, had run enough errands to endear himself to the staff. "My boss-people of Washington DC" he called them.

Jacob's grandmother had told Barbara that the boy was learning.

Truth was, they were spoiling him with game tickets to the Verizon Center to watch the *Capitals*; or entry fees for game-nights downtown; even membership to the Potomac rowing club; the bicycle club; volley ball on the Mall...

Today they were hard at work on Matthias case. Barbara was sorting through boxes, papers all over the place, even a few personal items left from her last trip down...

Across the landing, in the style of a drawing room with Louis XIV desk and grand piano along with a law library, filing cabinets, sideboards, shelves and boxes, was where Barbara worked.

"So, what have we got..." asked Barbara.

"Matthias says that the community in the law suit, bases their case on the hazards to their environment, citing it as too 'eco-sensitive' to tolerate construction" said Amanda.

"We however…" said Barbara "have found evidence in the records that shows the United States attempting to build a bridge in the area at the turn of the last century, chiefly for railroad use."

"That reshapes the argument…" said Amanda. "If we can prove that 'Progress' was already on the books, then their case for preserving an undisturbed environment 'never before developed' is rendered moot, right?"

"Right."

Barbara was thinking "But if its *coastal* waterline that must define the history of that era, and if the sea-level was higher, then the threshold for 'set-backs' was exceeded. If the sea-level was lower, then the natural shoreline showed no change in two centuries."

They both paused, and a thought hit them both simultaneously.
"That's what the boy was trying to prove, isn't it?" said Barbara.

Amanda nodded. "He must have understood that…" she paused "That's why he went out in a rigged dinghy to image any shoreline fauna that showed older undisturbed vegetation…"

"Right. Until something overwhelmed him, and he lost his ability to handle his boat…He fell overboard, his body sent adrift …Two days later washed up on a beach…" said Barbara. She looked up at Amanda "What would cause that? Why? What happened out there? What was he looking at?"

What Barbara was hunting for was evidence that could crack through the argument for the prosecution. But the incident of Jacob brought them to a pause, inevitably. Even Matthias was getting no further.

Amanda was close to feeling overwhelmed. For two and a half days they had poured over papers, maps, documents, statements. She left to make fresh coffee next door.

"I have it." announced Barbara when she returned.

"What?" said Amanda, hoping that it wasn't one of Barbara's ideas of what should be the case rather than what could be proved.

"Evidence for the defense." she declared "I give you this." she held a postcard.

"What is it?" Amanda looked at the postcard. It was the picture of a ceramic of the 19th century.

Ornate and faded, it resembled a religious icon of the Greek Orthodox Church characteristic of Saints enshrined in celestial bliss. But it wasn't a holy icon. Rather, it was of such poor quality that it looked like...what, a prize in a shooting contest?

"A duck?"

"No. It's a bird." corrected Barbara defensively.

"Ok. A bird then. So what is it doing amongst his papers?" asked Amanda.

"*To the Tsar of the family, your loving grandmother*" read Barbara, turning it over. "Well, maybe it does look like a duck..."

"Umm"

"It is *yellow*, with a beak..."

"*Barbara*?" said Amanda, frustrated. They were getting nowhere.

"Ok...I have no idea. But it was valuable to him, and it's even copied in pencil as an illustration sketch in his notes." She shrugged "Sentimental reasons?"

Amanda groaned. "Okay. So what else have we got amongst his notes?"

Barbara looked up to reposition her dark rimmed glasses further up her nose. "So it's not the most compelling piece of evidence ...I know. But I just know it means something, alright? After all, it was in the box of items he took with him. Right? A box still on the boat when it was recovered..."

Amanda sank into a chair feeling either frustrated or fatigued, she couldn't tell which. Either way, the expression was enough. Barbara was a terrific associate. Full of energy. Ideas. Playfulness. But she was also exhausting. Purposefully, sometimes. And Amanda knew not to argue back. New Yorkers always had to be right.

"Ok. So maybe it's not the world's greatest treasure, but it a sign of ...of...his care" finished Barbara. "It was amongst Matthias' box of things. *Things*, as in evidence for the case he was building"

"Give it here" Amanda stretched out her hand. "I'll check it out..."

And that's where it stayed. Sitting on the sideboard of Amanda's office two weeks after the paperwork was cleared away, copied, a report written and the evidence ready to send to Matthias. Once the boxes were cleared away, Barbara would have left for New York - her own inbox piling up there.

Below her the offices were filling up quickly with other pressing objectives for other clients.
Amanda looked over the balustrade from the top floor, a cell phone headset on her head. She could see all the way down to the entrance of the historic building where a checkered parterre could easily host two Medieval court jesters.

The grand marble steps, appointed with red-runner carpeting, coiled exquisitely up Regency brass railing to surround a cut-crystal chandelier. She saw a hand on the rail – staff, one of her research team ascending steps to the upper offices of the four story Beaux Arts Building. A lovely place to work, they all told her.

But as she was about to ask the receptionist on her cell monitor if Barbara had left any messages, her eyes suddenly narrowed.

"Janice..." she asked into her cell phone earpiece "What is that package at the bottom of the steps...?"

* *

Emergency vehicle sirens wailed through streets as if the prevailing song of the city.

An orange light lit up at the console of the Traffic Controller's Platform of Ronald Reagan National Airport. The potential for danger was always there, but not until it turned red.

At Union Station the trains went on Alert; the Subway and underground traffic connectors flashed. All subways turned amber with warnings-of-delays at all stops of the Nation's Capital.

Equal to a snow storm with the potential to shut down the government, a traffic jam brought everything to a halt in Washngton DC.

Tourists at the Tidal Basin had to wait for their Tour Bus; the National's Baseball game posted a delay, and everywhere the frenetic whistling of Intersection pedestrian police tried to untangle the gridlock with whistles and arm waving notwithstanding.

The city was taken hostage by police sirens, fire trucks, traffic lights and circling helicopters. Washington DC was not a city that took kindly to unknown threats and alarms. Of any kind.

If the security of a building - any building - had been breached with a possible bomb threat, then that was a different conversation. Everybody was angry.

The White House was less than six blocks away.

A bomb squad was parked outside Amanda's building. So was half the city's *Emergency Preparedness Contingent.*

Only when the remote controlled track-wheeled robot backed itself out of her building on an awkward ramp did the police allow Amanda to approach. They had questions. The staff were kept on hold for questions, and the ambulance was on standby for bodily damage. But nobody was hurt. There had been no explosion.

News of traffic delays disseminated across all channels, one TV station even sought some news for New York. But it was tamped down to prevent undue alarm across the airwaves from the Nation's Capital.

Worse. Traffic lights in the city was running slow. A surge of cars had come to a stand still. The evening agendas of millions of commuters, that night, would be delayed or scrubbed.

Amanda was embarrassed beyond measure by the time they were done. Not until the suspicious parcel was considered a non-threat was she was allowed to take calls. The first was from Barbara.

"And I thought New York was bad. *Ugh*." said Barbara, arriving at Grand Central Station. "I called his grandmother..." she said, reception cracking up. "She searched his room...Overnight Delivery?"

A bus roared by.

"Did you receive the Duck?"

* *

It was a yellow bird: On a pedestal of metal forged brass, its tiny shape hardly recognizable in the grime and clumsy moldings that held the thing together.

Supposedly, the branch that held the bird was of a slender nature, for it had been bent and lay awkwardly on the 'tree knot' beneath it, as if such artwork had to be shaped into anything so simplistic. And it gave the bird an off-balanced look, falling off its perch, so to speak.

The post card that they examined in their office was a picture of something real. Something the boy kept at his grandmother's place in New York.

Yes. Barbara was right. It did have something...

What?

Officially, in their decision to extract the threat from the building, the Homeland Security had found an abundance of technical elements present as tell-tale signs for a metallic home-made bomb. And while it was early ascertained by experts, using their technical gear, that the parcel might not have contained a bomb, a 100% degree of certainty was insufficiently determined.

From a distance, the man smirked at the news. It was easy enough to place a package in the Central Hall of the building.

This was not a threat.

* *

Congress was not yet in Session.

"Ms. Delaney. We have a question for you." said the Senator.

The resistance was palpable, but Amanda knew that unless you allowed for these objections to vent, the matter could be entirely suppressed and fester, unresolved. Better to suffer headwinds than to send the entire Subcommittee Statement to the bottom of the Potomac River where Senators had a way of sending things they didn't like.

"I didn't expect a return call" wailed Sarah over the phone. "They've called me in again to testify further."

Amanda took the news like a man. Together, they dedicated a full day of questions and answers in preparation. Plus, they called in another Attorney Bob Erickson to accompany Sarah at the questioning. Matthias came as well.

But they all knew that Sarah, a well qualified and steady lawyer, would attend to Sub-committee objections resolutely. She had an innate third-sense of timing, and she was the best person for the job at the moment. Still... Hot seats at a Senate Hearing was not for the faint-of-heart.

 "Look," said Matthias "It's not a court of law..." "More like a damned tribunal" interrupted Sarah

"Right." he smiled. "It's more a case of being on the record for public show. That's all. For them it's worth political capital. For you, it's a few hours of discomfort."

"Say *that* again." agreed Sarah.

"At least it's over" sighed Amanda.

"Yes" concurred Matthias. "You walked through a deep valley, Ladies. But you pulled it off. Well done. You satisfied their questions with your testimony in good standing..." He turned to Erickson "Your company came out ok."

"We did indeed" said Erickson, shaking hands.

Later that evening, as Sarah stepped into the cab she turned to Amanda. "Thanks...for everything." Before closing the cab door she added "I'll call you."

Amanda waved.

* *

Trevor was reading the report on his laptop screen. He didn't much like what he was looking at. But Alex had insisted he review the data. The geological record was pointing to a destructive level of Methane.

The Ridge geyser had turned into a dark and angry plume of methane rising from the seafloor and growing in diameter.

At least their primary mission had been complete and the *Cherokee* had turned back. They were still on the seafloor of the Arctic.

The deal was to complete scientific research together. But Robinson was getting anxious by the hour. The lights flickering with tremors and electrical static. It made him extremely uncomfortable that both submarines were in such dangerous proximity. Especially considering the cargo they were lifting off the bottom.

Trevor read on.

"Although carbon dioxide persists much longer in the atmosphere, the Intergovernmental Plan on Climate Change stated that methane was a full 72 times more powerful than it should be. Already, it competes with releases of gas build-up to the most catastrophic wipe-outs of life in planetary history..."

It was time to talk to Robinson, decided Trevor. They should break silence on the matter.

He sent a message to meet...*As if Robinson didn't have enough on his mind.*

"Tonight. At 2100 hrs" came the reply.

Trevor reviewed the material again. It seemed unfeasible, even if the opinion of a respected scientist.

"...Data closely linked to British documentaries of Permian and PETM mass extinction events..."

It took Trevor by surprise. The enormity of the report was alarming. He gathered his thoughts for a political recommendation, and would send a coded message...

He called Alex in again. "How long, Alex... do *you* think before we have a this – quote '*massive explosive release of Methane?*'"

Alex did not want to speculate. It was too awful to contemplate. It was not what good scientists did, he said. He looked down and fiddled.

"Alex...?"

The scientist looked up at him, opened his mouth then hesitated. "I know what you are thinking, Trevor...But this has nothing to do with saving my professional reputation already."

Trevor placed the clipboard in front of him, the newest telex information pinned on it.

"Tell me Alex. *How long before you think we have a Methane Release?*"

"*I don't know.*" snapped Alex. He walked against the wall, frustrated.

"Alex, please... We aren't playing up here. If we have to warn the world, then so be it. Our lives are not indispensable. We have a duty to perform....So tell me."

"What do you want me to say? '*We have an extinction event to occur next week at 8.oo pm... after the dinner, or ...before the concert?*' How crazy does that sound?"

Trevor waited. He leaned forward against the table and folded his arms.

"It could happen tomorrow..." said Alex softly. "It could happen next year. But it will definitely happen... in my lifetime."

Trevor looked at him. Alex was at least seventy years old.

* *

Amanda was washing her hair when she heard the news on the Weather channel. Tom Whitaker of ATTV Channel News:

> *"An earthquake with a magnitude of 4.5 hit the Gakkel Ridge at a depth of 2 km this morning at 0600. The location is shown on the map showing its proximity to the Arctic Circle. Some scientists ascribe the frequency of these earthquakes along the Gakkel Ridge to be related to global warming wherein the earth's crust is expanding by forces just beneath its surface."*

Amanda's thoughts went to Trevor. Was he there by chance? Was his duty aboard a naval vessel placing him in harm's way?

Was this predictable, frequent, or did it take them by surprise? She sat to watch the rest of the news report.

> *"With us today we have two meteorologists following the stories of the Arctic news along with Dr.Roger Sanders, our weather channel expert. What do you make of these earthquakes Dr. Sanders?"*

> *"I am concerned" he said "The above image shows large methane releases over the Gakkel Ridge, it is a fault line that crosses the Arctic Ocean between the northern tip of Greenland and the Laptev Sea. Methane readings registered as high as 2395 ppb at 586 mb, - an altitude that shows high methane readings originating from the Arctic Ocean. I do believe we may have a crisis in our hands..."*

> *"Thank you Dr. Sanders. We'll be back in just a short break. Stay tuned, ladies and gentlemen."*

Amanda watched at least a half dozen commercials. The station came back, then played straight into another set of commercial breaks. Finally a commentary on the local weather.

She waited. Policy news about Flood Insurance; more headlines from Washington DC and then more commercials. The program closed with a story about a plane crash in the sub-Saharan desert, four people died. Dr. Sanders never came back. Amanda knew why.

Like all others, he had been gagged. Alarmists were not welcome on national TV channels. It was bad for business. Bad for advertising. Bad for TV Stations and bad news for the Hedge Funds that owned them.

She turned off the station and tuned into her playlist.

* *

A sleek Limousine turned the corner and stopped at the foot of a building that rose thirty six feet above street level. The wind was whipping into Brookfields Avenue at First Canadian Place.

A woman stepped out, followed by a man, both wearing dark overcoats and stylish scarves to protect them from the weather. Sun glasses obscured her face, hair in wind-driven riot.

From her office suite at the 32nd floor, Lauren Papendopolous looked out her window. She could see clear across the city of Toronto. She stood at what must have once been a platform precipice when under construction, before glass walls closed in the building. At its highest levels, the building thinned into a tower.

She stood barely breathing. Even as the grey clouds cast her profile in reflection off the glass. She stood in darkness, a silhouette caged in a transparent tower. She wore a black Lanvin dress and polished heels, her leanness the dominant contour of her body.

She would not have the lights on, she had said to the cohort who escorted her to her floor. She entered her office, the wide double doors slowly shutting behind her with a soft click.

She would not be long in her office at all. In fact, she would leave very shortly, she said. It was Sunday. Her desk clear of much paperwork, thanks to her staff. Or her janitors, she didn't know which.

Alone inside her glass cage, she looked around her, her breath shallow, eyes half closed.

Her office was vast and sterile. A lavish ornamental display of orchid, positioned at mid-center on a stand in her ultra modern office, sickened her. This was a ritual she forced herself to do. This was the cost of climbing up the corporate ladder. An office at the top spot of the building.

She closed her eyes. She was afraid of heights, and she was rarely there. She had to demonstrate that she appeared at her corporate offices, on occasion.

She worked out of her Townhouse on 2st and M streets. With only one student for a secretary. There, she held no office meetings. No office parties. No office personnel. And no office camaraderie.

Still, she kept her office here, just to show that she could hold the standard. But not for very long. And only once a week. She chose Sundays. Her Assistant was a young man who escorted her to her office, and would tend to collecting messages and memos left for her by her staff to pick-up when she came on the weekends.

He would be sitting outside her office. That way, the word got around that she was truly, in circulation.

But when panic gripped the claustrophobic woman, little beads of perspiration rimmed her hairline; dampened her neck and made her makeup run. Her face could look ruinous in just one second, without notice, and without control. This she would avoid at all cost, and she used the private quarters attached to her office for refreshing before remerging.

The last six months had not been easy. The memories of it all raced through her body like ice and left her wet, sodden, overwhelmed and helpless. Every single day had been a struggle to regain her footing. And by God, she was not about to lose it again.

She took a step back from the glass wall. The city receded to her. Her fear of heights remained unconquered. But she had managed to mask it.

The facts that surrounding the rise of her career to this very floor of the Canadian stock exchange, where she belonged, would remain silent. How could she forget them? Their memories came back to her with overwhelming clarity, and often without warning.

The phone rang, and she jumped. It rang again, and she approached it. She punched at the speaker, still standing, her fingers tightly twisted together.

"What is it, Sonny?" His name was Gary Summers.

"Well...err.." he cleared his throat. "The company that reported the oil spill is actually one of ours. Rather, one we own from an acquisition some ten years back..."

She said nothing.

"Yes Ma'am. You err...asked me to check while I was here?" he said, his young voice loud and resolute.

He was an American. She hated Americans. She said nothing. Besides, she knew all this.

"The Oil Field Lease shows that Bottom Rights are owned by a British company insured and capitalized by a Bank that owns the Canadian stock exchange. And that, as you know, *we* own." he finished triumphantly.

"Really?" she managed.

"...Oh No. I'm sorry...I got that wrong..."

 She hated bunglers. They caused problems. She sighed audibly.

"...It owns *us*. I mean," he corrected. "The leased rights are owned by a British company, right? And *that* company is insured by a bank that owns the Canadian stock exchange...." he said.

Idiot, she thought. She disliked being jerked around - Let alone misinformed. She felt angry. "Our bank?...Don't be a fool. Nobody owns us but our own stock holders."

"No, err...the Exchange." he said "The Canadian stock exchange that...that...err owns us." clearly he was flustered at having offended her. Worse, he'd have to repeat it all for her, with lightning sparks coming through the intercom...

"Give me *everything*." she said, and slammed down the phone so hard he heard it all the way outside her office where he sat.

"Who is the Principle?" she said, coming out of her office.

"A Mr. Trevor MacDonnell, President of the Board"

"Give me a full profile on him can you?" she barked.

Within minutes she was striding passed him at the outer office and opening the giant glass doors into the hall for the elevator. He was still ripping off sheets from a printer that showed the company information of the oil field. He managed a quick reach for a white catalogue-sized envelope; stuffed the materials inside and rushed to join her as she stepped into the elevator, his coat left at his seat. He knew to call in advance for the Limousine, perhaps already waiting below: The rear door should be held open for its passenger descending now, he hoped.

He never saw her face. She turned away as the elevator descended, and he would have recoiled at the sudden paleness and dark eyes full of fear. He did see her clutching the envelope as her hand went up to her forehead to push away some hair. She held her silk black scarf to her mouth, as if to buffet against the wind outside.

She stepped into the Limousine finally, dismissing him standing on the curb, sans jacket in a cold blow with pencil and pad in hand to take notes if it pleased her...

He did know that she had spent the night at the ground floor of the Five Star Grand Hotel. A perk, he decided for the half hour of office attendance per week. In the morning she might reappear in grand fashion, perhaps even with a cup of coffee in her hand. Someone on staff invariably would see her in the hotel lobby, and her presence in the building would be reported as if it were breaking news.

* *

A meal was sent to her room. Then a cart arrived as Room Service with Coffee, Perrier, Drinks and cocktails.

She did not look for entertainment. She did not look much at the file, even. But she had to make decisions now.

She was alone contemplating that night about what had happened. She had to take matters into her own hands. How could she scrub it from her mind? Now she must act with calculated precision.

It had all started with a boring Annual Meeting of Stockholders: Oh yes, for Lauren those events were clear as day. They were the peaks and valley of the year's events. As an ambitious career woman, these events mattered. How could she forget that cold feeling on the morning of the day they were driven into an unexpected situation just before the Annual Meeting. It surfaced suddenly in the preparatory in-house briefing.

The day had started well enough. The limousine had turned the corner of York and King Streets as always, let her out at First Canadian Place.

It was then a festive occasion, the Annual Stockholder's Meeting. She spotted a few of them arriving from the airport.

She had walked into the building teeming with people in the Concourse and took the elevators up to the modernized great Lobby where once stood the old trading floors of early Exchanges. At the top floor, her own corporate offices were to hold a briefing.

The elevator, she remembered, rose higher and higher. All seemed calm. She was standing behind men, clutched at the rail, her eyes darting nervously as the floor levels ticked passed. Ten. Fifteen. Twenty First. Twenty Fifth. Thirtieth. By the thirty-first floor a haze of moisture coated her face and she all but pushed her way out the door of the elevator to escape the confines...

Ted Eastman noticed that it took her several seconds to regulate her breathing. She went to the Ladies Washroom and emerged fifteen minutes later, ready for business.

 "What's the matter with Lauren?" Eastman said to Hightower, she overheard.

Lauren was actually trained in Media Investor Relations. Originally trained in business journalism, she had migrated into larger finance. Hers was the job to maximize any details for publicity that could be found in *any* transaction, barring secret negotiations.

On that day, secret negotiations were in the deck of cards, but the hand that played them surprised her. They were rigged for someone's advantage: At the briefing she discovered that an offer by a foreign stock exchange was on the table for their stock position. 6 Billion dollars for the purchase of the Exchange in a merger acquisition.

Eastman and Smith unwrapped the details to the full board of Directors seated around the Conference Table at the briefing. They were here gathered in private before going downstairs to address the general Annual Meeting, yet they were stunned.

"This is not a happy day, Gentlemen" began Eastman. "Our bank has had a long and hard climb to reach this point, and we shall be out-bid by a foreign interest in a Take-Over bid..."

"A Take-Over what?"

Eastman left his place at the head of the conference table to show some charts, then waited.

"With the acquisition of the Canadian Venture Exchange by the Toronto Stock Exchange under the parent TSX Venture Exchange; and the subsequent acquisition of the Montreal Exchange, the stock exchange of Canada had grown to be one of the world's largest trading exchanges, as you know."

They were watching him.

"Especially for gas and oil companies, of which our bank is the main vehicle for clearinghouse trading....

"Thus, when a foreign Stock Exchange Group announces it would merge with the TMX of Canada, it represents a combined equity market capitalization of some $6 trillion, the second largest in the world. Naturally it would assume the banking function that they presently enjoyed..." he said, stepping away.

"You are joking, right?'

"No way."

Eastman had said enough to stimulate vigorous chattering and argument within the gathering, and it was fifteen minutes before they settled down. Everyone knew the deal.

" As you know..." he proceeded " a similar offer has been known to us. Just two years ago it came in, and we were the ones who recommended to the government that they block it..."

He stood very still, facing the numbers. "But not this time." he said finally.

The question before them - the *only* question before them, was how to inform the stockholders waiting downstairs with the information.

"As you know, they should be informed *immediately* - according to Security and Exchange Commission Regulations" he said.

"This is another Take-Over Bid." said one member seated at the table.

"Not necessarily." said Smith. He looked at Hightower who stood up.

"We can frame this is a *bonafide* Merger offer, with a fair valuation. And we *are* low on cash. We have no choice." said Hightower. "They will discover this anyway within six months as we submit our filings report.

"String them out." said one. "Let them pay for it through their last teeth..."

They discussed the matter, and the argument went round the table. They could string out enough law suits to buy time...Even if only for aggravation value. However, if done *intentionally,* that would officially constitute malfeasance and deliberate manipulation. Besides, the stockholders downstairs would plead for better dividends....

"It is their money" said Hightower, finally. "They have a right to know. They should be informed. And immediately, if we want their continued support. In fact, it is precisely this conclusion that our competitor expects us to arrive at."

Eastman nodded in agreement.

"*How* they respond is the issue..."

"So, how to present the bitter pill with whatever else we know and do well..."

Smith looked at those assembled around the table.

"If there was one thing we know is mining exploration: Exploration has not even begun. Our resources, on paper at least, remain largely untapped. Leases, while seeing a severe and perverse 'hick-up' in North America politics against drilling and mining, have setbacks. Our Bonds are suffering repercussions on market exchanges all over the world. But we have prospect."

Oh yes. Lauren Papendopolous remembered that meeting well...

"What remains unanswered is a strategy. Or, what is the Board was going to do about it?"

"Perhaps we offer to partner..." said Hightower.

"We shall put in a rival bid." interrupted someone else.

Smith walked up to a blackboard and made a revelation of numbers. They were staggering. The outside offer is too sweet for stockholders to ignore. We can't compete."

Some in the room murmured. "These are numbers greater than those of a nation's GDP"

"I propose this. The offer on the table by a rival is as follows. One billion, with the TMX shareholders receiving an enormous amount each per share. The special dividend, further, can be doubled. And the combined exchanges, plus banks, pledge to maintain the dividend at least as high as the current value, as a guarantee."

They were wowed.

Eastman nodded to Lauren. "You got that?"

In less than one hour the shareholders downstairs would be informed. It was her job to broadcast this offer with as much fanfare as possible.

This, he concluded, would put an end to any talk of takeover bids.

"You okay with this? Can you deliver the message to the stockholders..." said Hightower catching up suddenly with Lauren as they descended. Then he saw her face.

"My God" he said "Are you alright?"

It was Hightower, she felt certain who did it. He had declared her unfit for a public presentation, and he had turned the public dissemination over to Eastman for the rest of the stockholder's meeting. He alone had seen her greatest vulnerability...

He alone should pay.

In less than six weeks, she would be ordered to a full examination; diagnosed with a condition that would preclude any further advancements at the firm. Not that it would hinder any man. No. Just women in this conservative Canadian environment dominated by business men.

She had to act immediately.

She smiled to herself, thinking of her early first instincts when she sensed danger:

Later that night, at the formal grand ballroom, she turned to her friend Roger LaMaas. It was a lavish Gala event, and they danced. They talked. The target of her threat was Hightower.

Oh yes. He would pay, she remembered that night.

He held sway for the evening, the bastard.

Later, she would have hers...

Hightower. An apt name, she mused.

* *

Henson did not like the report he received. He promised to pass it along to Argueta. He should see this.

He sat in his office in Colorado and looked out the window. The Rocky Mountains, draped in a mantle of distant snow, were ethereally rimmed in purple hues against a rich blue sky.

 But for how much longer? UK scientists were reporting a huge dome of freshwater developing in the Arctic Ocean. The bulge, they explained in their paper, was some 7,000 cubic km in size and had grown in just the last decade to 15 cm.

He took off his heavy eyeglasses, hunched forward on his elbows, and tapped the table with them, his thoughts far away. That mean that strong winds in the Beaufort Gyre would now be creating a clockwise current in the northern polar region. This would force the water to concentrate and *raise* the sea surface height...

He resumed his reading.

Whereas spacecraft and satellite data confirmed a 'doming effect' in the region with perception of cracks, leads and frequency metrics of ice floes, the recent trend of rising was alarming: A full 2 cm per year.

This part of the report he dwelt on. Maybe there was an error? Maybe it was a modeling composition that needed adjusting?

The water in the Arctic was freshening. And whereas normally freshwater came from the Eurasian Russian side of the Arctic basin, strong winds and current were now transporting freshwater into the Gyre. The result was freshwater pushing into the Atlantic Ocean.

The consequence was staggering. This condition might at any instant induce a *counter-flow* of currents in the Atlantic Ocean. A *reversal* of what was known as the 'conveyor-belt mechanism' of currents circulating in the Atlantic.

Henson did not have to read the rest of the report. He knew what would happen if the currents started to enter the North Atlantic in large volumes. The weather patterns would alter.

Those Atlantic currents would pull warm water from the tropics and hold mild temperature at the extreme northern European latitudes: Once warm water was made to well up from wind-driven changes at the surface, the loss of seasonal ice cover would accelerate in the Arctic. At that tipping point, there would be no going back.

Scientists were now claiming that it was imminent. There had been disputes about this reversal. The Arctic summers could be ice-free by 2013. What the European Geosciences Union (EGU) annual meeting were implying was a tipping point during that year.

Henson decided to make the report available to one man first. Then it would be his responsibility as to who else should read these findings. It would be his call, yes.

They should soon dwell on what North America should do to protect itself when the sequence began…

* *

Argueta didn't have to spell it out for those at the Pentagon. The results were sobering.

Degradations to the environment usually were viewed as opportunities. This was no different. An ice-free Arctic represented opportunities. The most immediate reactions came from the Russians themselves. Then from the Canadians. The Arctic region was full of mineral deposits.

What the United States should be concerned about was losing the natural ice barriers across its northern border for part of the year. This he had to impress upon the White House.

"We know the evidence is showing a balding of the Arctic cap" he said, having the attention of the chief of staff. "Basically the policies have to be made are the policies nobody wants" he added "What I mean Sir, is that this could happen sooner than we expected. For the national interest, defense maneuvers must be included in our planning."

Argueta stopped there. A political officer would know how to proceed, surely. He would detect the words of warning from the scientific and military communities.

Argueta was met with silence. He understood. Silence, at the end of a presentation usually meant No. After thanking him, they said their goodbyes.

That was a week ago.

He was up early with a coffee in hand. The sun was now behind tall trees. He pushed out the screened porch door of his weekend mountain retreat, as he called it. Around him was a woodland of Western Maryland.

Why should he care? He was trained to be a soldier, after all. He descended the wooden steps and walked down to the lake, waterfowl calling.

* *

Arguetta re-examined a report that lay within his reach. He was familiar with it in general terms. But he needed to refresh his thinking if he was going to take any action. It began with information consisted with a communique.

According to the communique, the fault line that slipped was not just in the Berring Straits.

"While it poses no alarm, it is possible that it opened a seam in the earth's crust. That makes it a new seam along the northern rim of the Atlantic ocean.

"We know that two miles beneath the surface of ocean, the fault line caused a small tremor that went almost undetected. Generally remote and largely ignored it is an area not known for tremors.

"...However, what escaped us at first was its growing link as a hairline crack to another fault line that ran the entire length of the Atlantic Ocean: A fault line that continues, if allowed to follow its natural course, half way down the globe. The Atlantic Fault Line.

"...The tremors occur down the Atlantic to the San Salvador Fault Line -beyond the plateau of the Bahamas, which joins the Puerto Rico Fault line along the Ida.

"At San Salvador there are no signs of tremors. Evidently, all disturbances penetrate beneath landmasses that are submerged. But it is being monitored.

" We do know that from just beneath the landmass, off the Bahamas, a protruding undersea ridge extends twenty-five nautical miles northeast. There, on geological maps detailed bathymetry now shows a sudden dropping off from the North American Continental shelf. Underwater cliffs plunge into the deepest part of the ocean. There, the seafloor drops to an abyssal plain over a mile deep, producing current anomalies that remained unexplainable.

"Historically, we have records of magnetic anomalies. Known to bedevil ships and aircraft, the area is nicknamed the *Bermuda Triangle* as it produces electromagnetic disturbances.

"To scientists, these records show unpredictable and dangerous destabilization potential. But of greater concern are its effects to the flow of ocean currents.

"Beneath the Bahamas shelf is the edge of the Atlantic tectonic plate, extending to the Puerto Rico Fault Line.

"Poorly understood, only one scientific theory is circulating. It suggests that beneath the Fault line there exists a sudden upsurge of magma, a substance of such magnetic pull that it may be the cause of distortion to geomagnetic fields in modern instrumentation.

"For North America, such phenomenon off the coastal shelf remains unacceptable. It is well documented that during WWII, German U Boats lingered off this subterranean cliff undetected. Today, such a prospect would lay open much United States intelligence related to long range ballistic missiles from a nuclear submarine. "

Argueta paused to light his pipe. The evening had cast long and brassy shadows across the woods, and rays of intermittent sunlight penetrated through the trees. He sipped at his scotch and proceeded with his reading.

"Ancient lore has it that such an effect made meteoritic materials seem heavier, as they did in early records describing a fiery magnetic shower over the North Anatolian Fault off Turkey -famed site of Atlantis.

Possibly, offering explanations for meteor showers of destruction that fell over Sodom and Gomorrah, interpreted as a sign of the Wrath of God in biblical texts.

"Today, if an earthquake would run unfettered down the length of this continuous fault line, it would be an earthquake on a scale close to a Level 10.

"An earthquake of such a magnitude and danger at the seabed would leave the San Andreas Fault disturbances behind in record; pushing the survival of the continent to its most extreme.

"However, that would not compete with the upwelling of magma that would oscillate up the magma chamber. If such an eruption were to occur, as it has in its last 'super-eruption' record that resulted in an Ice Age, the planet would be again plunged into an extinction event.

"So far, it is known that if oscillations within the magma chamber increase in resonant frequency, then an eruption will ensue."

Argueta looked out the window and barely saw the light of evening anymore. He took another sip, the ice cubes melting.

"Moreover, the magnetic affects upon nuclear powered military vessels is yet to be tested."

This, Argueta had to know.

A slippage of the Fault Line caused by an earthquake that is travelling long, he also knew, was only the beginning.

* *

Robinson and his Exec officer were in discussion when Trevor stepped in. Robinson turned to him.

"They want me to take on some of their cargo." said Robinson.

Trevor looked at him.

Robinson was referring to the Soviet's submarine's supply of weapons. Notwithstanding their joint recovery-mission, this was utterly out of the question...

"They claim they're loaded to 75% burden."

"The rest?"

"At the surface, they've handed off some weapons into the hold of the *Cherokee* - departed at 0200 hours..."

Trevor knew the *Cherokee* had reported malfunction. Plus surface weather. Wind and ice had accumulated on the ship to within their weight-loading capacity.

Trevor wondered why a Soviet sub of that size would expect a lower class NR to accommodate, knowing very well that it was not outfitted to carry such grade of weapon on board.

"Desperate." said Robinson, reading his eyes and walking away.

Trevor and the Exec Officer were alone at the chart table. "How are we supposed render assistance?" asked Trevor.

"They want us to strap their damned warheads to our hull and sail home."

"Good God. Is that possible?" asked Trevor. The idea was too ludicrous, if not self-destructive.

"Anything is possible. We've communicated our response. They are considering other options. We suggested leaving them down here...for a later pick-up if necessary."

Robinson returned. The answer came in.

"They agreed. They will leave six weapons down here on the sea bed."

 "Birds with fleas or without fleas?" asked his Executive Officer.

"Without fleas." Robinson turned to Trevor. "That means they are disarmed..." He led the way down the companion adder one deck. "But I don't like it one bit. It scares me to hell..."

* *

Robinson crawled into the viewing space himself to see the weapons laying on the sea floor like six pieces of cordwood.

"It looks stupid as hell..." he muttered, wiggling free after half an hour.

"We shall escort them a stretch across the Ridge, then bid them farewell...We aren't particularly deep here" he said to his Exec officer.

"Right."

"This is one hell of a mission" said Robinson turning to Trevor. "That's six warheads *without goddamned* accountability...Something fishy is going on. I don't like it. I don't like it. I don't like it." He repeated.

He was hailed. "Captain. Visibility is so bad, hardly able to define her hull..."

They followed the dark Soviet hull at less than 200 feet off the bottom. Then an extraordinary thing happened.

* *

The submerged Soviet vessel had sailed into a sea of bubbles so dense that she almost disappeared from any visibility. Her signature fell off the radar at the radio and radar station of the NR2. An eerie silent static followed.

Only two crewmen at the bow of the NR 2 saw what happened through the Forward portholes.

In toy-like motion, the Soviet submarine ahead of them seemed to pitch forward, then roll slightly to portside before plunging radically into a vertical dive as if entirely without the buoyancy of the sea. She dropped, bow down, her stern lifting, the vessel gaining speed as it hit the seafloor.

There was barely enough visibility to make out what happened. The entire vessel crashed with such impact that the bow dug into the ocean floor, burying itself into a cloud of debris that blossomed like a mountain.

The submarine's weight crushing down upon the bow forced a buckling and crenellation that stitched up the hull until it sheered open and crumbled in two sections. The forward section of the hull buried by the rest of the hull, even as the current made it bounce before settling.

At impact, a display of light rays and flashing were emitted from both within and without the structure, the submarine swamped of its contents.

* *

At full reverse, the added thousand feet distance between them helped. At 2,000 feet distance, the Soviet submarine was seen igniting in an underwater explosion that set off a sonar signal the size of a pressure wave.

The *NR2* was almost bounced away as the impact wave hit them. It sent the crew and equipment flying, some dangerously articulated.

They were still in reverse mode when a second wave followed a few minutes later. By the time the third wave hit them, most crew on board had braced themselves. After that, the oscillations dampened out, and the ship stabilized.

"Damage?" yelled Robinson...

On board the NR, an alarm to battle had been called. Under strobe, damage control was already underway, bulkheads sealing off...

"This is the Captain" announced Robinson, his ship resting gently on the bottom.

He paused, as stunned and breathless as any man. He took a deep breath. "We are at least afloat." he said, he voice somewhat calmer. "All injured to be reported. Damage and systems report ASAP. I have issued a distress call for assistance. Stand by for further instructions..."

Six hours later they surfaced, and, as remote as the possibility was, they searched for survivors of the damaged vessel below.

The NR sustained no life threatening damage. But they stayed on station, observing.

The next morning they received orders.

Moreover, Robinson had made a decision.

* *

"What happened…?"

"At least two reports indicate methane bubbles rising caused the density of seawater to drop. She lost buoyancy so spontaneously that she dropped into a hole, and her nose hit the seafloor too suddenly to survive the crash…."

They said nothing. But the sequence of events gave them all pause.

That she crashed and exploded without warheads on board was a miracle.

Moreover, the incident occurred some distance from the location of those weapons posited on the seafloor.

But the next decision was Robinsons. He had decided to go back to the bottom and clean up. "We're going down to retrieve those suckers; strap them to the hull and tow them home if we have to. Piggyback."

It was done with the aid of a manipulator arm and six crewmen rotating continuously.

The extra weight was noted. Robinson sent out a message to the approaching US Naval surface combatant, a Frigate.

Two other surface combatants received orders to reroute and assist the NR2 as escort. But it would take several days to rendezvous.

"Make for the Bering Strait, if you please." said Robinson finally, standing at the C&C.

* *

Chapter Six

Washington DC

Jefferson smiled as he read the letter from his friend.

In those whirlwind years of drafting a Constitution, so elegantly wrought, the matter of running the country arrived with little to fear.

Yet, there should always be fear, he asserted.

Fear of things omitted; fear for a Nation without a standing Army; fear of an empty treasury or commerce unprotected on the high seas.

Above all, fear for a new world still in the maul of a medieval hunger for resources. Such were the obstacles watched by old enemies measuring their time. At any moment, there might be opportunity to re-emerge and regain dominion, if not plunge newly formed republics into uncertainty, disarray and dispersion.

Especially if an emerging nation faced unrelenting weather; inadequate finances, or showed insecurity in a new world without civil authority.

America had its challenges. Independent planters; Indian tribes fiercely resisting, and foreign armies attacking...

Still, for Jefferson as President, it was survival. This, as Europe was shedding an agrarian subsistence existence for a modern economy of Imperialist expansionism.

The letter before him was from a Frenchman Archard Fortescue, member of a scientific society embraced by Benjamin Franklin. He too had recognizing the need to modernize and advance.

At Monticello, Jefferson was busy, his friend knew. For the *American Society for the Promotion of Useful Knowledge,* the future could be conceived by capturing the past - Such was the unearthing of archaeological mounds left by Native Indians on the land.

However, as the letter revealed, there was trouble. The French, ever advancing their interests on the American continent, had forged allegiances with the Native American tribes during the French and Indian Wars. Canadian colonists fought alongside Indians against English mercenaries. But as France became entrenched in its own Revolution, the need for money at home outweighed its uses for a footprint overseas.

Jefferson seized the opportunity.

The currency of traffic, trade and treaties on American soil was common to Jefferson and Franklin. French land grants; land trade, continental purchases in America were viewed as profitable territorial expansion for the American colonies. The Louisiana Purchase opened up vast lands for the thirteen colonies. The heart of the continent opened up down the Mississippi. To the West were... untold riches.

Jefferson sent Lewis and Clerk on an epic expedition, and Jefferson came to recognize the benefits of working with the Chiefs of Indian Nations, like Chief Canasatego, leader of the Iroquois tribes. Negotiating treatises and *Takings* on the part of the colonists rested on ancient laws of conquest, trade, assimilation and negotiation. They were shaped by culture, written by law and supported by societies - slave owning or free.

Jefferson, during his short term of his office, discovered that his priority was to hold a sovereignty together. He gave it shape, order and direction. Then, he held fast to his convictions, even as poetry transformed dreams into investment realities.

For now, he must make choices. The rest, he hoped, should develop from the foundations of a Constitution, even under the test of time. The northern boundary especially.

Individual claims of land, private ownership and patent rights were used as the basis for credit. Equally, the Federation, in the acts of statehood, should amass wealth. Did that make them competitors for resources on this new continent? If so, then let it be by *Takings of Preeminent Domain*. And at fair market value.

He grinned. At least there was no Monarchy to claim royal ownership over all lands, people, resources and trade...No. Not amongst the colonists.

He looked up at the trees. Red, yellow, purple and orange colors surrounded him. This was a good land. The soil was good. He gathered his fingers behind his back, his thoughts still unresolved. Should he initiate the mapping of the northern boundaries? Should there be further disputes on this soil?

His triumphs were sufficient for one lifetime, he decided.

New boundaries should now define his Nation.

Let it be so.

* *

The Continental sea shelf off North American had been in place for over 6,000 years with little erosion. Known on maps to border the eastern seaboard in a beautiful blue shape, it hugged the curves of the shore like a woman's body dress.

It teemed with sea-life; human life and traces of countless ocean voyages and weather.

Yet large volumes of sediment, eroded from the North American continent during the Quaternary glaciations, lay unevenly deposited at the margins. Once, at full maximum extent, continental glaciers had reached the shelf edge off Nova Scotia and supplied sediment directly to the outer shelf and upper slope.

At New England however, the glaciers had not imposed upon the shelf-edge, rather, large rivers had transported glacial sediments to shelf-edge deltas. There, quaternary deposits of inter-bedded silts and sand reached a thicknesses of 400–800 meters under the outer shelf and upper slope. Then it thinned out upon lower slopes of the Continental shelf and into the sea.

From this glorious fairground, Atlantic currents circulated in belts of motion that brought seafood; water-mixing; clouds and climate stability to the entire Northern Hemisphere.

On this day, echoes of subsea disturbances inundated side-scan sonar profiles of the mid-Atlantic, instruments of scientific measurement. Mass landslide movement was detected as it slewed down the slopes of the Continental shelf. The slide had followed two others...

Southwest of the subsea Baltimore Canyon, the large Baltimore-Accomac slide, and the Albemarle-Currituck submarine slide had occurred. They registered large debris-flow complexes. Instruments characterized the event by high backscatter in images showing mosaics on the move.

Echo sounding profiles were even more astonishing. They showed hummocky topography, and inward-facing scarps that lay along the boundaries of the debris-flows described a ground that was shifting.

Two scientists observed from Norfolk.

"Here, we're seeing the depression of the slide regions...which suggests displacement of rise sediments in addition to mass movement of sediments that come from the continental slope..."

"Do we have any ships out there?"

"Only commercial traffic...barges and the like."

"We should warn them of any wave action - might become choppy for large containerized cargo ships travelling the channels off the coast. The sea passage route is relatively free, there are no fuel carriers..."

"So what do you think this is?"

"Turbidity currents associated with the mass movement. Let's look up."

He called the meteorological center for mid-Atlantic weather. A fair but faint weather Front was developing off the coast. Thin cloud-cover described a moisture variance in wind change. But no precipitation was anticipated. No wind velocity to speak of.

Still, they sent out a general Sea-bottom Disturbance Alert across broad band airwaves.

To be sure, at least the Coast Guard would be alerted if any incident at sea caused them to deploy for rescue and searches.

* *

At the Smithsonian National Zoological Park in Washington DC, the apes were having lunch.

Two glossy-coated apes looked up, and the third stood up on its two feet, sensing something in the air...

Simultaneously, all three abandoned their food and climbed to the top of their tree-structure in their park zone, waiting.

A flock of flamingos flustered and rushed to regroup themselves for a mass flight formation.

The lions stopped pacing and with large paws reached up against the walls of their confinement, as if stretching outward.

At the North Nuclear Generating Station, a slight power reduction was detected. It was August. A shuddering followed, and then the vibrations registered within the reactor monitoring devices.

Two nuclear reactors started to shut down.

The managers panicked. They ran for the alarms systems to alert personnel for override. There might be a margin for analysis. But it was too late. The nuclear reactors had self-regulated and adjusted to shut-down mode.

Within minutes, the facility off-site power was lost.

Two of the managers fell to their knees, realizing that were it not for the built-in safeguards required of the US Nuclear Regulatory Agency, the facility would have been caught without off-site power, rendering all nuclear fuel rods without power to be kept cool.

They evacuated the plant of all but essential personnel.

 At lunchtime, Amanda was driving along fast moving traffic at the Tidal Basin of the Jefferson Memorial when the traffic lights of Washington DC all switched off.

Around her, an assortment of glossy cars, tightly sealed for air-conditioning, all applied brakes. Others, if older models, had windows creeping open and strands of music filtered the air around them.

Clearly, something was wrong. People started running out of the US Mint and onto the grass mall.

The earthquake that hit Washington DC at 1.50 PM EDT occurred in the Piedmont region of the US state of Virginia. The epicenter was 38 miles northwest of Richmond and 5 miles southwest of the town of Mineral. It had a magnitude of 5.8, an intensity reading of VII on the Mercalli scale.

For hours after the main quake, aftershocks ranged up to 4.5 Mw in magnitude. It was an intraplate earthquake.

The earthquake, said the News dials, was the largest to have occurred in the United States east of the Rocky Mountains since the Giles County Virginia quake of 1997

The quake caused landslides 150 miles away, and rippled the ground in waves within the Virginia Seismic Zone. The earthquake occurred beneath the Earth's surface, emanating from the mantle's continental collision that created the ancestral Appalachian Mountains.

While no deaths were reported, the damage came to $300 million first count, of which one third was insured. Landmarks were yet to be inspected.

The White House; the US Congress on Capitol Hill and the Pentagon evacuated of all personnel, as did most government buildings.

 Washington Metro systems trains operated for the rush-hour at reduced speeds as tracks and tunnels were inspected for damage. Subways, constructed upon soft swampy sands in the basin where the city lay, showed less stress and more flexibility within the structural allowances.

Amanda called the children.

Gwynie was at school where they had exercised a Fire Drill to vacate the building. Sandra, at college was far away from Washington and did not feel much impact.

Amanda called the house and found little affected there. Mrs. Carlos had just arrived; the dogs had just been walked and safe, waiting for her in the enclosed porch with their basins of fresh water, snacks and toys.

On the news, reports came in showing gas leaks; pipe damage and water bursting as being the most visible.

But the damage was deeper and silent.

The Washington monument sustained sufficient damage to be shut down indefinitely.

At the highest point of the city's ridgeline where stood the Washington National Cathedral, three of the four spire pinnacles toppled and damaged some of its colossal flying buttresses. Without insurance for earthquake damage, the National Cathedral launched immediately a campaign to raise funds for repairs.

At the Smithsonian Castle, five of the decorative turrets toppled, and over fifty jars of rare and preserved specimens of the 19th century fell from the shelves in the Smithsonian's National Museum of Natural History, their gene-banks erased.

Maryland, Delaware, Pennsylvania saw damage to historical sites dating from the thirteen colonies era.

The damage was widespread along the Atlantic seaboard.

Wall Street workers in New York evacuated into the streets as the skyscrapers above them weaved and whipped.

New structures under construction, like the monumental suspension bridge of the Delaware River at I 295 had to go back to the drawing board for structural damage.

From the West Virginia Office of Miners' Health, Safety and Training, a statement was issued declaring that West Virginia coal mines were fully inspected and considered safe following the tremors.

The quake was felt as far away as New England to Canada, and as far as the communities on Lake Michigan.

Remarkably, people remained calm, if redolent of terror attacks at the Pentagon of 9/11.

More than anything, defiance had become the hallmark of Washington's citizens as they conducted the nation's business.

Amanda's thoughts fled to Trevor. She wondered where he could be, and if he were impacted... Or even if he was aware of the situation in Washington DC?

Would he worry for his family? Did he wonder at their welfare when hearing the news? *Where was he?*

By the time the international community became aware of the quake, most people had gone home and settled down.

Barbara called. "I'm having a drink." she said.

Amanda laughed.

Later, Amanda caught the moon nodding wildly in the breeze through trees outside her window.

She missed her husband, his letter with her.

"My Darling..."

* *

Tectonic plates moved unstable submarine soils. The seabed roiled and had folded upon itself as the tumbling occurred.

The continental shelf changed its shape, filling canyons and sheering off the slopes that sliced into the deeper Atlantic ocean. Live disturbances curled and rocked the seabed as suspended sediments, turbidity and rolling earth swirling into the water column and shifted to new settling, releasing displacement forces that redirected the ocean water normally flowing.

In the disturbed swirling of angry waves, the hazard was only just beginning. A wave of amplitude three-sometimes eight meters had developed. It travelled, gathering speed and distance. By the time it reached the Newfoundland coast as a tsunami, it had a run-up of 13 miles.

The instrument system GLORIA, a side-scan sonar imagery table later showed a detailed mapping of the effect as being outside human knowledge.

* *

Amanda rubbed her eyes. It was two oclock in the morning.

She read her last email:

> *Amanda, This might well be the only explanation for laws on the books today with regards to "Takings"*

She was puzzled. How does this factor with the case at hand?

How to make a case without a base understanding of what constituted territorial *sovereign* domain, and what constituted *private* lands? Did the "takings" of land affect the takings of human rights - something upon which the very ink of the constitution was rendered?

"*...the pusuit of happiness*" What did that imply? If they were *not* able to pursue happiness *before*...?

Why?

Evidently their happiness was denied when the monarchy stole their endeavors of labor, lands and rights? So, if the moral obligation of individuals to claim and defend their owned endeavors, lands and rights, was guaranteed under the constitution, then they were also free of *Takings*..

Takings, then, had its limitations. How to account for the Amendments that followed? Clearly, it was a matter of doctrine...

So, if the case made against Trevor's company for damages could *not* be tied to territorial rights...

* *

Lauren took the call from her Limousine. She was in New York on her way to the Metropolitan Opera. There she would join a party of interested investors in her new venture.

"What do you mean "unclear?" she asked, leaning forward to inspect the high instep of her diamante stiletto shoe. "So *what?* ...We paid the damned fool enough. Enough to put his family on Millionaires' Row somewhere. Explain how the explosion leaves questions..."

She was not happy with what she heard.

The damage from the rig's explosion was bad enough, but insufficiently defined to lay blame to any one particular company. Sure, there was debris, and a few telling photographs of the US Coast Guard Cutter in the area of the oil rig's demise. But since it had not yet been tethered to the ocean floor, the matter of a "floating" platform oil rig - as opposed to a "fixed" platform oil rig, drilling from specified leased land *within* US territorial waters was more technical than practical.

She was angry. The idiot had managed to blow up the rig -himself included, before it was approved by the Department of Interior on paper: Without those Mineral Mining Approvals, it could take up to a year to achieve a argument against the Administrative Parent company, let alone its Insurer.

No. This did not suit Lauren Papendopulus. She said as much.

What was troublesome was the question of the lease itself? Something within the process was stalling the matter. Had it been considered by the US Department of Interior or not? And if not, why not?

The answers did not suit her.

Evidently, the lease bottom had generated some debate. It lay partially un-surveyed. A domain that remained outside the territorial United States, being offshore.

The Limousine turned the corner and slowed down.

"Find as many connections as you can to its operating procedures, like names, dates, officials, management, business plan, financing and corporate ownership. Especially parts and suppliers of subcontracted arrangements, like shipping and rights etc. etc. Then go to work."

"This should tangle them up for a while. We start our litigation for failure to perform and produce a product for which we have made future contracts on...Plus serious investments."

A thought came to her, and here she knew she had it nailed.

"Who is the Insurer?"

She smiled when she found out. It was the British company - around since Scottish colonial ventures in the 17th centuries. *God how she hated those legacy companies.*

"Find out all there is to know about them. Who is the management? The CEO's..." She paused. "Oh yes...you did tell me." she calculated a second. "The same group who owned major stakes in the Canadian Exchange? So, let's begin by throwing enough litigation to tie them up for a while and cramp their style. Go deep. Get personal. Find out who's who. And go for it. In fact... mortal thrusts. Get it?"

Her evening went well. Only once did she consult her cell for a call back. None came, and it annoyed the hell out of her that some young professional somewhere who was given instructions did *not* provide her with a minute by minute update.

Well, it was early in the night. God help him the next day. In fact, she would become his most favorite caller. Impressing young men was her forte. She prepared to step out, smiled at the reflection in the Limousine window, her red lips and pulled-back dark hair presenting a manikin on the red carpet event.

Just so long as she was not tracked or questioned by her investors: Hazardous environmental conditions was something they fled from.. Something that could run deep into your company finances - with lasting damage. Economic and environmental impacts were considered as hazardous to the financial position of a company as the toxic pollutants they produced.

She'd call her Assistant at breakfast, a young man. Dawn.

Perhaps catch him in bed.

* *

What Lauren could not know was that the Mining Lease purchased by the company of the rig was on the desk of three key officials at the Department of Interior.

Only a sketch of the mining plan was before them. Unusual. Since the BP Oil Spill, their methods and inspections were meticulous. Proof of the seabed condition; its plans for mining, and the *quality* of the Reserve was as important as the engineering itself. That is, *if* the platform was fixed.

At the heart of the question was how much Royalty payments could be produced for the government from corporate mining? Everybody needed energy. Especially the United States. But what disturbed the Senior Director were the drawings of the bore hole itself. It showed a distinct angle.

 He put down the file and walked to the coffee machine and poured. Surely there was a way to capture some Royalty?

Not only was the seafloor *not* officially within the territorial United States, but the oil reserve itself led off considerably into International Maritime Waters, even if accessible now by Artic melting.

 How was it that a British Insurer would hold it in bond? *Unless they owned the sea bottom.* What assumptions of ownership were they claiming, exactly?

He needed to check the Statutes on maritime commerce and Territorial Rights of Reversion. If no evidence for ownership could be produced, then no responsibility for damages could be asserted...

He checked his watch.

 He would make his call later.

* *

Amanda felt frustrated. She readied herself for the day, and the question remained on her mind.

How to press on with her small initiative in a non-profit world rooted in public funds? Should she discover parallels?

How did the case of Virginia get a subpoena for "Takings" from private owners who sued, and the survey lines unfolding to be in *another* State of sovereignty altogether? Or the case of a mining claim in Nevada whose mineral deposits were actually in Utah?

This was beginning to sound like Frontier living.

"Gwynie." she called out, hearing Clara down in the kitchen already. "I'm taking Gwynie to school today."

 She would take Gwynie to school today before going to work. She hoisted up her hair, dabbed her lips with quick color and folded the bedding for Clara to freshen before leaving the room.

"Where's my sleeping angel?" she asked softly as she opened the door to the child's room .

Gwynie sank under her covers with a giggle, then roared out like monster "*Whoaaaah.*"

"Oh No." wailed Amanda, her hands to her cheeks "Help."

* *

Argueta got a full report of the explosion. Was it a legitimate incendiary accident? Or a hostile act along the northern border?

He was ill at ease with the prospect that this was a natural phenomenon rather than a man made assault: How many events would have to be checked if 'accidental' along the back-door to America no longer sheltered by the Arctic ice cap? Never mind that on the other side of the balding border was a nation with the largest nuclear arsenal on earth, the Soviet Union, once an avowed enemy? True, now a staunch ally, and nothing to fear as a nation, but unstable. Internal instability could lead to external surprises.

What if some lunatic...He stopped himself.

He had three meetings scheduled and he hurried down the hallways of the Pentagon, his thoughts miles away. Then again, he was trained as a military strategist: It was expected of him to outline any concern of this nature. Northern defense was particularly his concern.

How in the hell had things progressed so quickly down this road?

He abhorred the way an environmental movement had found its way into the highest levels of government, even now reaching for the hearts and minds of everyday kitchen table-talk. In fact nothing could be further from the truth. Science; cyclic climates, over-population did nothing to mitigate the dangers to American safety.

Was it possible even? He wanted to swallow the thought. But it would not go down: *Environmentalism could become communism.* He could hear his old mentor and professor speaking now from the Academy

Podium. An old codger from the Cold War, they later laughed.

Beware the enemies of the harmless. Those early training lectures echoed for every Admiral on every ship on every mission, he knew.

The matter stalled on his mind all through his meetings. It could be anything really, the enemy of the harmless, the enemy who saw opportunity across a northern border without defenses, or an enemy from within seeking advantage of natural resources and contract concessions to deal with municipal budgetary needs?

Of course, much had to do with politics and the democratically elected will of the people. That he would uphold unto his last breath, regardless.

But he was worried. He tried to understand motives and searched for any deception: Basically, all that environmentalism meant was the stewardship over resources. Not a bad aspiration for a nation enjoying the fruits of its bounty.

But what if there was something else? What if the resources were being acquisitioned for other agendas? Or something else? Or *someone* else?

He checked his email. The Server was down again. Updates. Cyber security had been breached, they told him. Routine rechecks for the day, he was told. -Find something else to do until 1300 hours.

Lunch.

He made his way down to Ground floor levels to exit the secure premises of the Pentagon. Something was off, he thought.

"Hello Arguetta." chimed a passing Army Colonel.

He smiled.

His vehicle pulled out of the underground parking garage and drove out the secured gate of the Parking field.

The sun was bright over a blue Potomac River, gleaming off commercial aircraft landing and taking off at Reagan Airport. A green Jeep was behind him.

He turned into MacDonald's on Jefferson Highway and ordered at the drive-through window, slowing for pedestrians and service. A quick coffee and a chicken sandwich. Of course he could get the same food on the premises of the Pentagon. But he wanted to get out for some air and clear his thoughts... At least while the Server was down.

He drove into the Security Gate of the Parking Lot and gained admission, like everyone else. Strangely, the green Jeep was again behind him, though it veered away at the gate.

His duty became clear. He'd task for more research at his office, then he'd consult with scientists and contracting specialists. He would offer an official recommendation for a policy change regarding the northern frontier.

That was his job title, after all. Advisor.

* *

George Svalkov was on the phone to America. He loved being on the phone to America. He was being interviewed by a journalist from Washington DC. He must explain a recent article published by the journal Nature Geosciences.

"Excuse me" interrupted Sonja Perkins from the Washington Post "But how does this relate to the weather, exactly?"

"Well...you understand... We can tell from the modeling that when freshwater enters the North Atlantic...it affects the circulation that alters not only European weather patterns – because these currents...."

"Could you repeat that for me, please?" she insisted, the small time delay across international calls was causing them both to speak at the same time in overlap.

"...It...it pulls up warm waters from the tropics that helps the winter temperatures of European latitudes..." The pencil he was holding flipped off his fingers and rolled off the desk.

"Hello? Are you there?" He leaned down and the phone line seemed to go dead "Hello? *Hello*?..."

"Yes. Yes. Hello..." said the journalist. "I have what I need for my editors. Thank you for your information." she added.

"Oh...you are welcome. Err... Hello. Hello?" Actually, he wanted to say more.

The European Space Agency paid him well, but damned if things weren't grating on him. These calls, for example, did they have any idea what it all meant? Dear God.

He put on his overcoat and turned away from his desk, the office lights already dimmed from an office vacated half an hour ago by fellow employees.

He walked out the office in Paris and made his way to the nearby train station, the weather cold for late Summer. What he *should* have explained is that... is that, is ...No. He would have said it in a *fancy* way...No. He should have said...He handed his ticket to the kiosk master and entered the turnstile.

Ridiculous. Stupid. He spat on the pavement.

What it was that the world was asking, these days, was only for *Sensationalism.* That was all she wanted, that girl. What he should have done is explain it like this: "What we see from the high altitude Spacecraft are the measures of ice floes and their thickness..."

She should have interviewed him like a scientist. Instead, she pushed him on, like a schoolboy, with an *"Ooh, I see."*

 "Is the planet getting warmer then?" she wanted to know.

What did he answer? "It is the amount of fresh frozen water-melt that we note, especially in the last twenty years..." he continued. "Well of course." he said "the planet is getting warmer. It is the rising water level, it has been climbing at the rate of 2 cm per year"

She was pleased, evidently, with what she heard. And thanked him well enough.

But he could have kicked himself for not explaining it fully. And he did try "But what the model predictions warn is more ..."

 "Thank you Dr. Svalkov. You've been pretty helpful. I do have enough for my article..."

"Wait..."

He sat at the rear of the train all the way out of town brooding, his thoughts turbid.

 Science, he decided was being played for political ends. It was the appalling trend of countries with economic interests to take statistical findings and make political hay from them as a distraction for siphoning off funds...

He got out and walked. He crossed him arms, as if to shelter himself from the cold. Cold, rather in his mind. Because what they did not understand, these policy-makers and economic people in countries, was the real possibilities of cold and its consequences. Being a Russian, cold was entwined with its history and traditions. But these bloody Europeans and Americans...they had no idea what the cold could do. No. Not even in their imagination. What it could do to a country... To a people. *Or how vulnerable they were.*

And he wanted to laugh. Not even the surface cold.

The train ride out of Paris lulled his thoughts until he was almost in a state of reverie.

Raised a Russian boy, he wanted to be a scientist because he dreamed of changing the world. By understanding the environment, perhaps you could invoke greater understanding...

Hell. These Europeans. What did they know? He got up. This job, it was mingled with such frustration that he would quit. Go back to Russia and paint. Like his grandfather, a Russian Painter. In the tradition of the Russian greats. The great poets. The great artisans...

Paint. But paint what? Beautiful flowers that would no longer bloom? Skies that would no more be blue or white...or...

No. He could not quit his job. He would stay. Even if his apartment was so grim. Yes. He would stay. He was a Russian scientist.

And the danger too great.

Reverse the conveyor-belt direction of Atlantic currents carrying temperate water to warm the shores and the globe would plunge quickly into an ice age...

If that happened, even the hand of God himself could not change the course of history of the record...

* *

Two days later, George Svalkov got a call from the Vostok station in the Antarctic. "Hello Igor." he said.

Igor was his friend. Someone with whom he had attended university - and a fellow trainee for cold weather survival and endurance, someone he could talk to.

More importantly, someone who could always put him in a good mood about issues and values and whatever else the Vodka provoked. He put the caller on a speaker phone.

"So, how are you doing down there in the most difficult place to work on earth?" he asked

"Oyo, not bad, considering...Although I would do anything to have your cozy premises up there...and cozy apartment..."

"and cozy women." interrupted George

"Of course." laughed Igor.

"Well don't worry. The only cozy women I get calls from are young 23-year-olds wanting a good story for their media on global warming."

"Bahhh...Be careful my friend. That is a hot issue."

"Yes. I know. And grossly misrepresented. All we don't need is some career politician to make decisions based on propaganda instead of science...Speaking of which, what's all that good news you have down there? Tell me."

"Oh, I can't tell you enough: Our scientists have drilled into the Lake Vostok, a huge body of liquid water buried under the Antarctic ice as you know."

"Yes. Yes. Some[JC1] 300 sub-glacial lakes existing on White Continent." said George.

"It is our first penetration..." squealed Igor excitedly "and I can't tell you about the abundance of microbial life forms new to science.."

"Perhaps God should have called you Adam."

"Oh. Oh. Oh....it's too, too much to say...You have no idea what we can see. We will be able to biologically evaluate the evolution of living organisms..."

George was smiling. He loved to hear his friend drone on about the wonders of the earth, science and the Antarctic. But he also knew that where scientists went... politics followed.

The Russians clearly had an eye for the two poles of the earth: A wealth of natural resources rich in minerals including oil, gold, gas...That meant world dominion and financial power, he knew.

Still, he was surprised by Igor's sudden change of tone "So, what's going on in your neck of the woods?"

"Well, you mean other than the cloud-whitening ideas?" asked Goerge

"Yes."

"Well, its bullshit, honestly. What a preposterous idea. To put dust particles into the stratosphere to reflect sunlight like a cooling volcanic effect is Mickey Mouse. Disastrous for the Arctic, I tell you. It would increase the temperature at this pole by 10C."

"My God" said Igor.

"And what if they put up the wrong sized drops in the dust particles? Huh? Those bloody idiots – it could unleash results in climate... The idea is to keep the Arctic iced up. Not heated."

"No" said Igor. "I was referring actually to the heating bloom you have spreading down from the Fresh water into the Arctic. I just saw the charts this morning. I should bring my scuba gear for the beaches of the Bering, eh George?"

"I'll take a look. And to keep you informed" said George.

George and Igor had a good laugh before hanging up. But George was alarmed. Igor was telling him something.

George turned to the charts. Sure. Sure. The Atlantic was heating up from a slug of something that looked like an algal bloom spreading south. But then again, as they said in Boston about all things alarming *The British Are Coming*.

Then he saw the chemical breakdown. He paused. *Methane Gas*?

Now that he was thinking about it, he considered it strange - the absolute *absence* of knowledge about methane. Yet methane could create a cloud released from seepage from the earth's crust, they said.

Satellite tracking had no way to see it visibly as it moved around.

What did this thing mean then?

* *

The check came in. It made Amanda smile. The Law Firm that sent it to her on behalf of the corporate client attached a Memo "For services rendered in full, and with complete satisfaction." Eddie had signed the check. He added a note. "Good Job. With thanks."

Amanda held a staff meeting.

As always, they gathered in the conference room for the morning meeting, and she waited for everyone to get in and settle down, coffee in hand.

"I have some good news." she said, waving the small piece of paper. "Firstly, the check from our client - with their thanks for a good job."

"*Yeah.*" they all cheered. Some congratulated each other; others joked, and a few shook hands and hugged in the ebullience.

Amanda was beaming. "This check will pay our bills for a year longer..."

"Can I get a raise now?" said one voice in the background... They laughed.

"Of course you earned this, each of you. I thank you for your hard work; long hours and excellent effort. Thank you Jim, you focused on the client's needs with an overall management plan *upfront...*"

He nodded. "Thanks also to Bob, *you* helped him keep his focus when things seemed to be going backwards...Sarah, Mary, you did the homework, the research and the industry-survey that was needed..." They grinned.

"Charles, Ed, you kept us legal when we got squeamish; and Evan, you kept the financial projections and issues manageable when we felt a little overwhelmed by the project...Amy, *you* kept the place running; the phones answered; the bills paid; the coffee pot fresh and the press releases under control as the media pounded on our door. Thank you."

"Yeah." they cheered again, satisfied.

"Seriously. This task was one of the toughest this firm has ever had. So, well done, everybody."

Amanda waited, they chatted. "There's a bonus in it for everybody, plus one week extra for vacations by year-round; and a little something else besides..."

"First, I have more news. The assortment of industries that we included in our presentation on the Hill have each come to us for retention, generally, on more work... down the line... as their rep."

"*Alright.*" they grinned, understanding that more retainers for professional services meant continued employment at a place they each considered to be the best.

"So, you'll be pleased to know, we have a few more years of employment ahead of us." said Amanda.

She looked up and added. "To celebrate, as my thanks, I'm arranging for a small party for all staff. A *Soiree* formal event - Friday next in Washington."

"*Ohoooo?*" giggled the girls, excitedly.

"So Gentlemen, bring your ladies. Wear a white tie. And Ladies...Let's see some evening gowns for Dinner and an Opera at the Kennedy Center."

They loved it.

Certainly as a capital city, Washington DC had it share of sports events, museums, entertainment and festive ornamentation. But above all else, it was a city of inhabitants who cherished the performing arts.

Amanda's invitation hit the spot for the occasion.

* *

At the Roof Top Restaurant elevation, the sun was on its descent, flooding the elegant reception area with iridescent golden glows. There, they gathered for champagne and h'ors d'oevres.

The festive affair was beautifully arranged. The ladies wore evening gowns and arrived on the arm of the man they loved, each to walk down a small red carpet. The men brought spouses. Flanked by friends and staff, all were greeted with applause and music.

Amanda and her Personal Assistants handed them each an envelope containing a bonus check as they passed through the receiving line.

In addition, the men received an Express Intermission Bar Service card for drinks; the ladies a small prize of Chanel products, some powder and lipstick, others perfume, each beautifully gift wrapped in silver-lame ribbon. The room was full of excitement.

The Roof Top Terrace at the Kennedy Center was fully prepared. Seating was arranged in an enclave hidden by elegant partitions and subdued lighting.

They sat at circular tables piled high with formal place-settings of crystal glass, silverware and stunning floral arrangements. A team of chefs were to serve a short menu of specialized items for Amanda and her party.

The Maitre D' knew Amanda. Together, they had pre-planned a well scheduled dinner before the start of the Opera. Tonight was to be a glorious evening at the gleaming Kennedy Center for the Arts located on the banks of the Potomac River.

On the menu was an assortment of Caesar Salads; wild mushroom soup; Beef Tenderloin Au Poivre; Muscovy

Duck Breast or Salmon; herbs and vegetables and later fresh-made Tortes, Pies and Ice creams Crisps au liqueur of several varieties.

The party was filled with laughter, toasts, tale-telling and congenial sharing of the menu that crossed the table in odd sampling...such that Amanda looked up at the waiter pleading for patience at her playful lot. Clearly, they were all having a wonderful time.

Coffee and treats followed quickly, the Opera soon to commence. The ladies retreated for last minute coifs and nose-powdering. This night, they all said, was one to remember.

Opera House seats were found at about the mid-point of the Orchestra Level. They took their place in a row, and the theater went dark. Amanda sat on the end aisle seat next to Eric, their youngest Intern. The evening treat, she had insisted, was for *everyone* on the staff. Eric included.

They waited in the dark with anticipation.

 An actor in costume of the 18th century dashed out on stage and then attempted to rejoin his troupe behind the curtain. A spotlight found him and followed his frustrated attempts to find the opening of the curtain. The audience laughed. He crawled under the curtain on the stage, embarrassed, and the orchestra began its Overture.

The musical conductor, his podium rising from the orchestra pit in the darkness, came to light.

Gradually, as the audience became drawn into the music, they realized that the conductor himself was in costume delivering the comic opera. The *Marriage of Figaro* may have been based on the libretto of *Lorenzo Da Ponte,* but as the conductor turned to smile at Amanda's party, they realized that his role was not just of a conductor, but of composer Wolfgang Amadeus Mozart.

He was playful, the orchestra running away with his composition, and he thrilled the audience.

Finally, the curtain opened on the first actor – the lowly Baber of Seville measuring space for a bed for his upcoming marriage. The nuptial bed, he was trying to say, was too small…

The audience recognized him and broke into laughter.

Amanda glanced down the row of seats watching the opera and found them all enthralled. She was pleased. As music swirled around the comic crisis for the play by *Beaumarchais,* she knew she had made the right choice.

When the play first opened in 1786, Mozart himself conducted the orchestra. Mozart was challenged to use only original composition throughout because his patron, Emperor Joseph II, was himself in charge of the Burgtheater. He was concerned that the performance would be too long for his Court's attention.

"To prevent the excessive duration of operas, without however prejudicing the fame often sought by opera singers from the repetition of vocal pieces, I deem the enclosed notice to the public that no piece for more than a single voice is to be repeated as to be the most reasonable expedient. You will therefore cause some posters to this effect to be printed."

The result was a wealth of creative ideas and clever musical arrangements that marked Mozart forever as a musical genius. Nor did the Opera of the *Marriage of Figaro* diminish through time.

As the Acts progressed, Amanda noticed the faces of her colleagues and friends seated beside her in the reflection of stage lights, all of them lost to the wonder of the musical genius.

 How lucky she was, she thought.

The Intermission came only too soon. Eric followed Amanda out and went to collect some drinks with his ticket. She asked for a Ginger Ale and lime.

Outside, in the grand central foyer of the Kennedy center, beneath the bronze statue of the President, they mingled.

"Amanda. Amanda."

Sarah Delaney introduced her husband Tom and another couple with them; Jeffrey Watson and his date, a South American girl, Elisa.

Sarah and her husband again expressed thanks for the work of her research group. It had been a huge success at the Congressional Hearing.

 "It was an event." said Tom, chatting in the melee.

Amanda was surrounded by her group, and Sarah looked on enviously as they all bobbed and weaved around her passing drinks and laughing.

"I wish I had a job in a place like yours." said Sarah.

Jeffrey Watson extended his hand to Amanda between the shoulders of two people, the crowd pressing. That's when Amanda recognized that Sarah's party comprised of the senior partners of the firm *Delaney, Watson and Jacoby*, her client.

"What a performance." said Amanda over the crowd noise.

"Wow. It certainly is. I love it..." giggled Sarah. Tom waved at someone and turned. Jeff Watson was looking at her, the two shoulders parting.

Eric reappeared with his hands full.

"Our Intern, Eric Svorgenson, visiting from Finland" said Amanda by way of introduction "Mr. and Mrs. Delaney; and Mr. Watson and Ms. Elisa..."

"Oh..." said Eric gallantly "May I get for anyone else a drink from the bar?"

"No thank you." they all smiled.

"Yes please." said Elisa "but only if you let me come with you for a special order that I wish to have...?"

"Of course" he said, Amanda left holding two drinks with lime."

"Are you mothering again Amanda?" laughed Sarah.

"Tom." yelled out a man from two heads away. Both he and Sarah spun around and shifted off, bumping Amanda's arm to send one lime spinning to the floor.

"Here..." said Jeff Watson to Amanda "Let me give you a hand... " he relieved her of a drink and stepping back into the crowd plonked it on the silver tray of a passing waiter, his face winking back at her with an expression of *she-looses*.

Amanda sipped her ginger ale, wondering at the dispersion of her group. The noise surged as the lights dimmed. Obviously, her *Soiree* had been as success, if not yet fully executed. Still, with some relief she felt her social obligation completed: Transportation remained available for all who needed the limousine, but she felt now relieved of her duty as host.

"I fear we have lost our company in this crowd." said a voice behind her. She turned.

It was Jeff Watson. "Seriously, allow me thank you for representing our interests so ably before the Senate Subcommittee..."

"Sarah did a great job. It's not the easiest thing to be placed on that hot seat. Above all, you had better be prepared with answers..."

"Yes. You did that for her. It was potentially a political minefield" he added. "I want to tell you that we have decided to retain your firm for a long time to come...Your timing was good. You read the political thermostat well."

The lights dimmed to mark the end of the Intermission.

"If I don't see you again, please accept my card. I am free to be consulted with any questions you might have. Anytime." he said.

"Of course. Thank you" she said.

They drifted off, and only when Amanda finally made it down the aisle to reclaim her seat did she find another person in it. That person was Elisa - fully attended, it would seem, by Eric.

At first, Amanda felt annoyed. But then, seeing that there was enjoyment all round, she felt able to entertain another option for herself, and she encouraging the girl to stay.

Amanda withdrew. She politely watched another Act standing at the rear of the theater, but ten minutes into the final Act, and Amanda decided to call it a night. Her feet ached, and frankly, it had been a long day.

She checked out her coat; unsubscribed from the list of Limousine passengers for the night, and walked to the Elevators for the ground floor level. There she waited.

"Fleeing the scene?"

She turned. It was Jeff Watson.

"No not at all…" she said courteously "Just a decision to leave before the ending. I've had a long week."

"I see" he said, entering the elevator with her.

"Can I give you a ride home?" he asked. "My car is here, and I've been dismissed by my Date."

"Oh, I'm sorry…" said Amanda. "Eric should know better than to intrude on your evening…" "No. No. Elisa made her decision, that's all."

"Alright then, I was going to take a cab. I'm in Chevy Chase. Is that out your way?"

"Not at all. I'm going to Potomac."

Having negotiated the traffic crowd through Georgetown and up to Wisconsin Avenue, he turned to Amanda and said "Tell you what, since we are a pair of escapees, why not have a quiet *Apre*-coffee somewhere on the way to close out the lovely evening?"

"Why not?" she agreed. She would need to get to know his company interests as her client, anyway.

They picked a little Bistro and she tiptoed in by lifting her evening gown silk skirt off the parterre. The management never blinked. Washingtonians could be at dinner at the White House one hour; a Press Conference the next, or at the fish market buying lobster for diplomats the next…That was the city for you.

"Your staff seemed to be having a lovely evening, all of them…" he said. "Do you arrange such an event often?"

"Only as a treat really. We get so busy actually, it's fun to have a reason for gathering like this for a night out…"

"Quite right." he said. "We should do more at our group…"

A waiter came out. "Care for something to eat?"

She was still full, and settled for a cup of cappuccino.

"Your err...husband is not with you?"
"Trevor is on duty overseas at the moment" she said.
"I do miss him terribly."

"I understand" he said, ordering the French Onion soup. "You don't mind?" he asked.

"Not at all... Please go ahead."

"I'm famished. We skipped dinner to come here tonight..."

They chatted well into the morning hours. There was much to discuss. The Senate Hearing; the Industry, the cause of the dilemma for which they had to petition...Even the Congressmen themselves who asked questions came under review.

By the time he dropped her off, she felt that she had told him more about her life than she intended.

Further, she regretted not making more query as to the nature of his firm's work.

But then again, this wasn't the time...

* *

Chapter Seven

Amanda awoke to a least a dozen messages of thanks and expressions of appreciation by everyone on the staff for a lovely evening at the Kennedy Center. They were fun messages to read. Including Eric who sent an apology for displacing her seat...He went looking for her, he said.

What Amanda didn't expect was a ten o'clock delivery of flowers at her door.

She thanked the delivery boy, read the note and placed into a vase in the kitchen in the basement.

Perhaps, she decided, she had been too frank and open with her hospitality last night. She hoped like hell that she had not encouraged thoughts of any promiscuous relationship. That would be the very *last* thing she needed right now.

More than anything, she craved news about Trevor.

Amanda needed to finish up her work for at the Firm. Even if only for a few hours, she picked up the file that was on her desk.

The complete list of attendees was in it.

Rebecca in Toronto had done a splendid job of taking the email names and linking them each to their various interests and corporations.

The list was endless. She searched through names, groups, corporations, organizations and sovereign entities. Capital and financial support services was represented from all over the world. The Arctic Mining interest of Canada were amongst the largest and newest ventures represented. These investments were all insured by Sterling Insurance of the Highlands.

Trevor's firm, Amanda knew, always guaranteed success for his clients. Regardless their losses.

The file also contained photographs of the stockholders. The event too. The stage, the presenters, the speakers, the entertainment. Even the mid-day luncheon was in one image. Others showed the orchestra at the Banquet dinner and Gala Awards Ceremony. Clusters of celebrity and social gatherings had been photographed.

Amanda could not find her. She was nowhere in the images - the woman who had thrown-up. The young lady whom Amanda had taken to her room for some rest...the woman who quietly disappeared without a word? Not even a thanks for sending up the Nurse. Rather, the Nurse found the room empty? *Where was she in these images?*

Amanda read the dossiers of others who attended. Surely they had common interests, let alone much capital invested. What backgrounds did they come from? What was at stake for them, she wondered. Trevor would be interested.

* *

"Following your readings last week, what I need for you to determine…" asked Amanda of her class "Is whether the Revolution was induced by *tax* requirements from the Empire - or by internal strife?"

One hand shot up, a Californian. "Both?"

A student in Economics spoke "…But surely that throws into question the sovereign rights of the colonists, and…and… the resources they used as collateral to back loans from the Empire?"

"That's a good proposition." encouraged Amanda.

"But ask yourselves: Were the boundaries established as a loosely knit Republic amongst the thirteen disparate colonies - now states?"

Silence.

"Also, consider this: What about the individual? What agency did he have? Or, how about the *rights* of the individual?" suggested Amanda. "What informed them, and how far back in tradition did they go?"

"Remember, the First Amendment established the rights and statutes of all Americans at the time. Much like the first Mosaic Laws for societal organization, the Constitution gave birth to American citizenship, including the right to the *pursuit of happiness* etc. as the first words of the document declare…"

Amanda waited.

"Further, there is the question about the right to better oneself in the new world? Did individual citizens have rights to own any private territorial holdings? Did that mean freedom to engage in Enterprise ventures, patents, and trade in free market capitalism?…."

"And what of any conflicts internally? Did previous pressure evoke concerns about monarchical Authority? Did the Federalist Papers show that rights of central authority should not interfere with the States' authority to self-govern?"

The class understood and was sufficiently contented to begin the test.

She smiled.

"OK. So, I want clear arguments and well-thought out logic as you present your cases." said Amanda.

They took to their questionnaire. Amanda gave them time and strolled to the window.

 Outside, and not far from her classroom window, the river was calm. No wind. Just a gentle breeze, and a sun setting on an evening of warm-scented air for early fall.

The sounds of laughter carried clear across the water. The sailing team was finishing up, all boats approaching the dock for berthing. It was a calm enough moment, no further practices scheduled.

Amanda leaned over a tad. Could she actually spot Sandra her daughter walking about? There would be waterside gear-checks, some dingy paraphernalia - something the team did in abundance and with much pleasure. At college age, they were all young adults, clearly able skilled in competitive sailing as a sport.

A few girls jumped off their boat and headed straight for bathrooms, shedding safety vests and seal-tight sailing gear as they went, receiving for their daintiness the taunting laughter of guys. But only on home turf, Amanda knew. When at Visiting Matches, the Mens' Team was highly protective of their Womens' Team as fellow crew.

Amanda looked around her class, all heads bowed and in deep concentration, but for one or two. She checked her watch.

Outside, by now it was clearly after hours, and the dock coaching staff leaving...

Sandra was team captain for the day and acting as a substitute coach. She approached the docks with the chase-boat in a soft idle churn, having towed the last of the dinghy's in off the river.

As the vessel came into view, Amanda was surprised to see that Sandra had Gwynie her sister seated beside her. Gwynie looked like a large beachball engulfed in an oversized swimmer's safety life-vest: Gwynie was supposed to be on the lawn with their housekeeper, Carla. Instead she was out on a boat with a sister.

True, today was Visitors Day. Reserved to show parents, donors and patrons a tour of the campus, guests had been invited onto the premises to enjoy events; observe the teaching; view the gyms, inspect the boathouse as a peek into life at the college...

Evidently, for an hour, with her mother teaching and Carla – who had come down with Amanda today to watch over the child, Gwynie had been whisked on board by her sister for a ride.

Amanda turned back to her class, all engrossed. No questions. No issues.

She had to suppress a smile. Gwynie was so bundled up in her life-vest that her fair curls and little hat was lost inside the puffed up flotation device. *Safety first*, insisted Sandra, always.

 "*Gwyneeeee*" sang out the team of sailors as they approached, waving. The child giggled shyly.

Sandra was almost at the dock, the lengthening evening shadows settling upon the river.

Sandra never saw it coming.

A speedboat flew out of the darkness with such velocity that the motorboat sprang upon her before she could react to avert a collision.

But a collision was not intended. The fast moving vessel had enough power to swerve away suddenly like a slalom and send a wake strong enough to heft the sailboat aloft and off its center of gravity for a total capsize. The speedboat roared off down the river.

It happened so fast. Sandra was thrown overboard. And so was Gwynie.

The head that popped up was Sandra's "Gwynie?" she blew out, splashing.

One of the boys dove from his boat before the wake reached his dingy and swam beneath the wave to vaguely spot Gwynie underwater landing on the bottom mud. He grabbed her life vest and hoisted her upward.

Amanda did not see what happened, having strolled away from the window. But she heard some commotion and returned to the window. A cluster of wet sailors and a melee of soggy girls huddled over Sandra who was holding Gwynie tightly in her arms.

Amanda could not make out the meaning of what had happened. But when she saw Clara flying down to the dock, she realized there had been an accident.

Amanda gasped. She looked to where pointing arms flailed, a place further up the waterfront. Then she spotted a glint of reflected sunlight off glass from the Parking Lot. It came from a pair of binoculars observing the episode.

They came down from the face of a man seated in his car. A face she had seen before. She was horrified. A green pickup truck, a green Jeep with Maryland Tags that ended with SKI.

It pulled away abruptly.

* *

Finally. Some satellite tracking data from France. Igor was frustrated, as he walked back to his building.

He had to call them up to resume their input relays. Why? Because an unfavorable political election occurred last week which terminated the funding of things...

He made his way down the hallway of his office complex. *Who were these people to play football with scientific data systems*? He paused and pulled out a cigarette. He missed the cold days of Russia. He inhaled.

...And now he was guardian of the warm days of America. What was happening in the world now?

Anyway, this was a screw up. No way that any of this garbage made sense. So, he'd call France again tomorrow. He stubbed out his cigarette with a heavy hand. He had quit smoking anyway.

All night he stayed in his Lab to make the call and maybe catch them in their offices during banking hours. How quaint. Bloody socialists, the French.

Except that the *Receptionist* there...*Eheh*...well, who knows? Everyone is screwing with everyone, he concluded and turned his attention to his computer to view the data. Finally he shut it down and decided he'd get more sleep in his bunk at the lab before dawn, such as it was in the Arctic.

Only he didn't. He was up again one hour later. At first it looked like a faulty image. It was a dark lake of water in the North Atlantic. How it got there was something else. Was it even was water, he pondered.

He called George. Surely another tracking satellite would have showed something? At least Igor was awake at this hour of the clock.

"I was hoping that you would say something soon..." said Igor, implying that by scholarly courtesy, this was strictly George's domain of analysis.

"I see this puddle as a blemish in the North Atlantic that appears from nowhere" said Igor "I'd say it's about 150 kilometers wide, and maybe not even water..."

"We do see a notable change in temperature around it, so it could be a natural gas seeping from the bottom of the ocean."

"But it's the size of a lake?"

"Yes"

"It could be methane. Then it could be oil. An oil slick?"

"Then they can burn it up easily" said Igor.

"I'd be relieved it was some goddamned oil spill from some cargo ship that sank from an iceberg."

They laughed, both knowing that this was quite different. For one thing, it was too large. They both knew that igniting oil spills to burn off was less popular than closing airports and grounding half the airplanes of Europe for a volcanic eruption in Iceland.

But more importantly than its presence, a horrible idea was lurked behind it. And they both knew not to say it. Especially without knowing the source?

"Look, I'm reading the French tracking data, and they remain clueless, as always. But what I want from you Igor, is the threshold readings of salinity spreads. Can you send me anything? Let's be sure we know what we're doing before we tell anyone."

"Of course." said Igor.

George feared the worst. After all, it wasn't every lifetime that witnessed the melting of the Arctic. He had been wondering about things for a long time. He wasn't sure about the timing of this event. Should he report this? Was he supposed to inform his authorities?

* *

In one of London's tallest buildings, the Investment Firm and brokerage offices of Klugberg and Freeman were marked by new and modern furnishings.

Jeff Bingham, representative for Trevor MacDonnell was being feted.

Not only would his company receive the benefits of their investor's venture capital for the project, but government guarantees had been awarded as a token of confidence from several European governments.

Trevor's banking group would ensure the rights to a new drilling lease of the Arctic region of the North Atlantic. More importantly, an agreement had been crafted amongst them that half of the proceeds from the drilling venture would go directly to retire some of Europe's most severe Sovereign debt.

"I dub this venture, The Redemption Project."

Hurrah.

Jeff was grinning. "Just don't be calling us hard-core socialist...."

Laughter

"As you know, we are hard core free market capitalists..."

"Just hard core..." yelled a happy voice from the rear somewhere.

He smiled good naturedly and proceeded "But these are difficult times: This deal - is no more than a strong sense of obligation and understanding about what is important in our lives. Trevor MacDonnell would have it no other way. So..." he raised his glass "May they use their futures wisely."

"Here. Here."

"Well done."

He would be leaving the building offices, his tall frame and silver blue tie complementing his eyes and grey lined temples.

The high-rollers would follow up with a week of appreciative gatherings; parties, opera excursion and club luncheon events. The Media would dissect the Announcement with meticulous attention. This was London. City of innovative thinking. City of London Merchant Bankers.

As for the rest of the various administrations, staffs younger and new to the world of venture capital, they would celebrate with bonus monies for their families. Those unattached would party long into the night.

"Damned noble thing to do" said Jim, his best friend since University.

"Well, I hope it is." said Jeff, collecting his coat and receiving airline tickets from his Assistant for Washington DC. "I need to speak with his wife..."

"Since when does private equity help out the state?" laughed Jim "I can't believe it."

* *

Igor called George again.

"You'll never believe what I've found" he said. "Data from Peru of all places. Seismology graphs that coincide with your lake, which has dissipated, by the way. So, it's not worrisome..."

"*Hah.* I know what it was. It was an iceberg that wicked up an oil spill, and then travelling south, melted entirely to leave only the oil slick..."

"So I always knew you were a slick sonofabitch." laughed Igor.

"So..."

"Yes. So, there have been a few tremors, and of course along the Atlantic ocean ridge"

"Yes."

"But the turbulence, while evident and not particularly alarming shows a regularity that actually has a defining line, George"

George did not answer. He could have laughed. He could have waved it off as inconsequential. But they both knew what Igor was saying.

"It's the fault line that's long...These quakes, they leave Washington behind..."he said, both of them having long ago agreed that Washington was a city that deserved a good shake-up. But statistically, they knew it was nothing to sneer at.

George knew that less than six weeks ago, an earthquake had been registered in Canada. More recently another, further down. These were registering – along with wave action now being recorded for tsunami data - entirely down the Atlantic ocean crease where tectonic plates met. That meant a fault line in the seam of the earth had opened up, and would produce a mega volcanic jolt somewhere.

"God."

"Well, that explains the oil spill. There is a seepage that someone in Washington wants to blame on someone in a corporate board room... Like BP. In fact, it is a natural rupture that is effectively even wicking up icebergs."

They laughed, nervous. And they said no more. "I'm still waiting on new salinity charts...which I'll send up to you." promised Igor.

They hung up. No need to say more.

Igor trudged to his hut where the lighting was softer and the air warmer with coffee and food. He wanted a place to read. And read *carefully*. He clutched notes in his hands. He wore fir gloves and parka survival gear. He was looking down, and one of them fell out of its pouch. He stooped to pick it up, and touched the metal clip board with his skin. He was distracted, and nothing happened. At any other time on the Arctic, the contact might have peeled away his skin. He looked at his hand without injury. Things were definitely getting warmer, he noted grimly.

The salinity of the Atlantic ocean however, was altogether a different matter.

He trudged on.

* *

When the news reached Toronto Canada, the reaction was very different.

"The Redemption Project?" repeated Lauren. "What kind of goddamned name is that for a Venture?" She punched the speaker Off.

By the time she got the full file on the project, her mind was already racing ahead.

Lauren paced her dark shiny office, her thoughts miles away. She did not like to be interrupted. She did not like people milling about in her office. She did not like people. Period. Especially the kind who pandered to your good graces because you were worth a few Billion.

No. This was serious. Finally, she made a decision. *There was no way in hell that this firm was going to get the rights to that lease.* That lease belonged to her. The oil belonged to her. The bottom of the sea belonged to her, and even the goddamned Federal Reserve of the United States would belong to her before long. What she needed was that lease."

She reached for her switch "Get me Desmond and Una. I want to have dinner with them *Tonight*. Make the Reservations at the Marriott, downtown. I'll spend the night. I 'm flying to Washington in the morning. Book me a seat by mid-morning"

"Yes, Ma'am."

* *

The wave that hit the coast of Newfoundland was large. Sediments, rendered unstable by the release of gas hydrates, had generated a silent tsunami.

Once the tectonic plates began straining, it was only a matter of time before the slippage would cause an earthquake. The subsidence release in Virginia was so pressurized as to deliver a subterranean shock wave offshore to produce a landslide off the continental shelf.

The wave's amplitude was small offshore, yet long, - hundreds of kilometers in length. It formed only a slight swell, 300 millimeters, above the normal sea surface as it started to roll out, then grew in height as it reached shallow water.

By the time it reached land, it was two hundred meters in height and washed over everything along the northern coastlines within minutes.

Fortunately, there had been inclement weather, and beach visitors were few. Loss of life was minimal. But those that stood in its way had no chance of survival. Neither did the town, nor the roadways that housed the tourists and allowed rescue.

More worrisome however, was the Nuclear Power Facility that was not as updated as it should have been.

Two US Navy military carriers were in the vicinity. They were called upon by the US Government to survey the damage and offer assistance if needed.

They transmitted their message by radio, and redirected their mission. Their original course was to enter the Bering Sea.

Both surface combatants had been on their way to assist a disabled submarine on its slow track home with a burden of cargo...* *

Amanda took time from a Research Report to turn to something a little less serious. It had been a long week since the accident. Happily, Gwynie was fine.

The country was no longer at war with the British. Aspiring for industrial developments and finally feeling a little security, America had its own Treasury, currency, and Navy. Women in carriages enjoyed wealth that came from overseas as trade and exchange. Cotton, timber, metals, tobacco. Ships shuttled to and from Europe in a merchant fleet of sailing vessels. Plus a domestic industry was flourishing, even as inventions raced ahead in developing new industrial technologies like Walking Beam engines, steam power, rail, and even telegraph...

"...The oyster boats went out at dawn under sail. Long pincer-like tongs were then submerged to the riverbeds strewn with oyster seeds in the Chesapeake Bay. Pulled up by hand, a nest of oysters could be gathered from the bottom of the bay and dumped on the boards of their vessel in little time. One sorted, they were put into bushel baskets and by noon, a boat could be fully laden. The hulls were typically log built canoes of some size called Chesapeake Bay Sailing Log Canoes. Masts, rigs and boards hoisted sail and used ballast to stabilize their vessel on the bay. Because their secret, over the centuries, lay in their draft: They could move along the shoaling waters of the great estuary and up into sandy tributaries for oysters without going aground.

"It was the custom to reward the first boat to dock with good money, and racing back fully laden with glistening and tightly sealed fresh crustaceans was profitable. Especially in a burgeoning consumer market with commodities now fetching top market rates for such popular shellfish.

"Still, items accidently lifted off the bottom with a load of oysters were left dumped alongside the boats at the docks. Such was the case of one article coated in seaweed and barnacles, tossed aside on the local dock. When dried off by the sun, the item took shape. It was a box.

"An Annapolitan claimed it, cleaned it up, then sold it to a local hardware shop where odd pieces of dislodged cargo often strayed. He recognized it as a possible item that had sunk from the hold of the *Peggy Stewart*, something that occurred in the town a long time ago. And it survived.

"A Representative House Member of the General Assembly in town for the session, walked by the hardware shop and spotted it. He appreciated its intrinsic value as an item of trade, now memorialized as a fashionable virtue. It indicated the tribulations of a young nation. As a token, and cleaned up, it was taken to Washington and given to the President.

"The staff had it restored and repaired by a silversmith. Following the Louisiana Land Purchase from Napoleon, and with the final payments that followed, it was sent it France as a token of thanks and remembrance.

Amanda put down the article. She would call Barbara that evening.

* *

George was asked to submit his report to the Pentagon. To Admiral Argueta. United States Coastal Defense and Atlantic Environmental Advisor.

"There is concern that melting Arctic glaciers and sea ice may raise sea levels around the globe. If enough freshwater is introduced to the North Atlantic, there could be a shift in ocean currents, let alone an increase in water temperature.

"That the sea level is rising is a given. Land is slowing being submerging on the fringes of the water bodies all over the world..."

 He wrote.

"...Habitat is changing, especially in the Artic where the permafrost layers are giving way to marsh grass and open land areas for much of the year. Species cannot survive. Many of the migratory birds have changed flight trajectories, if they still exist. Extinction of species are frequent over the last two hundred years. So systemically are crop failures, population increases and even world wars changing the agricultural habits of man, frequently turning to fowl and fish as an alternative, regardless their role in the ecology..."

He hesitated. Then pressed on. "We should anticipate Melting ice caps."

"That means an infusion of fresh water" Again he paused.

 "In the Atlantic ocean such freshwater intrusions hold a steady standard of bi-blow currents with salt water. This affects the clouds, climate and general surface circulation of temperature. If the currents change, and the Atlantic fails to perform with extant ocean flows, then a reshaping of climates shall occur.

"The 'conveyor-belt' of warm water keeping the Atlantic circulation of currents are well known: West from Africa to the Gulf Stream Current eventually caress North American shores and re-crosses the northern Atlantic to keep northern Europe encased in warm maritime shadows.

"Change that 'conveyor-belt' circulation and you change the world temperature. In fact, if the ocean water level temperature rises, we should expect an immediate ice age..."

Finally, he came to the most difficult question submitted by Arguetta. *Is this global warming, how should it affect policy?*

"Global warming is not the scientific argument, and neither is it the fault of industry: This is a geological cyclic planetary condition, induced by solar flares; electromagnetic subterranean pulls and heat barriers induced by human populations. It would happen regardless."

Had he said too much? Was it appropriate? He was asked to offer an opinion. Should he do so?

"It is therefore logical to say that the issue is being *used* to exploit policy by special interests, including environmentalism seeking to inhibit free market capitalism for socialist purposes, and for centralized control of ownership of resources....A utopia of global dimension for the survival of a few, untested by cultural traditional of Western civilization rooted in early Judeo-Christian teaching."

He concluded. "Once those currents change, we're looking at an imminent and sudden ice age. Policy should reflect a preparedness for extending present liberties on earth, not bury them."

Argueta promised to be back to him for more explanations.

That was two weeks ago.

George disliked to wait.

* *

Amanda had the piece examined at the Smithsonian Institute.

Age had taken its toll. Some of the platinum was bent and misshapen. Its tiny casings appeared to be bereft of their jewels. What was most puzzling was the crusty corrosive marks at the banding.

In its heyday, such a bird would be set alight in reflection of lighting. Glimmers of shine; cut crystal - tortoise shell jewels and tiny diamonds would set the piece off.

"It was old. Yes" said John Mac Callister of the Freer Gallery. "We tend to see cultural gems trying to tell cultural stories. But damned if I can tell what's going on with this piece...I'm sorry. I'll love you to tell me though, when, and if you find the full story"

"I understand John. Thanks for looking into it with some care. Your leads are helpful. We'd like to make a small donation to the Museum as a token of thanks. Is that alright with you?"

"Absolutely." he said "You are a classy lady. And I'd be happy to sit with you anytime. Keep in touch Amanda."

She did find the full story. It came from Archives of private collections in New York.

It was, in its own way, tied to the American story of immigrants at the turn of the century. In fact, it spoke of turmoil in Europe - turmoil and conflict that left Europe divided, and policies that had brought consequences of untold misery.

She was determined to see this through - For the Firm. For the boy's life, and for all that she held important, she decided. *Because if you didn't find meaning in life,* *then life wasn't worth living...*That was something Trevor told her.

Too many had been denied the luxury of choice. Young or old; choices made for an individual whose will was blocked by other doctrines of ownership, public or private.

And by greed. Too many had been killed or damaged for greed. So yes. This she must do...

Besides, she had promised Barbara. The grandmother had kept it for Jacob.

With books spread out from the south window to the door, she was drawing a picture of social history from WWII. The question she had to answer, after it all was narrowed down, was *why*? And what did the bird mean?

From the caliber of craftsmanship, the item was made in the custom of the 17th century - commissioned for a Royal family in Europe.

"Greco revivalism" in style, it was doubtless intended to adorn the home of a Duke. In its finest moments it was clearly a bird of some elegance. Even as age deadened the lightness and its shape become more prevalent than its effect. Still, to Amanda, it started to hold almost magical properties in its delicate bearing and color.

It seemed to have a flat bill. Not a duck. Not a wader of any kind. But a bird of flight. And so bulbous that it needed help, evidently. For it had a small handle at the banding, as if the delicate fingers that held it should have something to pull. Like a toy.

Still, the puzzle of corrosion could hardly be ignored. What metals had corroded, if they were indeed precious? It has sat at the bottom of Annapolis harbor for years. This she had to keep reminding herself.

The stones themselves came from Siberia, the curator told them: The Caucasus or the Urals. It had agate, Siberian jade, other rocks...There was a message there.

It would take a little time to unearth. She started the research.

Two days later, Amanda had the full story.

* *

"One more squeeze on buyers...and the whole market will dry up." said Jack Chester, taking advantage of the ear of a Congressman able to free up capital.

The sky was bright blue and cloudless, the breeze off the Potomac river wafted briskly across the marshy area of Wilson Bridge in Alexandria Virginia.

On the higher ridge, at the Fort Hunt Golf Club , the Greens fairly shone in the glimmer of sunlight with nothing less than an invitation to play golf.

Rain had pushed up the grass to sharp blue edges, and while a little taller than normally allowed by Club standards because of wet soil, it left a nice feel to the swing of a golf club.

The two men playing golf were not happy.

The game started out easily enough -the Congressman bragging about his victories on the Hill this week; and the investment broker on his Fees from real estate transactions this week. They had a lot to chatter about.

The market was good, the broker told him. Fed purchases, which was aiding big banks by buying their bad loans and flooding them with money, was having its effect broadening balance sheets. They were lending.

The Congressman was interested. He represented a district known for its high-end income producers. They worried about an uneven housing market.

He got the full story and listened carefully. If the housing market was good, so were the fees of those adding commissions. As he saw it, that left the market either feasting or fasting, depending on which properties were selected.

At the Eighth hole, the Congressman stood at the tee, and glanced up at his own house perched on the ridge, partially hidden by trees, but in view. It was a convenient place to live while in Washington.

"Wish I could sell that damned thing." he said, delivering a blow with his club that sent the ball one hundred feet into the air.

"I've told you I could get it sold Harry..." said the broker.

"Yeah. Yeah. Yeah. I know. It's just that *she* won't sell..." "Seriously?"

"She's got the place littered with antiques – '*Investments*'...It's a goddamned warehouse."

"Well. It is Art. It is beautiful, and the house location is good."

"We've been here for over twenty years."

"Why not ask her to let it go?"

The Congressman looked at him, waiting for his shot to end.

"And tell her what, Jack? That I'm down a few hundred thousand on campaign funds? Another one hundred fifty on expenditures that cannot be expensed out? And what about that the loss of my investment in the Hedge fund that ran me a bullshit line that doesn't end? It set me back, I'm telling you."

"It was a bad deal."

"More like a bum investment that took out a million...."

"She doesn't know?"

"She doesn't know *squat*." said the Congressman. They walked. "And she must lose her home over this?"

Jack spoke softly. "You know, it's hard as hell being a wife in Washington DC. Either you're a career woman and earning a living, or you're a volunteer soliciting funds for this, that, and the other cause..." he said.

"It's true, Jack. She's helped me enough on the campaign trail over the years. That much I'll give her. But you're right. It's hard as hell being a wife in this city. By the time you've competed your service on the Hill, you're out of money."

They finished up the hole.

The Congressman spoke next. "I'm counting on you to make a case for a Dividends Release on that offshore drilling platform. God knows, the company is able enough. They've enjoyed enough Mineral Managements Contract concessions to mine off our coast for generations..."

Jack laughed. "Pittance...really, considering their global reach today. The sun never sets on their operations and mining profitability."

"But there's pressure, right?"

"Absolutely. It's a fossil fuel energy company, and a favorite shareholding strategy in the portfolio of any large Investment Fund Manager - both here and abroad. But yes. There's pressure to rein them in..."

"I'll talk to the key Congressmen weighing a bill to waive compliance requirements. The Carrier cartel is bracing for a fossil fuel emissions ban, they fear heavy fines from their profits. The Waiver however, will leave their profits untaxed. Tomorrow, I'm at the White House dinner. God knows the President is staying away from any decision on *that* one."

"I don't blame him. It's a political liability if he doesn't veto the bill. But it'll deflate his income to pay for his social programs, let alone inflate pass-alongs..."

The Congressman gathered his clubs.

 "Americans are still reeling from the last round of health costs...This may just shut down the shop, I fear..."

The Congressman was puffing from the exertion. He looked down at his ball, not exactly in the rough nor under the trees, but where the grass was weedy and the ground uneven. "I know" he said, aligning for the shot. "Still, I need the money. I need the investment dividends to come my way..." He delivered the shot. "Or, I need to press *against* passage of that pending bill for the Carriers. ...See to it, will you, that I have a good offer for this house?"

He called it a day and offered his resignation from the game.

 "Right." said Jack Chester, knowing when the argument was over. "How's about a bite to eat up at the Club House?"

"Nah. I'm done here..." came the response.

* *

Chapter Eight

St. Petersburg, 1917

By the time that Peter Faberge received the bird, he understood it completely.

Being a Russian and trained as a goldsmith jeweler, he recognized the message that this bird must portray.

It was of Russian breed, the type that only lore and legend described from the great forests of the plains of the Urals. Here was a statement from a Russian landscape that should leave no doubt as to its origin: The stones themselves came from Siberia, a display representing the Caucasus and the Urals. There was agate; Siberian jade (nephrite); rhodonite; malachite; aventurine quarts; rock crystal, obsidian and bowenite - a variety of serpentine.

The craftsman was a Parisian who first added those gems. Originally, the artist was Russian. Yes? Or maybe he was shown a portrait of colors that he should copy. Either way, they were vibrant and well proportioned, and he must copy them. That was his commission.

The feathers, supported on engraved gold trellis, were set with gemstones, and the chest carved from nephrite, placed in rock crystal and skillfully arranged to contour the head and beak of the bird.

Now that Peter and his brother worked at the Faberge Firm developed by his father, he had full responsibility for the piece. Not only should it reflect the natural environment as a symbol of beauty, but the very coloring of the regions from it came should tell of great wealth derived from those hills. Especially since his own father had been of the Huguenot traditions of Europe, where gems and brilliance of the Orient were recognized.

He was to alter it.

Outside St. Petersburg, anarchist gunfire and Palace Guards could be heard. He remained focused on the task at hand. These were changing times, he knew...

The hours passed as he worked. He added to the translucent enamel guilloches ground with sunbursts in a sort of revived quatre-couleur gold work. He had a free reign over the work since the gold fretwork had been long ago developed by his family. Still, it was tense.

Tsar Alexander III patronized the Faberge firm, and even made him the Official Supplier of the Imperial Court. Already, Nicholas II ordered work for the Dowager Tsarina Marie Feodorovna and Tsarine Alexandra Feodorovna.

He understood the growing influence of Italian Renaissance and Art Nuveau stylistic subtleties. It had helped grow the business. He had several. As their Franchise grew in popularity, he filled his workshops with skilled artists, allowing the Imperial Warrant of the Appointment to be stamped on his work, recognized as the Romanov double-headed eagle. He knew that before long, after the Revolution, a Committee of Employees would take over. He would then leave the country, he decided. But this...

The artwork alone was in value far greater than the gems. He would leave the crude settings in place rather than deface the sculpture with the kind of ornate fretwork that the Russian Imperial Household had so come to love in their affecting of French designs.

But what puzzled him was the motive behind the commission to work on this sculpture: He was to cut it half and remove the internal workings of what was once a clock. He puzzled. Shortly after that, when a small delivery was made to his shop from the Imperial Palace he understood the full meaning of his commission.

The work was complete and prepared for travel.

By the time the King of England received the gift from the Russian Tsar, the ravages of a full scale war had wrapped around every corner of Europe: Monarchies came under attack; their holdings seized; land and wealth was taken by a growing labor movement that swept clean the political landscape until gradually, fierce dictators emerged to replace the monarchs of Europe.

King George would not have England succumb to such a fate: He would do what England had done since the beginning of time, distance itself from Europe as an island state.

Further, he dropped his German Heritage name of Saxe-Goethe inherited from Prince Albert, husband to his mother Queen Victoria. He adopted the Royal Household name of Windsor as the official name of the British Monarchy. He would have nothing to do with the demands of Europe, nor would he suppress civil unrest with violence. Instead, under the advice of

Parliament, he drove himself to acts of charity, making it the hallmark of his reign.

It saved the English Monarchy.

 Outside, the disadvantaged, the poor and the unemployed coalesced around labor movements as an Industrial Revolution roared into train tracks, motor cars and fossil energy.

The ceramic jewel was sent to him by Tsar Nicholas of Russia in their darkest hour. It sat alone, neglected and out of sight, a horrifying reminder of what lay in fate for monarchs who disregarded their peoples.

Shortly after his death, it was said, after he uttered his last words to his Nurse, the bird was snatched as retribution by a young girl on the cleaning staff of the palace, wife to a man on the streets unemployed.

"God Damn You." the King had said to his Nurse as she administered the morphine that would end his life once and for all. *How could anyone say that to his Nurse after a lifetime of loyal service to the Royal Household?*

The young girl who stole bird migrated to America with her husband: In New York it was sold to a pawn shop, later bought by a Russian Émigré.

* *

Amanda was outside beyond the kitchen porch trimming her plants when Mrs. Carlos appeared. There was a phone call for La Signora…

"Hello?"

It was Jeff Watson.

Amanda relaxed a little. It wasn't often you got phone calls this early in the morning.

"Good morning. How are you?" he said cheerfully.

"I am fine, thank you, Jeff. It is a beautiful day. I was outside pruning… What's up?"

"Uhm…nothing much" he said slowly "just an invitation to the White House, that's all…"

"An invitation to the *White House*?" repeated Amanda.

"Yes. For the most beautiful and capable Researcher in Washington. A garden party on the front lawn Friday afternoon 4.00 PM. Cocktail Dress. Care to go?"

He totally surprised her. Amanda's soiled hand raised to her forehead and a dark stain of potting soil streaked her face. "Wow."

"I gather that's a 'Yes'?"

"For what occasion? I mean, how am I invited…?"

"Well…We're on the Guest List, and I asked to have your name affixed next to mine as consort. Is that OK?"

"Jeff err…How exactly does it relate to our work?"

"Well….Let's see: For one thing, you were instrumental, as far as we are concerned, in successfully   making   a   case   to   introduce legislation...Secondly, you get to meet most of the Congressmen on the Committee. Finally, if that isn't enough, I get to introduce you to the President and the First Lady...?"

"Jeff. Thank you for your thoughtfulness. I am most grateful. Can you give me a chance to respond when I look at my calendar?"

"Respond? *Respond?* What's to respond when the White House calls? Don't you want to meet the President?"

"Of course I do, Jeff. It's always an honor. But actually, he already knows Trevor and I...It's just that I'm trying to get a grasp of whether it's appropriate or not for me to go..."

"I see. Trevor is at sea, right?"

Amanda paused. Yes, she thought. He is at sea.

"Besides..." continued Jeff "We want to make sure we bag that legislation. Remember it is in the interests of us all, n'est ce pas?"

"Well of course it is Jeff. We do collaborate. It's just that..."

Amanda had walked into the library with the phone and glanced at her calendar. "I'm busy on that day."

"You're *busy?*"

"Yes."

"Look" he said suddenly "I'm in traffic. I'll call you back."

It's not that Amanda waited for his call. It's just that she anticipated it, and she was a little disturbed.

One the one hand, going to the White House with a distinguished Gentleman who had enormous pull on the Hill was one thing...On the other, attending the White House to advance your own Firm's business was another.

She couldn't quite differentiate between which...

* *

Jim received a report that truly surprised him.

Jim may have been Trevor's best friend, but he was not above a little innate competition with the man. Hearing this report was of particular interest to him. The question is, did it lay open Trevor's scheme and leave him vulnerable, or did it have a means of being contained?

The real question remained with the Americans. Where they up to the challenge? Should they be confronted? Would it embarrass them that the rights to their lease had been given to a British Firm with the intention of aiding European debt? How well would that go with the general American public? Rather, how much political capital was at stake here? Certainly, Trevor would be talking with them...

He should talk to Trevor about it, at the very least. That is, when he returned. He and his wife had a home in Washington DC, and with their youngest still being in school, he spent most of his time there. Word had it however, that he was on a Special Mission.

No. This was opportunity to advance oneself, he decided.

He would approach Henry Demsworth himself with this information himself. It would give him great pleasure to be in the company of the Minister, and perhaps add to their already warming relationship.

Yes, having friends in the leadership ranks had its privileges, and he certainly had paid enough for them.

He asked his secretary to make the appointment for a call to the Prime Minister's Office. To ask for an appointment please.

Trevor could be informed...in due course.

* *

Lauren insisted. She wanted to press her case to the key Congressional Leaders of the United States. They promised to weigh her appeal.

Her Canadian company should receive the rights to the drilling lease off Canada, an offshore drilling contract that was now awarded to Trevor's *Redemption Project.* A Letter of Commitment had been promised.

The European company that had been awarded the contract by the US Government was to pay its royalties to the Americans not in Canadian Dollars, but in US Dollars. There was a difference.

Trevor's bid to aid ailing sovereign debtors was compelling since many of any of them were US Investors.

Lauren Papendopulous, dining with three key Congressman on the Appropriations Committee was in a full sway of a power-broker's look. Her hair swept back in silver status-blond; the dark suit and pearls, and makeup suitable for any Photo Opportunity. Seated at the candlelit table of the Mandarin Hotel, she leaned forward to deliver her most promising *coup de grace.*

"Gentlemen, I shall buy your Treasuries and your Debts as my payment."

It seemed like an offer they could not refuse.

* *

He was puzzled.

By the time Jim strode into the Prime Minister's office, he did not know that the matter was already officially known. Or that Trevor had been informed with a message directly by the Prime Minister himself: The Americans were considering awarding the lease rights to a Canadian company.

So Jim felt rather foolish. He was at somewhat of a disadvantage. What was he here for? Rather, why had he not talked to Trevor, already?

The Minister would have liked an answer. So Jim made one up. "I believe Sir, and I've heard this only through the grapevine - no official information exists, but the Chinese are the intended buyers of the product, once it has been extracted from the ocean floor."

"Really?"

Jim had no idea. The Prime Minister had been informed by the Ambassador in Washington that the Canadian Company which had been given the lease was receiving some very special dispensation from the US Government.

The question was, why?

This disappointment they both shared in common. That, and a warm brandy of Scotland's finest brand.

* *

Argueta sat at his desk at the Pentagon and put on his reading glasses.

Why were so many North Korean fishing vessels suddenly so interested in trawling off North America? They were clearly pinching the territorial offshore boundaries...

This was not their habit. Nor their ship types. Not even their kind of seafood harvest. He put down the satellite images. Too many for coincidence, he thought.

But until explanations could be offered, intelligence was not something you shared. What were they up to? Did the Coast Guard have any ships deployed there at the moment? The Navy? If he was wondering about America's northern borders, this was now a new development. Normally, the seas were too frozen for passage.

He turned to the matter on his desk next. Was there any Security risk with this intelligence? He should read the full report.

For seven years now, one the world's largest oil drilling companies had been planning to drill a well in the pristine Chukchi Sea, Alaska's Arctic Coast.

Billions had been spent in securing leases, and years of environmental hurdles had been addressed. Then there would more time, cost and infrastructure necessary to bring the oil to market, he knew.

Further, the corporation had spent money and years collecting 3-D seismic data. A fleet of seventy new Ice Breakers had been built. It had "undertaken the most aggressive and comprehensive reforms to offshore oil and gas regulation and oversight in history."

"A Christmas Eve" moment, as the Governor of Alaska said in his official Announcement when the award was made to the company. A royalties agreement had been achieved to satisfy both the state and the Federal Government

But something was troubling here.

Not only was the sea itself presenting its set of challenges - such as the ice being the thickest in a decade, but problems were cropping up for the 4.700 ton oil-spill containment system, but there other storms: The Administration now thinking of turning down the *Redemption Project.*

Why? It was to provide for America 400,000 barrels of oil per day.

Argueta went over the numbers. He understood how the Nation was still dependent on foreign oil imports that left millions of Americans out of work and begging for government aid. Especially since the Federal Government could not even sustain its own Defense budget.

It was as if a campaign had been aroused to incite activism and resistance.

Since when did the Administration cave in to demands from activism or threats?

Why was the drilling season so drastically shortened? Where did the objections come from?

Already, the Environmental Protection Agency was dragging its feet.

And the Coast Guard was nit-picking. It delayed the final oil recovery barge from leaving the Pacific Norwest for fear of a potential storm. "The ship might drag its anchor." Permits were to be waived only when it is found that technology does not exist to meet the extraordinary requirements of the EPA. *That was utterly ridiculous.*

Argueta fumed: Yet the US Navy was supposed to support with Emergency patrols off its northern border *without* Appropriated money from a Congress - money diverted to Administration whims of policy? Frustrating, perhaps. But not his duty to question.

Still, he had been asked to review public activities that suggested deliberation of attack or threat to the defense of the nation. Especially regarding the northern border.

New objections had came from in from the Inuit Native Americans demanding more accountability for drilling in the proximity of their hunting grounds.

Other environmental groups were coming out of nowhere citing concerns over walruses, beluga whales and seals. Even for Penguins, migratory birds and other historical weather birds that flew the Arctic fringes for hatching young in other regions like Russia and Asia.

Argueta looked down a list: And who the hell were these so-called 'Advocacy Groups?' *The Oceans for Wilderness? The Pacific Packers. The Fish of the Sea Society. The Transpacific Carriers of the Americas?*

One name jumped out. *The Sowaldi Group.* What was *this* name doing on this list?

Known as terrorists in Syria, Asia, Afghanistan and Europe, this group had no interest and no business on this list. Argueta was buzzed.

"Time for your Two o'clock at the Navy Yard Sir" said the Lieutenant on the desk phone. "Will you need a car?"

"No. I'll take my own. I'm going home after that, thanks."

"Yes Sir."

On the way he made a decision. He picked up his cell.

"Amanda, would your Group be able to do some research for me?"

* *

The Touring coach was full. Amanda had packed Gwynie's backpack with a few surprises. Amongst them three simple rag dolls with a pouch that looked like a burlap sack.

Gwynie was seated in the front with two friends. Each child had a rag doll, the pouch invoking curiosity and interest. In it were swatches of gauze, gold and print fabric; pieces of string; buttons, Velcro and a smaller samples of soft leather.

By the time the rag dolls had been dressed; undressed; interchanged and fashion-enhanced with cloth dresses, buttons, string belts, fastened-leather shoes, hats, shawls and Velcro-appliquéd wigs, the boys on the bus had not only ceased to agitate the girls, but wanted to get their hands on the rag dolls for their own fashion imprints.

A mother on the bus gave Amanda the thumbs up sign. "Brilliant."

Four mothers and twenty four children were on their way to a field trip.

The day was planned for Historic Mount Vernon, south of Alexandria, Virginia. From McGlean, the ride took almost an hour.

Arranged by Amanda, what started out as a half-day summer excursion for a few children in a van blossomed into a tour bus event subscribed by twenty plus school families.

Mount Vernon was the home of George Washington, she told them. First president of the United States and Army General who led the colonies to victory in the battle for Independence from the British in 1776.

The children stared at her, and Amanda smiled.

Historic Mount Vernon was a popular place to visit. Excitement began as the bus pulled up to park in a woodland thick with old and mysterious trees; cobble-brick walkways and stone enclaves.

Once inside the main gate, the children rushed into the Entrance and looked up. The Gift shop. The Book shop. The world of another earth surrounded them with strange stuff. They had never seen such a wonderland so full of unfamiliar things. Here, there were horses and wooden stiles; over there rotating weather vanes and birds in clocks. Dolls. Guns. Arrows. Toys and pulleys and trains; kites and hoists; wheeled sleds and stuffed barn animals.

Once first impressions sank in, more subtle items came into view. Real items that entertained real boys in that period of George Washington. Some put on the hat. Others touched the sword.

For hunting from the early 17th and 18th century an array of early colonial guns, powder horn; arrow-heads, sticks for whittling and slings and stones lay prone. Some opened books of game birds, animals and feathers... *Oh boy.*

For the voyager, it was all there, they squealed. Adventuring pouches for messages and signals came in signal containers for carrier pigeons. Carry-boxes for pencils, quills lay open. Paper, wax seals, letter openers, ink wells, code books and leather-bound pouch scrolls for military orders and secret maps.

For cooks, they stood amazed. Wooden vessels and wares of the Welsh spoon were highly carved. Decorative bowls, shiny silver, pewter mugs, ugly - *ew.* faces on tankards and ornamental instruments of all kinds and shapes filled the tables...

For gardeners, there could pick from shelves planting seeds of colonial flowers; discovery pictures; treatises of magic balms and lore mysteriously tied with clues and string... Gwynie found a garden book with a bunny.

Amanda's group of children were transfixed, each using their budget to purchase an item or two. Those who did not choose something could come back later, - or not purchase anything if they didn't want to, said Amanda.

The morning of magic passed swiftly.

Children ran down historic pathways of cobble brick. They crossed plantation greens that marked early colonial life of America. They entered barns, chickens, stables, horses, herb gardens, pottery sheds, orchards and old tools in the Foundry and Milking sheds.

There was little need of supervision, said the parents following. Many sat on benches, glowing in the calm weather and enjoying the park setting.

 For children it was an atmosphere of farm life from early America, and it was bliss, they discovered. One by one, the tensions of modern life could almost be seen shed from their young shoulders.

Still, Amanda also saw that the heat of the day was wearing them out, and she worried about hydration.

"Lunch time." she announced.

If the afternoon was to be dedicated to touring the Historic Mansion where Martha Washington lived, then there was time for a break.

Within minutes, her posse were seated beneath trellised vines in an open veranda munching lunch sandwiches, chips, apples and pop-sickles. Deep sucking sounds from straws and slurping kept them occupied as crows filled the treetops and sparrows hopped around the ground cleaning up food crumbs...

"They're *enchanted*." said a voice behind Amanda.

She jumped. "Jeffrey."

"Hello."

He stood there, his hair swept across a tanned brow, his eyes blue and smiling. He wore a casual knit Sports shirt, khakis and loafers, as if on his way to a golf game.

Amanda looked around and signaled to a parent across to the next group seated. The parent signaled back to accommodate. Amanda retreated from the children.

"What... err... What are you doing here?" Amanda led Jeff out beyond the lunch area.

"Why, thinking about you of course. I thought, why not go? I could actually be with you...?" he teased.

She looked back at the children.

He leaned in. "You seem to be either entertaining...or feeding others Amanda Wells. Do you always make things happen for everyone else but yourself?"

Amanda was puzzled. "Aren't you supposed to be at the err...White House?"

"Aren't you?..." he answered.

She looked at him, trying to understand his tone.

"I came to find out *what* it was... that made you turn me down... for the White House."

"How did you know where to find me?"

"Mrs. Carlos told me. She thought I was one of the parents coming to join you..."

They walked towards the Museum Entrance, away from the children. It was obvious that he was not at all being clear.

She opened her mouth to speak when he grabbed her by the elbow and backed her into a brick partition garden behind the Administrative building. Above them dense trees overhung with shade and heavy foliage.

"Jeff..." she began.

It happened very suddenly. He had her against the stone wall, his hands travelling up under her arms to fold her breasts, then up to her neck where he held her throat upward and landed a kiss on her lips.

"Amanda..." he gasped. "I'm besotted by you..." Again his lips came down, her neck held fast by his hands.

With as much grace and respect as she could find, Amanda dislodged his hands from her throat, slipped from his grasp and stepped out into the open, her breath deep and longing for air. She stood there, nursing a raw elbow, waiting for him to emerge.

He came out, his eyes down, searching for words. "I'm sorry...I'm sorry." he said.

She didn't need to say anything. Her body did. She stood facing the main Exit area.

"I'm leaving. I just ...I'll call you...I'm sorry." he said again, and left.

Amanda retreated. It was a good hour before she joined the troupe at the Mansion Exhibit.

Her head was reeling. *Where had she lost her focus? What had happened here?*

Only just before leaving, when Gwynie reached up to hold her mother's hand did Amanda find some semblance of recovery. She paused thoughtfully, and looking into Gwynie's eyes realized that she was not the only one unsettled.

Trevor was the one who gave them all equilibrium. Without him, they were disoriented.

Had she done something... *misleading*?

* *

Lauren was particularly pleased with herself. Not only was she achieving the drilling lease Off-shore in the territorial waters available to the United States following the Arctic Ice melt, but the rates of exchange were nicely falling her way.

What the hell, she was in the banking business after all. What else did stock exchanges exist for?

She dabbed her red lips, saw a beguiling face in the mirror, put on leather black pants that resembled a cat suit, and landed a chiffon shirt with leopard skin shades. The total effect was professional while evocative. This she had mastered as a young fashion designer long ago.

Actually, by the time she discovered the power of clothes, she had already outgrown her interest in the industry and shifted into the financing of the garment business. Outsourcing manufacturers quickly followed overseas...

This, the board would admire. Wait till they received the full information. What the company would receive as benefit was substantial. Attached of course, was her bonus payment.

The last thing she needed to worry about was the Memo received this morning. It amounted to pressure that politicians came under when scrutiny was focused on matters of banking. Could she sweeten her offer?

Really?

If the currency rates were off their mark, and Canadian currencies outpaced American then so be it. She had promised them the going rates, right? So that's what they would get.

If the credibility of banker's lending rates rested on some lame administrative oversight group that failed to notice special trades at special rates, that was not her fault. It bothered her not at all that the result implied only one thing: Fixing the interbank offering rate, Libor. And if the British Bankers' Association that oversaw the Libor noticed nothing, then all the more stupid men they.

The rates offered to the Canadian dollar exchange for borrowing were lower than others. From that she could garner millions of dollars in profit on top of the sales of the oil from the wells.

All she had to worry about now, was how to keep the Americans on their toes. She would apply some pressure to serve her interests.

She picked up the cell and made a call.

* *

The Senior Program Manager did not like the data. An earthquake in the Washington DC region had always been considered a remote possibility. But August had changed everything.

Even with the epicenter of the quake being in the center of Virginia, the quake left the Washington Monument cracked; the Whitehouse damaged, and the National Cathedral raising $50 million in funds to repair fallen gargoyles.

 As for the rest of the city, the underground Metro; The Capital, and all residential apartment buildings were yet to be inspected.

But the quake was felt as far away as Connecticut...

A routine estimation figures issued from the Nuclear Regulatory Commission came nowhere close: The odds of a quake that might cause damage to its facility was less than 1:1 in 100,000.

Well, *guess what guys*, he thought, marching down the hall way with his charts.

His cell rang out. Would he be back in time to buy some vegetables? His wife wanted to know before the ball game tonight started for the kids? If not, could he pick some up on the way home?...

Yes. He put away his charts, got rid of his overalls, and less than an hour later, made for his Jeep outside in the parking lot.

He was to report his findings to the Department of Homeland Security. That was the drill for anything that threatened the seat of government. His responsibility was considerable. He was Senior Manager for the Calvert Cliffs Nuclear Power Plant, a critical source of energy.

Outside, similar thoughts were on the mind of another man, a visitor, Victor LaMaas.

He observed the well-maintained fencing; the fresh paint on the premises and the insignia of the nuclear facility as he drove by on his way down to Southern Maryland where he kept a beach house. It was an impressive facility, as a plant.

He knew that joint venture between France and a renown Icelandic Energy corporation had successfully coexisted for years. The two 2700 megawatt thermal Generation II loop pressurized water reactors that they owned and operated stood at Calvert Cliffs and served the Mid Atlantic region of the US East Coast.

Unit 1, a fully operational plant, used a General Electric designed main turbine and generator. Unit 2 used a Westinghouse-designed main turbine and generator. Heat produced by the reactor was cycled back into the Chesapeake Bay which became the cooling heat-sink for the plant.

The pressurized water reactors operated 692 days non-stop to serve the greater metropolitan areas of Washington DC and its suburbs. It's capacity ran at 101 percent.

A third nuclear reactor plant had been proposed to the facility.

Objections came because of the cost, and because threats were cited for a dense population area.

 The Nuclear Regulatory Commission defined two emergency planning zones around the nuclear power plants: a plume exposure pathway zone with a radius of 10 miles presented exposure to inhalation and airborne radioactive contamination, and an ingestion pathway zone of about 50 miles that would contaminate food and liquids with radioactivity. Washington DC was 45 miles away, and included a population of almost three million people.

When initially built in the 1970s, the two plants cost 766 million USD. While the initial applications for the third power plant was approved, and the cost of the new facility would be almost 10 Billion USD, the government asked for a Guarantee Fee of $880 Million USD *upfront*. It stopped the venture from breaking ground.

The chief environmental matter of concern, according to scientists at the Johns Hopkins University, was the blue crab in the Chesapeake Bay.

LaMaas had to smile. This was a value system that appealed to him. But then again, that was not his mission. His mission here was to create an incident that would put pressure on legislators in Washington DC.

He had planning to do.

He would report to Lauren tomorrow.

The Plan was preposterous. LaMaas understood Lauren's goal.

On Lauren's instructions, he had already applied a little distress to the family of Trevor MacDonnell.

Evidently, the stakes were getting higher now. As was his fee. So, the plan to execute further damage was clearly on the table.

First, he had to shut down the source of information that was keeping this danger alive. That source, evidently, lived in Washington DC. It didn't have to be spelled out. And no tickling around the edges.

His moves would have to be more assertive and final. No longer was he to frighten people off. He was to kill.

* *

Argueta called Amanda.

"The tag number that ended with SKI which you asked to investigate turned up a man by the name of LaMaas. He comes from a famous Afrikaner Diamond family: He's a US Citizen, living in Southern Maryland. He works in the area, and there seems no cause for alarm. I am sorry, but his presence there was completely coincidental."

He paused

"I'm sorry to leave you without helpful information. Yes. You must have had a fright...wait, hold on Amanda. - (*yes, thank you Mary, I'll take that call as soon as I'm finished here...*) Anyway, all is well. Your daughter is undamaged and safely at home. I will keep checking on the name though. So don't worry..."

Amanda knew when she was told stop being an alarmist. "Of course. I understand. Thanks for checking..."

That was that.

Whatever happened at the college was as coincidence. Period. Put it out of your mind, she decided.

OK.

* *

It was Saturday, and after an early walk with the dogs, Amanda was in the kitchen reading the paper over a cup of coffee.

There was a massive amount of work to do in the garden today. Gwynie appeared with a trowel in her hand.

"Right then." said Amanda. "To our troops all waiting for us in the field..." she laughed, snatching up Gwynie for a big hug and a toss.

Truth be known, Amanda was not a gardener-born. The real surprise was Gwynie who seemed to have a child-like instinct for looking at the picture of a plant on a packet and knowing where to put it...At least, close enough to the plan.

The Tudor House in Washington DC was a charmer. There, in the hot humid, hot summer climate, gardens had a way of flourishing in wild and wonderful ways. Over the years, theirs had lapsed. But remarkable hide-away places in this city garden flourished.

Principally, there was once a knot design that had prevailed. "Shall we make a Bunnykins place Gwynie?" asked Amanda.

Gwynie lit up. She knew Bunnykins. Her egg cup; saucer and bowl had Bunnykins. She had a garden book with a bunny too. She thought about it and nodded solemnly.

"Then Bunnykins it is." cheered Amanda.

They planted evergreen herbs at the outer geometric beds and enclosed the knot.

"This way, we shall have green things to look at all year round, don't you think?"

Gwynie agreed, if still a tad dubious about her mother's concept of Bunnykins, who should be left outside in the garden at night.

Together, they turned over the soil; un-potted the herbs; stuffed them into mulchy holes and watered. They planted creeping juniper first.

 "That's *Juniperus horiontalis*" heralded Amanda to her daughter aiding with an absent expression of delight on her face. Behind her were trowel and mulch in the wheelbarrow which she loved digging.

Next came Rosemary. "Wowsmry" repeated Gwynie.

 "That's *Rosmarinus officinalis*" said Amanda, tickling. "Now, here...we put Thyme."

"Iym" repeated Gwynie, the surveyor.

Side by side they dug at the seed bed. "What would Bunnykins like to hide in?" asked Amanda.

"These." yelled Gwynie. She pointed at a tray of bedding wild flowers. They were bright, white and yellow.

"...this then, is Angel's Trumpet - *Datura inoxia*"

"*Da..oxiaa.*" repeated Gwynie, approvingly.

"And here... we shall put a small statue of Bunnykins, yes?"

Now Gwynie jumped up and down. She got it. All the things in the knot were for Bunnykins. The statue on the central dial was for Bunnykins.

"I want him to... the...to...sit.. *here.*" said Gwynie.

Her view would be perfect, decided Amanda. For Gwynie, Amanda wanted to create a safe area with a presentable garden. Their land was large enough to support a small meadowland background. This could be their spot to delight in. So, with symmetry in mind, she had allowed for some variation that gave Gwynie a place of delights in the garden. *Her Secret Garden.*

"A visitor for La Signora." announced Mrs. Carlos. It was about Three o'clock in the afternoon.

Sarah Delaney appeared. "I'm sorry to intrude...I had no idea you lived in such a wilderness here." she teased.

"This is our daughter, Gwynie MacDonald."

"Gwynie, this is Mrs. Delaney."

The child beamed at her, smudgy-faced, frizzed hair and a weed in her hand.

"Mrs. Del...ey, Mommy's friend."

"What a beauty *she'll* be with those eyes..." said Sarah.

It was almost nine o'clock at night before Sarah slowed down with her incessant chatter.

"There is a Congressman opposing our bill in the Senate." she said.

Only after Mrs. Carlos had served dinner, and after Gwynie had been tucked away in bed *sans* her bedtime story, that Sarah Delaney began to make her exit.

With her coat on, Sarah Delaney looked about Amanda's home and remarked "You know. I envy you. You are so even-minded and have a decent life. That's nice."

Amanda felt a need to assuage her, brazen as she was. "Not as lovely as your house in Maryland, Sarah. It's a dream place, your house and gardens."

Sarah stopped suddenly, her bag in her hand. "Yes. It is. A dream place. But not a reality. We're falling apart Tom and I..."

Sarah Delaney walked to the door and was almost out when she turned suddenly and said absently "By the way, Jeff says hello. He enjoyed meeting you at the Kennedy Center. He wants to see you in his office next week. And he said to tell you that he talked to a man called Chester. Something about 'tell Amanda that it's all in her hands now...'"

Sarah kissed Amanda in perfunctory fashion, and left.

Amanda went pale.

* *

"I'm so Sorry Miss Wells" she could hear the words now echoing through her head as she walked blindly down 54th Street .

At the bottom of the building, she could see the sky if she looked up. The Offices of Klugberg and Freeman were lodged in the shadow of Manhattan's highest sky scrapers. *How could she feel so dumb?*

Mr. Taylor was unable to receive her.

She paused.

Usually, when Trevor's company conducted business with the law firm, they were attentive. They kept appointments. Particularly since he was one of their best clients whose interests they represented in the United States. Clearly, their fees reflected that?

"Was there any *other* partner in the Law firm that Amanda might like to talk to ...on short notice?" asked the Para-legal receptionist.

Their conversation was interrupted "Mrs. MacDonald, I'm Ben Phillipson. I am so sorry about this. Something err... happened over the weekend which Bill had to tend to immediately. I do apologize. Is there any way we can reschedule?"

Amanda's cab had already pulled up to the entrance of their building, waiting to pick her up.

"Nothing ...*serious* I hope?" she said.

"No. Well, actually, yes." he paused, evidently debating whether to inform her.

Here was the wife of the firm's best client and here he was *cancelling* her appointment without much to say.

Especially since she was coming on Trevor's instructions from his office in London.

He looked at her, and decided to be open -perhaps because of Trevor's predilection for boating.

"It's his Yacht, which he kept in St. Thomas. There was an explosion on board over the weekend, two people dead. He needed to appear before the local authorities to answer a few questions. That, and his concern for his crewmen. He also is talking to his insurance inspectors down there..."

"I am sorry" said Amanda. "Of course I understand. Please tell him not to be concerned about us. No, no need to reschedule just now. I'll be in touch in a week or two. Thank you for explaining..."

What do you do when your appointment with your lawyer is suddenly cancelled and you are standing at the foot of their building?

Go home? Why not? She had plenty of work to do. Instead, she walked about the city.

What a tragedy for his crew, she thought. She could imagine the consternation down there at the water's edge by the docks where the sea was so blue at Gregory East in St. Thomas. There, some of the world's most fabulous yachts were docked for the winter seasons....This she would explain to Trevor, she decided. Next time she talked to him.

She would calm her nerves at a little bistro and have lunch. *Au Giardin*, she picked salad, cheese roll, coffee and a delicate dessert, New York style. *And why not*?

This was the center of downtown New York where city traffic pushed breezes up streets walled by tall buildings.

Here, people talked, and jammed, and shopped, and rushed ...*What was happening to life anymore?*

She sipped her coffee and watched. The scene before her was amusing and colorful. It brought her back to normal. Here, life went on.

Two days later she was back at her desk looking over the details of a list that needed attention. Somehow, other thoughts were blocking her lucid logic. Trevor's office, whom she called, had asked her consult his attorneys in New York.

She also wanted to ask them about something else. She had a vague suspicion that there was an intruder...She decided against asking.

His lawyers were unavailable. How do you track that, exactly? She knew of her husband's absolute confidence in their abilities.

Her fears? What was he thinking? What was *she* thinking? Something *was* wrong. *What*, exactly?

She should be investigating the intruder herself. In fact, she made a decision to do so.

 She should have used her own lawyers in Washington DC. At least they had better offices; fresh coffee, lots of follow-up calls, and even a car delivery service to meet appointments downtown for certain clients. To say nothing of their influence on Capitol Hill.

After lunch downtown Manhatten she took the train back to DC at Union Station.

Barbara, she would save for another day. She had to get home today. By tonight, dawn rather, she would call Trevor's office in London.

* *

It was actually days before she called. In fact, she felt bad that she had neglected to do so. What was even more disturbing was that he had failed to call *her.*

Accustomed to getting his messages this separation felt strange. His messages used to be sometimes full of business, sometimes just quiet words of private longing. Either way, she loved his voice. She loved his words. She...

That was before the letter, the letter she still kept in her purse.

What explained his leave of absence? *Surely it was not a farewell. Surely he was alive.*

She paced the bedroom for an hour waiting for the clocks to turn. On Greenwich Mean Time, they were five hours ahead of US Eastern Standard Time. She should wait until the offices opened, at least.

She had called Trevor's cell at least five times. Clearly, his cell was elsewhere, and connections were being re-routed to somewhere undisclosed.

She had made attempts to reach him. She was tired of excuses from his housekeeping. From his office. From his partners...

No. This she had to figure out: He was in transit. But when? To where? How?

That night she never went to bed. By morning, she had made her decision.

Was this a legitimate absence of duty, or was something wrong?

Trevor, where in God's name are you? Call me. Damn it.

The next evening a decision came to her. It came to her from a recollection -of last resort.

But what if she sounded like a bloody fool?

She calmed down. She would wait and sound normal. She picked up the phone, finally, at five o'clock in the morning.

"The offices of the McGairney Group" said the efficient secretary.

"Hello, I am Mrs. Trevor MacDonnell...I wonder if I may speak to Tom McGairney please. I'm in the United States, and I have some information on behalf of my husband."

"Just a minute, if you please Mrs. MacDonnell"

She must have waited for a few minutes, precious minutes. Long distance minutes. An eternity, it seemed.

"Mrs. MacDonnell" said a man's voice suddenly "I'm so terribly sorry to keep you waiting. I am Tom's partner. I'm sorry to tell you that Tom is taken ill. Rather gravely, I'm afraid. He hasn't seen anyone in days."

* *

The days were filled with dog-walking and routine events around the neighborhood. There was Rock Creek Park that filled with bloom and greens as the seasons turned, a favorite place for walking with Gwynie and jogging when alone.

Meals were the sum of Carla's good work in the kitchen, and occasionally, a stop at a coffee shop or a mall was fit into her schedule. Once, she took Gwynie to the Zoo. On another occasion, there were Museums to visit at the Smithsonian Mall - an ice-rink to play around, and even a trip to Baltimore Harbor.

At home there were gardening projects, building and painting in the basement, and even a room to redecorate. But the hours passed slowly. Amanda felt alone, even as the phone rang less and her emails thinned out for the lack of new business...

What had happened, she wondered. What had changed. How she missed Trevor.

 In the days that followed Amanda discovered that at the offices of *Klugberg and Freeman* there was nobody willing to talk to Mrs. MacDonnell.

Trevor's corporate business was "confidential and proprietary" - not hers to ask about...

All she wanted to know was had they funded his newest venture?

That too was confidential, they had to remind her. The response that came from one Asian staffer was condescending and totally unacceptable. Amanda felt shut out.

* *

Chapter Nine

The fissure had opened up.

Deep within the ocean, the earthquake at the divergent fault line were caused by tectonic plate movement. Magma beneath rose to the surface to fill in gaps, causing an increase in magnetic pull.

 Especially off Bermuda. Recorded on sophisticated seismic instruments, those deviations once associated with altered state of magnetic orientation were reflected with leaps and pulls of delicate measuring needles.

The seismic activity was worrisome. The tremor was not unnoticed. But it had its sudden effect with little warning.

Those un-trained to adjust could be subjected to unintended consequence. Not that any US Naval ship could not be deployed elsewhere. The United States had to have eyes everywhere. The Straits of Hormuz. The Behring Straight. The Cape. The Pacific. The Indian ocean. But this spot was not the place for any US Naval combatant to be prowling around without cause, and without advance warning.

In this case, it was a joint UK/US naval sortie conducting subterranean coastline surveys of the Eastern United States, particularly off the ridge of Bermuda.

The R.N. Submarine *HMS Huntress* surveyed the ridge off the Caribbean and set to cruise speed. Her task was to search for indicators, anomalies and anything unusual to the Bathymetry of the continental shelf.

"Captain" reported the First Officer "temperatures continue to rise, and seem to sustain at a wider spread than usual, Sir"

Submerged, the submarine was familiar with the territory off the ledge of the Caribbean. It dropped like a cliff and plunged into the deepest part of the ocean. Something you did not want to discover by accident, the Captain knew.

Nor did he like to mystify his crew, many of them well trained and completely confident in the instrumentation and technology of the world's newest fighting ships.

Captain Brewster did not like the mission, actually. It's not that it frightened him, it's just that there was too much in the way of scientific information that he was supposed to report on and filter at one pass.

 "We'll run the grid one more time, and then call it quits. We have enough material to give Washington all it wants..." he said, turning over command of the charts to his Officer of the Deck.

"Aye Sir."

Captain Brewster made his way to desk. Had they covered the essentials? Telemetry. Topography. Atmospherics. Bathymetry. Temperature. Sonar re-imaging, and feedback loops that offered a clear picture of anything new...Had they missed something?

Clearly, the shoreline was showing signs of biological stress: A temperature change was sending all kinds of sea material through pumping filtration systems that put a load on the turbines. That implied unsustainability due to some event. He made some quick calculations and decided on a small change.

"Alter depth by 50ft" he said into his speaker to the Con. "Rise."

Normally, heated thermal vents at the bottom of the sea floor disgorging ducts of magma-heated steam resulting in warmer belts within the sea currents, including the Gulf Stream itself.

But for some reason, the temperatures had gone through the charts, and with reports of debris washing aloft, it was considered less a reconnaissance mission now as a serious survey.

The coast had experienced a small tremor and subvention in the sea floor as tectonic plates ground together. By itself it was not unusual. Nor was the movement of the subvention any different here than usual. But if the Navy wanted the very latest information on what things looked like down there, then they should have a fresh update. That was the thrust of his mission. And he played it by the numbers. Captain Brewster was almost done.

Captain Brewster knew this. And he wanted it all done. But the deviation was of concern. It was too drastic, and fluctuating.

Even the temperatures *within* the vessel were rising and requiring extraordinary adjustments.

Plus he was getting irritable. If he wanted to survey the ocean bottom, he would have picked bio-oceanographic-engineering as career. He was a trained military officer, with the command of a nuclear war ship...

"Sir."

He raised his head from his desk.

 "Our ballast bearing is unsteady."

Oh that great, he thought. Nothing like swimming blind.

"Blow the Port ballast by 10 percent only" he said, to compensate. He would veer to starboard after that, and exit the quad to close the exercise.

 The conclusion that he recorded and transmitted was that the activity came from beneath the earth's crust itself. He suggested that magma beneath the earth crust rose up to closer proximity of the mantle, creating a heavier pull of its magnetic fields.

Clearly an indication of magma activity and proximity were greatly indicted here...

 What he could not know was the extent of the subterranean disturbances. Certainly, a magma chamber had risen to the earth's crust. If he sought to compensate for the submarine's magnetic depth and and pull by relieving depth pressure he would have been correct. Understanding buoyancy, for a submariner, was everything. But he had underestimated its pull.

The zone he entered had created an anomaly so strong that the entire ship's steel hull had been placed within a force of magnetic field far greater than had ever recorded.

* *

Tuesday, just two days before driving down to St. Mary's College to lecture a class. Amanda needed to get organized. Gwyneth would be with her. The routine had become predictable.

Not too long ago, an incident had occurred at the docks. That was alarming by itself. But in the more recent past, Amanda thought she saw a car slow down at the Scenic Stop that she recognized once before. The scenic Stop was an observation park.

She had a thought.

Since a webcam scanned the waterfront, surely such a car could be retraced on a recorder? Something she hated to review unless by police permission. So far, she had not voiced her fears to anyone except for Argueta.

It had been such a grueling week chasing the whereabouts of Trevor that all else had been put aside. So far, she had attempted to do without causing alarm and entreating those in government authority.

Ok.

She would change things.

She made her plan. She would wait until Clara the Housekeeper left the house.

Amanda relaxed in the garden and surveyed the rose bushes, picking off a leaf here, a deadhead there. Gwyneth, by turn, played with Muffin the dog, first the orange beach ball; the crocket paddle and the wooden *boulle* that Muffin felt compelled to retrieve and deposit at her feet.

Finally, as the tall beech trees rustled in the evening breeze of Rock Creek Park, it was time to go indoors. The evening wore on, and together they gathered toys and made pretty the room. At bed time, with all her school clothes ironed by Clara for the next morning, Gwyneth and Amanda could enjoy cuddle-time together. Gwynie took her bath.

They picked a book to read, and finally it was time for prayers. Gwyneth fell asleep before Amanda reached the door and switched off the overhead lights.

Downstairs, Amanda poured herself a little after-dinner claret and sat in the study to watch some News. Then she got up, went to the kitchen and made herself a fresh pot of coffee. She had much to do.

She sent an email to her students to proceed with their "Independent Research." Instructions included dividing themselves into groups of five, selecting their particular topics for enquiry, and orchestrating their tasks accordingly. Their final list should be prepared and emailed to her in the morning, but with that gathering complete, they were free to adjourn without a lecture for their independent projects....Questions could be addressed with emails. She was available for anyone if they needed her.

Next, Amanda turned to the tasks of her office staff and sent out emails:

Could she have a status report from each one tomorrow *in lieu* of an office staff meeting? Further, she needed to delegate the responsibility of a new Project for the team: Who would be the Project Management? Who would support, and what components would each party be doing? She would assign her plan according to the feedback, and to be led by expertise on hand. TDC personnel only. Meaning only those with Top Security Clearances could touch this one.

She concentrated on Argueta's request: He wanted a full analysis and report to address the following issue: If there was a disaster in the offing around the Nation's Capital designed to put public pressure on the Administration for energy policy changes, what would be the means, motives and opportunities that might trigger such an event? Or, as he put it "What would happen to oil drilling decisions if alternative energy sources were a threat or caused sudden catastrophe?"

Clear enough.

She thought about how to proceed: She should ask Brendon to consider the effect of environmental laws that might affect offshore drilling now in place at the US Department of Interior.

She should ask David to consider new initiatives for border protection and military responses to national defense from Military Operations Archives.

For alternative energies and diversifications she would Susan to check on the Nuclear Regulatory Commission for anything new; the US Dept of Energy, especially its Lobby of hopefuls for new legislation.

Finally, she should have someone examine Emergency Preparedness. What were the new plans, who were the contractors, and what budgets we involved with which sectors, including the city.

She would need a brief political run down on which Congressional districts had similar energy concerns. This she could do.

Federal analysis for logistics, statistics, security and economics could come from Todd. That would complete a pretty comprehensive report.

She knew her staff well. She would get positions papers and a full research report with source notes from them all.

Satisfied, she filed her Notes for the morning; timed her email delivery request to each one, and started to shut down. Then she remembered something.

Ask Barbara for updates on the Coroner's Report.

She was tired and she closed up for the night, her thoughts far away...

Unlike most others, it was the way they worked in her office. With every consideration and courtesy, everyone was given as much privacy, respect and latitude as possible.

As workplaces went, it was considered awesome: Generous off-time was allowed when needed. Plus the occasional fun season tickets for the Nat's Baseball games in the Summer at their Southwest Waterfront stadium. Or Games...Even concerts. The result was a dedicated team of academic experts and scholars that worked hard; met their research deadlines, had a lot of fun doing it. They easily put out twice the effort and accuracy in findings than anyone else in town - complete with a knowledge base that made them the "go-to team" in town.

She had to smile. Many were all-nighters if they had to be. Others did prep-work well in advance of the deadline. And all respected the rules of the office, including client confidentiality. The result was work for the Firm coming in from law firms; government agencies; scientific divisions; policy institutes and global clients. Amanda should be proud.

In her bedroom she turned to her arrangements for tomorrow: She was not going down to St. Mary's as scheduled. Gwyneth and Clara would be coming with her to St. Mary's next week, and the opportunity was appropriate...

She needed time. And one more quick day trip to New York City. Satisfied, she put her affairs in order.

She turned to the matter of Trevor's absence. There were things that puzzled her. It was a little hard to be a player without the facts. Or rather without feedback from the corporate group in question. They were all silent, it seemed...

She switched off.

Yet as tired as she was, she could not sleep. Something was bothering her. *What?*

In the calm shadows of her bedside quarters, her thoughts floated as she dozed on and off. Then the reading lamp switched on, and it became lucidly clear –like an alarm that had strayed into the forefront of her mind, even perhaps ringing for a long time. Yet left to her own imagination, it seemed she had been entirely alone.

Trevor's investors in London were in a line of responses that were adding up: The first instance was from Trevor himself. It came in the PS of the letter he wrote. She had glossed over it as if were not her affair.

> *"Sweetie, I have to tell you that not only do we have a spot of trouble here with regards to the corporate investors, but to Mr. Becker himself..."*

Amanda sat up. Becker was dead.

She reached for some water. Of course it would upset Trevor, she understood. Trevor would miss Hans Becker, they had been golfing friends for years. True. What?

Wait. *Surely not...?*

What about his lawyers in London? What was that? The err... McCairney 'fraternity?' Did they have a position for him or not? Come to think of it, she hadn't heard it mentioned. Not that she was *in-the-know* on anything, but it seemed a little odd. And a little *sudden...* They were agents who used to flood Trevor's mail sent from London.

Neither were things any better in the States. The Firm in New York that handled his affairs – the lawyer to whom she was to turn for any family assistance, Taylor, was unable to keep appointments? His boat had an "incident?" What did that mean? An explosion? Sabotage...in the *Caribbean?*

Of course it would take him offline from his job in New York if two people died.

But where did that leave *Trevor*, exactly? What was going on?

Sleep.

 No conspiracy theories now, *please.* She could hear his voice telling her. She looked over to his side of the bed, silk covers undisturbed, pillow undented. *God how she missed his assurance. His lips on her neck.*

Fatigue found its way into her thoughts, and she fell asleep, exhausted.

* *

Chapter Ten

Amanda Wells and Barbara rang the doorbell of the boxy house in the Bronx. They were holding flowers, just as the sun disappeared over the horizon.

It was a Russian neighborhood. Iconography, lovingly displayed in the recess of windows, some graying with dust and neglect wore the symbols of remembrances. Very soon, the houses would be torn down; rehabilitated or replanted as parks, Amanda knew. Then the block would be re-posted as modern living quarters for those who could afford such proximity to New York City.

The Twin Towers, now gone, and the crisis that roiled Wall Street had inexorably given way to a slow erosion of localism. New forms of investment capital for new neighborhoods had displaced original dwellers of older homes with fabulous offers, even as Europe teetered in economic turmoil.

The woman that came to the door was herself a caricature of the Slavic grandmother, a red bandana around her face and her skirt-frock long and mid-calf. She had to look up to speak to them. When Barbara explained their interest in her Jacob her grandson, she invited them in.

"When was the last time you saw your grandson Mrs. Vastrovia?"

Barbara had to translate.

Two weeks before he died, she said. He had come to visit for the weekend, he and his friends who came often for family reunions. Her eyes gleamed in the recounting.

Jacob liked to visit his grandmother. He had his haunts and friends in town too, all coming around to the house on weekends when there was food, family and fun, she said. Then they would go off into the city together, especially if there was hockey match, to play at night...

Amanda had to smile at the savvy: *How would she know where they went at night*? She eyed Barbara, who whispered "When no one is watching, they all speak in Russian..."

Amanda changed the subject. She brought up the bird. Had Mrs. Vastrovia seen it?

The old woman lowered her eyes with a small flutter, then looked up, her face flushed. Yes, she said. It was a family heirloom.

You see, it was *her* family that once owned a goldsmith shop in St. Petersburg. At that time, her parents had told her, each piece was commissioned by the nobility. That was a source of great pride and revenue for the family. Like the work of the Faberge Eggs to the Imperial Household...she waved her wrist in wonder and amazement: Who could forget the stories, the tales, the details and the accounts of *how* the piece turned out? How it was made. They would talk endlessly about its progress and workmanship. What metals had been employed in the commission of their work: Gold. Silver. Gems... What skills, scrollwork, detail of the old tradition, or the new...

Best of all, when her father came to the table, the children and family were all in awe as his creative abilities: *Oh.* How they valued the workmanship in the family as matter of pride, she said.

Mrs. Vastrovia fairly sparkled with the childhood memory.

Finally, when asked about the yellow bird, she looked up with eyes full of wonder. Who could not forget the story of the yellow bird?

Barbara implored her to elaborate.

You see, the bird had a secret. It was a secret that nobody knew. It held a secret so precious that only the goldsmith and the Patron could speak of it. For he came to the shop himself - a man in his carriage. A code of honor that the goldsmith took with him to his grave. Alas, a grave dug too soon by the Russian Revolutions; the wars, and the economic transitions that occurred in the history of Europe.

Yes. The bird was famous in the family: It held good fortune, they said, if it kept it's secret hidden within its beautiful chest.

Amanda assured her that if her grandson had reconnected with it, he would have been proud of it. It clearly held great meaning for him.

The old woman brought them sweet tea and crispy baklavas. Then she appeared with a large book - A book the boy had with him the last time he visited.

He needed it, he had said, for his next expedition.

Amanda had to smile. That was how he described his work on a research project. In older pedantic ways, as if to heighten his stature in her estimation.

Except that he forgot it, said the old woman. Too big for his tiny car, she said, her eyes playful.

Barbara and Amanda enjoyed the tea and biscuits. They emerged refreshed, as if they too had visited family.

It was dark when they left, and it was decided to spend the night at Barbara's place.

Only outside, where the sky of New York had darkened to deliver a silver rain did Amanda realize that if she discovered the meaning to bird's secret, she would know why the boy had died.

They examined the book, she and Barbara. *Birds of North America*, with a few pages notated for places, scribbles, details and notes. Quite an avid ornithologist, he was. One in particular was circled in large pencil rings. The North Carolina Snipe: Extinct.

Barbara and Amanda must have had the same instant thought. It was just like the bird his grandmother had in her possession when he died. But curiously, it was painted a different color. 'Extinct.'

* *

The documents sent to her from London stunned Amanda. They related to Trevor's corporation.

...."result of damages, cited, recited below...

Amanda could not believe her eyes.

> *"...extinction of a rare bird and endangered animals if the project were to proceed in a zone known for its unusual nesting grounds..."*

Later that night at home in Washington, an even more profound question crept into her consciousness.

Why?

In her bones she felt that there was a connection between the boy's research, and, somehow... her husband's Corporate investigation.

She emailed Barbara that night while the thoughts surged through her mind. Was there a smoking gun? Were there any connections?

Then it came to her.

Evidently, the boy had *sighted* the bird. *It was alive and thriving.* The species, evidently, was not extinct, as the book said.

Amanda just sat there, staring at the email. What a strange thing to send to someone in the middle of the night.

Her hand trembled as she hit SEND.

* *

Amanda received word that the case against her husband's company was proceeding in court. An injunction had been placed against the company that delivered the Jack Up rig.

Rebecca called. The report was appalling.

"...All further Mineral Mining Lease Rights were to be placed in a moratorium until the Department of Environmental Protection re-examined the application.

"..Further, other damages were to be cited as pending criminal actions against the company. Including the extermination of local resources, mining options, offshore marine life losses, toxicity and natural shoreline erosion.

"...An environmental assessment was to be conducted to find if any hurt had been inflicted on natural species of the region before the government would issue any further lease rights to individuals, private corporations or investment drilling on speculation off the Arctic."

* *

Lauren smiled. This would slow them down a bit. London had a way of dancing around the rules. This would arrest their progress. Even if Canada moved like the lame duck she invented for her venture projects at the expense of investors...

 Still, this was her company. The less competition, the better. Besides, she had bigger fish to fry.

She picked up her cell and asked for a call in to Washington DC.

She had favors to collect from certain officials: She hadn't been encouraged to buy all that US Treasury debt for nothing...

She was getting that lease.

With the London interests nicely On Hold, she could focus entirely on her upcoming profits granted by the US government in rights, leases and holdings offshore in the Arctic region.

Oh, and one other thing. It was time to separate her own interests from the company cover she was using. Time to own her own mega-fortune. Damned the bastards who built these tall edifices, she thought as she viewed her reflection in the highly polished brass face off 35 elevator buttons. She would raze the lot.

At the bottom of the steps, just as she was about the climb into her limozine, she got a call from her Assistant.

Trevor's company was counter-suing. Actually, it was his wife...

Right there, she knew a threat when she saw one, though not with complete certainty.

She dialed Le Maas.

 "You're going down there soon, aren't you? So trail the bastards."

"I'm going to Maryland tomorrow evening…"

"Proceed with your plans there tomorrow.

"Right"

"Let me know how everything goes. I shall be in the area myself shortly. I shall want to hear…"

"Yes Ma'am" said LaMaas, his lips tight. He closed off his cell with an efficient click.

He would be paid well.

* *

Amanda got a message the following afternoon, Jeff Watson wanted the meeting to be held the following day in his offices.

He held little sway other than belonging to Sarah's firm. What in the world did he want from her?

She went jogging.

Running did her good, she decided. She beat the pavement with rhythmic pounding. In fact, next weekend they would go to the beach and roast in the sun. Waves, sand, sun, sweating and crowds...

She turned the corner. Oh God, it would be so good to hear Trevor's voice. If he was alive...If...They were...

She missed him. She so wanted to find resolution...to ask...

That evening, she sat quietly in the study of their home. She remained stuck in the horns of a dilemma. Perhaps that was what he anticipated. That was his warning

... But follow your instincts, Amanda, and stay the course of your plans....

She was alone. For two days, she had left unresolved the issues that pressed most upon her conscience.

Amongst other annoyances, Jeff Watson was being intrusive. He was forcing her to face him.

Amanda knew Jack Chester. In fact, Trevor had used his services once before as a broker. But only once. His methods of investing, he told her, were too speculative and less than reliable: He reached into realms not entirely verifiable, citing companies for investment strategies not entirely reputable. Neither did he have a reputation amongst investors to stay long with clients nor with his own strategies.

Still, Trevor had given Jack Chester his chance, enabled him to enjoy a fee from it. But that was it.

 Chester remained a favorite with people. High stakes gamblers, mainly those for whom money was in plenty. Losses mattered little to many of his clients - the rush of investment and bragging was everything to them. Chester knew how to play the game.

The Congressman opposing the bill in the Senate was clearly using his services to dig himself out of a hole, that much Amanda now knew.

It threw her that he should use desperate measures. Jeff Watson was using his influence over the Congressman for her complicity to engage with him: The bill was surely too significant to be held hostage for some personal conquest?

Jeff Watson. In a personal way, Amanda found him attractive. Handsome. Powerful. Possessing all the attributes of a Washington player, and certainly enough in physique to bowl over any woman. But why would he even notice *her*? What was his motive?

She had become the focus of his attention since they met at the Kennedy Center. And his focus was beyond any reasonable expectation, that is, in the normal way of things. He was her client, by way of Sarah Delaney as senior partner. They were retaining Amanda's group for continued work.

Pending was a bill before Congress that they had been asked to support.

Amanda had a team to manage. And contracts for work keep them all employed - much less a professional reputation.

More significantly, she was married with a family and a life. Within the circles of Washington DC, she and Trevor were not without some recognition of their own...

But that was precisely his point. Trevor was *not* in town. Was this some *Achilles heel* for a scheme he had?

Besides having no room for another man in her life, Amanda found herself horrified that he should find a way to compromise the progress of the Bill if she remained uncooperative in his scheme?

Evidently, the Congressman would only sign this bill if Chester were able to pass big money his way by means of a timely investment. Jeff Watson knew this.

Easy to solve, as far as he was concerned.

If Amanda understood Sarah's message, then she was to see Jeff Watson in his office. Come what may.

Not that the consequences were even being considered, but the notion of being caught up in a game of this sort appalled her. Yet Washington was rife with them.

At stake was the risk of losing the bill; the contracts that would retain her Firm for work; the prospects of employment that would keep her staff with jobs...

How could this be happening? What in the world had she done to solicit the interest of a man she hardly knew?

Easy enough to give in. He was hardly an undesirable man to resist, but that was beside the point.

She wanted to talk to someone, her thoughts were too personal. Once you went down this road in this city, there was no turning back.

The thoughts settled by the evening. She took out her letter from the bottom of her bag.

"wet as a rat and idiotically mistaken...It is your pureness of heart that I fell for..."

It was against her principles – her agency as an independent professional were words that somehow got stuck in her throat.

Stay with the high ground.

She would go to his office, appear at the door and tell Jeff that she thought he had enough of his own influence to persuade the Congressman himself.

The Congressman had to vote his conscience. She would tell him that she was married, she was not interested. That she was hired to support their effort, not to guarantee passage of legislation.

Then, she would return to her Firm. *Tell them what, you idiot?...*She stopped. *That they're all out of a job?*

* *

Tomorrow Amanda had a class to teach. She had it all planned out. After morning school, Gwyneth was coming with her, as always. So was Clara, the housekeeper. There was much to prepare in advance.

Amanda was the first to rise to set the day in motion, sipping coffee as she did so. She now looked at her watch: 7.45 AM.

Today was Special Projects day in class. All night she had been assembling the child's school project, and the Exhibit was carefully loaded into the rear of the car for school: It was a cardboard-made theater of puppets held by strings. The puppets wore colorful costumes made of big letters. If they danced, they could spell certain words. Gwynie was excited and had practiced. The class would love it, Amanda and Clara had stayed up half the night constructing it.

Amanda showered, pulled on a suitable black skirt with a patent leather belt to match sandals, and ran a comb through her damp hair. She patted on mascara and lipstick, added a couple of gold earrings and a bracelet and dashed out the door with her bag and briefcase, cell phone already ringing. She took what calls she could on the way to work, then put away her cell.

Barbara would doubtless be waiting for her morning call in New York; and the staff waiting for a briefing before they turned to their research deadlines.

Also scheduled was a charity Washington luncheon followed by a meeting with Argueta.

After that, it was off to St. Mary's for an evening class.

The world rushed at Amanda the moment she walked into her building. The Receptionist had calls from

Building Contractors offering price quotes for construction improvements. Three clients were already there and talking to staff; Argueta wanted to postpone by half an hour their meeting this afternoon. This suited her fine, since luncheons were bound to drag on, and judging from the clients waiting to talk with her, an extra half hour would solve as lot of problems.

Barbara was good enough to wait. And the staff were holding their meeting without her as they went through the paces of who was working on what, for which client, and at what deadline.

Great.

Still, it was an hour and half before she consulted her cell, and there she found a call from the Elinore Swanson, Principle,of Gwynie's school: It left a message articulating the name of the school within the call back numbers.

Amanda dialed back immediately.

"No. No problem. And we did all so enjoy her theater puppet production. We spelled out all kinds of words, and the kids were making up new spellings just to play. What an ingenious idea. Thanks." She cleared her throat. "It's just that perhaps you should take Gwynie home. You see, there's been a rather nasty accident in her class involving two children at her little table, and I'd like to spare her the anxiety of it all for the rest of the day..."

"Nothing too serious, I hope?" said Amanda..

"No. Everybody will live. It's the parents I fret over. One of the kids had his front tooth broken on the head of another ..."

Amanda listened to the full accounting, as if the Principle was relieved to be telling someone she could trust, grateful for a patient ear. "So, it's Gwynie I was thinking of..."

"Clara has gone for the day, I kept her up all night puppet-eering, so I told her to go home for the day. I'll come round to pick Gwynie up myself and have her enjoy the rest of the day with us here in the office, if you don't mind"

"Perfect. Sorry for any inconvenience..."

"No inconvenience at all. I'm happy to oblige. It's a privilege that comes with having your own business...Don't give it another thought please. Half an hour...?"

Clara had been sent home directly after delivering Gwynie to school. She was to return later in the day for evening duty. This suited Clara better, her husband a night worker.

Amanda had less concern about Gwynie running around the building than the staff who took her presence in the building to mean that this was play-day at work. They spoiled her. They played peek-a-boo. Gave her candies... Let her type on keypads... Talk on cell phones. Play on computers games.. .Hide behind tall potted plants. Amanda even found Sam towing Gwynie for sleigh rides across a smooth marble floor in the lobby citing the magic carpet of Aladdin ...

Then here came Bill. Bill had gone home for lunch and returned with his pet *Arturo*. To amuse Gwynie, he announced. The sheepdog beside him was hot and panting like a full-throttled Boeing 747.

This was getting ridiculous

"More like the contented staff you keep…" admonished Barbara from New York, when she heard about it.

Amanda was fretting now about Gwynne's staying power; with her school routine and calmness surrendered to this bunch of office playmates, the child was wearing out, getting cranky and over excited. Finally, as Amanda found her dangling from a heavy brocaded curtain in the front office, she took her firmly by the hand and led her to her office where she had to have a half hour rest- break on the sofa.

Gwynie wailed. The cell phone buzzed. Amanda picked up, and Gwynie ran out.

Barbara had called twice. And on each occasion they had discussed the matter of the bird in the possession of Jacob when he died. Why had he cherished it so? What made him keep it? What was the meaning of the Bird Book notations? Part of his environmental assessment for the client?

Except that Amanda mentioned it was being argued at the case of the prosecution. 'Negligence' was hardly environmental damage. Still, it was clearly something he was stitching together for a report that he was working on when he died. If only they knew what the significance of the bird was.

"A secret" said Barbara, referring to the grandmother.

"Right…Anyway, the bird is still up here, secured in my office. "Rather, excuse me..err.." Amanda ran her hand through her hair, tired and distracted "I put it outside in the hallway. Gwynie is running around the place and I wanted her to take a nap…"

"Good luck." interrupted Barbara. "Send her up here to New York…I want her."

"His project went ..." The noise outside surged "Look, I'd better go. I'll call you later"

"Sure. Tell me how things go with Argueta this afternoon, ok?"

Amanda was barely off the cell when it happened. The whole antique oak chest on the top floor landing lurched out as the dog chasing Gwynie caught its lead around one of its sturdy legs.

The entire oak chest teetered and then settled back on all fours. But the contents on its surface were strewn. Including the vase of flowers that filled the elegant landing between the two top offices. One could see it looking up, through the upper balcony brass railing.

Only one item did not survive the lurch.

In horror, Amanda watched the yellow bird get lifted up and flung off the oak chest, over the railing and tumble down through the air for three levels until it crashed on the marble floor of the lobby.

It shattered into a thousand pieces of glass, crystal and silver.

For Amanda, the world stopped. Or was it her heart? So much was wrapped up in that antique ornament that it took on a disproportionate position of value. Even Gwynie started to whimper.

Amanda ran down the stairs to see it, as if chasing its course to the bottom of the building would somehow put humpty dumpty back together again. At the bottom, she froze, the bird broken, her face pale with shock.

Other than Bob who had the sense to pick up Gwynie and whisper softly. "It's ok honey. Just a broken pot. Don't cry." the place was hushed. If any phones were ringing, they were a thousand miles away. Then someone put their hand on Amanda's shoulder.

By the time she called Barbara, she proclaimed it a long day. But that was only half the tale. The rest came out slowly.

From the belly of the bird, that is, now shattered glass...an item went skidding across the floor and lodged under the plant.

"A silver *what*...?" screamed Barbara.

"A silver ship."

"what do you mean, a *silver ship*?"

"It's a battleship. Made of silver. Even with a name on its bow"

"You are *kidding,* right?"

"*HMS Liberty*"

"My God" said Barbara "I'm coming down Monday." and with that she hung up.

 The grandmother was right as she told it. It all made sense now.

Amanda lay in bed and thought about the irony of it all: Inside the bird given from the Tzar to the King of England was a message alright. As sign that asked for help from one king to another amidst war; revolution and revolt. They were taken hostage, the Tzar's family.

 A tiny model of the English Royal Naval Cruiser HMS LIBERTY. It was made of gold and enamel. The message was clear: It would sail the Crimea Sea and rescue the Tsar and his family from the Russian Revolution.

If Parliament was willing, as the record showed, the King was not. And whatever socialist movement triumphed, the same end came to both monarchs. One, at the hand of Revolutionary gunmen. The other, at the hand of a Nurse whose morphine was euthanasia.

Yes. It would be nice to have Barbara around. Otherwise, she would go crazy.

* *

The routine was nicely predictable, and sure enough, she picked up her follower when she stopped at the main gas station for a stop of refreshments, coffee and snacks.

He was as obvious as he was that night when Gwynie was overturned in the boat by a boat wake. He parked first on the Scenic Overlook, then back up the road. A dark green pick-up, a Jeep, watching with binoculars.

Was he anticipating some action? She'd confuse him.

So, let's see what you can manage today, she muttered, spotting it in the rear view mirror. Clara was besides her, Gwynie in the rear.

Once on campus, she picked the parking lot besides the Student Center, parallel to another dark vehicle, just like hers.

As pre-arranged, they all walked into the Center for a stop in the bookstore: Sandra was to meet them outside. Ensemble with other students, all of them strolling around the parking lot, making noise and commotion, Sandra was to duck suddenly into her mother's car, turn on the ignition, and drive the car around the other side of the building where Amanda emerged with Clara and Gwynie in tow.

She pecked her daughter on the cheek. "Thanks love. I'll call you in a few days…"

Sandra moved quickly out of the way, and joined her friends to enter the building where Amanda would normally be teaching her class.

Instead, Amanda left campus within fifteen minutes.

It was a move done of a sudden, with a class-change-up crowd milling through parking lots and walked to buildings: Something a parked observer would never have spotted from a few blocks away.

If he were waiting for her to re-emerge from her class room as lecturer, he would tonight be duped. What it gave her was time to stop into the Security center, and ask to see a tape of the night of the 13th, last months: A tape made by the Webcam on the waterfront. It had evidence, she said. He took notes.

Fall weather was shortening daylight saving time, and the cooler temperatures brought an end to water sports. Visibility was not bathed in the sunlight as it had been just a few weeks before. In fact, the foliage of the campus was so dense that in the multiplicity of fall flora; drooping boughs and swirling leaves, everything was a whirl in the lengthening shadows of the evening.

Amanda was well up Route 4 and entering route 2 by the time the class would be over. In fact, no one assembled in the room: Her assignment had been pre-arranged for library readings tonight. They were all online this week.

They had stopped at McDonalds. Gwynie had her 'Berger and fries, Clara happy to be camping with the family, she said. Before long, they were half way down the country roads that would lead them to their retreat, approximately two hours from the city.

It was a long drive, and silent. Gwynie had fallen asleep, Carla nodding off as well.

Darkness fell quietly upon the road ahead, and nothing but traffic lights and familiar junctions paved the way that Amanda took now.

That she had foiled him, she was certain. That he would be far behind was less certain. This was not a man without resources. And it was not as if they had lived a covert family existence, all of them, over the years. There was Washington DC where they lived, and places where the family went. It was no mystery that they owned retreat on the Eastern Shore of the Chesapeake Bay.

She paid her toll at the Chesapeake Bay Bridge. Driving to the Eastern Shore across the wide expanse of water was a thrill that could course through anyone with excitement, even at night.

Amanda did not want to alert anyone of their arrival. She fully expected the place to be locked up and abandoned. Not that the farm was ever abandoned. In their absence, the place was watched by farmers, friends, neighbors and watermen alike. All of them fans of Trevor and the family.

It was almost dark when they stopped. Amanda was the first to get out of the car, and she stood still, familiarizing herself with the grounds. Gwynie jumped out.

The house looked peaceful, undisturbed. A calm deep reflection of water on the bay surrounded freshly harvested crops, and the air was redolent with the sweet odor of cut field corn and tidewater marsh grass.

A sound shrilled across the sky, a sound that came with Fall. Canadian Geese were flying in from the colder regions to winter in the warm bay. Gwynie pointed up, their formation outline still visible in the receding light. They stared, all of them gazing up until nothing was left to see but the stars, wonder still in their eyes.

"Right then." said Amanda, fumbling for keys, whispering, adventure-like. *Schhhh.*

Only the hurricane lamp would be allowed on the front porch. OK?"

They nodded conspiratorially, Gwynie and Clara plunged into the spirit of stealth and abandon. They advanced like thieves in the night, all of them giggling and fumbling and casting about for ways to behave like co-bandits.

It was wonderful to be in the country.

The house was fully equipped and secure. It had a well stocked pantry of dry goods, which, added to the fresh milk and fruit that she had packed in a cooler the night before, would make for a wonderful pancake and fresh fruit breakfast.

The bathrooms had toothbrushes and towels; the drawers packed for weekend clothes of every size and description - something that never waned here in the country. In every room a community drawer had evolved by default - extra pairs of this, that and the other...Oversized for any fit, including kids, swimmers, joggers, and other houseguests needing Tees, sweatshirts, hats, overalls, baggy shorts and flip-flops...

Gwynie easily found her old favorites, and Clara was invited to use the guest room - a simple arrangement of beach furnishings and white coverings.

In her own bedroom, Amanda opened closets full of memories, which she had shared with Trevor - Items just stashed for the weekend with no particular structure: One drawer surprised her. It contained a white muslin and silk negligee that Trevor had bought for her in London. Knowing how she adored sleepwear, he had indulged in a Harrods's designer ensemble of nightwear - fit for a Hollywood film. She smiled to herself, the memories of those tender nights warm ...

Tonight, she would wear it.

"Mrs MacDonnell" knocked Clara. We turn on the water, yes? No water in the bathrooms?

"Oh yes." said Amanda remembering. The water was usually turned off when they left. It prevented the pipes from freezing and bursting during the winter months. Habits. Old habits.

How funny. She couldn't remember whether she had turned them on or off after their last trip down. She trotted downstairs, under the basement, Clara close on her heels, and found the main piping.

Amanda had pulled it off: A completely executed detour from Southern Maryland to their home in the country. Here they would stay, undetected and safe, without much exposure or noise.

Most importantly, without being followed by an assailant in a dark green pick-up watching them at the college.

Wow.

So far, so good. Her plan was intact. Now, she would take the old red Wrangler that was parked in the garage and drive it. Clara would take the car back to Washington DC in due course.

But sleep did not come easily. She drifted in and out of sleep. As a rule, everyone slept like a rock in this house. It was nearly dawn. Amanda awoke and looked about the room, so reminiscent of those weekends here with Trevor.

God how she missed him.

Trevor where are you now, she wondered. Married now for a number of years, their love ran deep - their passion still vibrant. Here in this house...their days had often been crowded with country activities and boating...He outside; she fussing with food in the kitchen and a porch full of friends and neighbors coming and going, kids everywhere trailing everything from fishing gear to rubber tubes for boat-towing down the river...

She peered outside, the river bathed in moonlight. Mists gathered at the fringes of the woods where soon deer might appear. It was dawn, yes. Strange that no hunters were out and perched in trees already -hunters with a license to kill game.

From across the river though, evidently some hunters must have disturbed a flock of slumbering geese: They were flustered like protesting ladies at a tea party, then resettled, one at a time: If things got too bad they would take flight for another river...

The fields, some still loaded with corn or soya-bean crops, were now getting sodden with moisture and threatening mold. This was definitely harvesting season. A good blow would dry them out one more time. Droughts across the country had affected the Futures Corn Market in Chicago, and this yield, per bushel, was now more valuable. Those farms with irrigation systems were advantaged.

As she mused, she knew that Trevor would now be standing beside her and gathering his arms around hers, a peck on her head. How fortunate she was to have such a husband...

Her mind was miles away when something caught her eye.

 A glint, maybe. Perhaps it was the pre-dawn light that caught a car's chrome surface. Or a window. Maybe nothing.

But in these remote regions, little surrounded them that she did not know about. Nothing was supposed to be there but farm fields and marsh grass.

She froze. Surely...*not.* No. the idea was too stretched. No one could possibly have *followed* them there?

She was about to dismiss it and return to bed.

Instead, she walked passed her bed and down the steps that led the kitchen. A secondary set up steps originally built for house staff in the 19th century led to the ground floor. Here, she and Trevor had improved the structure to add a stone tower and landing. But the old steps had remained. Simple and unadorned, just as they had been used a century and half before.

Just before the kitchen was a Utility entrance that held pegs and closets. From one hook she pulled a large silk stole, actually an antique silkscreen that served as a stole, complete with long tassels. She had bought it from a seaside bazaar long ago.

She reached for the upper shelving and drawers and found keys; unlocked the cabinet, unhinged a gun and loaded it with two shells from the drawer below.

She stepped out, holding her stole around her chest with her left hand, and a shotgun in the folds of her nightdress with the other. She walked all the way to the edge of the field where she was certain a car was waiting...

Half way out, as the dark receded, she started to feel ridiculous. By the time she reached the edge of the field, the gun was heavy, the folds of her nightdress wet with dew, and her hem grassy.

She reached the spot where she saw something form her window. Nothing more natural could have stopped her glancing back at her bedroom window from which she first spotted a silver glint. Yes. The view was clear.

Nothing. Nothing here at all. She looked about carefully, the field was quiet as a grave.

Nothing. *Nothing.*

She felt stupid as hell. If anyone saw her standing in a nightdress from Harrods, a tasseled silkscreen for a shawl and a shotgun – loaded, no less – in her hand.

God. What was she thinking?

Dumb. That's what she was. A total fool.

She trudged back. Again missing Trevor doing his man thing.

Fortunately, she re-stowed everything before anyone was up. But they all did find her at the kitchen table with coffee brewed when they awoke. She fixed them breakfast, and she had made a decision, she said. They were all returning to the city, she announced.

Gwynie objected. The look on Clara's face was puzzled. She swooped up Gwynie and upstairs they went to get organized for a return.

Amanda gazed out the window a little longer. Something was wrong. Terribly wrong. She felt it deep inside.

For one thing, *being* down here was wrong...No. she had miscalculated.

Then again, she was propelled by events that drove her on a flight to the hills, so to speak. What if someone had been waiting and watching for them at the college, the night before?

Following the incident of Sandra and Gwynie in the boat – something induced by another boat while a car sat in the distance observing?

No. Something was definitely wrong.

What a month. The boy's death being neither accidental, nor without meaning, something the grandmother confirmed with her information about him... Then reports from the pending case against the Corporation implying foul play.

Now she was getting angry. Where the *hell* was Trevor?

She must be going mad, she decided. False alarm. Still, they were going back today.

The farm manager's wife came in regularly to check on things. Amanda left a note.

Gwynie had found Brutus, the neighbor's Chesapeake Retriever who had come lumbering over for strokes, sticks and water splashing by Gwyneth, and that's when Amanda knew she had to call the neighbor and explain their visit.

Finally, with the car filling up with items now finding their way back to the city as the summer closed, she was close to getting tired, frustrated and close to... to... wanting to give up.

 She called her office and said she would pop in for an hour later in the day.

Then she looked back at the dock. How she would have like to stay, fiddle with the lines of the boat or the moorings; the boathouse and the toys stowed below decks for the season. Just stuff. Things you did...

She was about to climb into the Jeep when she froze. She saw it. Off in the distance, and damn it *across the field*... The sight bolted through her like a shock wave.

Parked. The green pick-up.

It was there. It had been there. It had been stalking the house since dawn.

"Clara" began Amanda. "Would you mind very much if ...if..." She walked around and asked Clara to have a word with her. Clara got out of the car, Gwynie strapped in already.

"Would you mind if I asked you to drive Gwynie home?" The look on Clara's face was even more puzzled than the one she had the day before. Yet it was full of concern.

"Don't worry, Clara. I will return in the Wrangler in the Garage. Trevor would have wanted me to check the boat, that's all. I feel bad that I didn't before returning to the city. It will take me at least an hour."

Clara's face cleared of alarm, she nodded, understanding these things. A farm was full of obligations. This she had learned over the years. And she was too polite to suggest that Amanda's behavior was less than normal, if not a little jumpy. That was the prerogative of your employer.

Amanda squeezed her elbow in thanks. As varied as her tasks had become as housekeeper to this family, Clara knew of their generosity and kindness to her and her own family. More than anything, there was trust between them. Of course she would take her instructions and leave. Gwynie was told that Mommy was following.

They left.

Amanda looked at the old Wrangler and hoped to God the Manager had not been creative with the gas in the tank, or rather, his teenage son. But the place seemed untouched. She went back inside the house, and would have reached for the gun.

Instead, the thought struck her that this was ridiculous. You don't take matters into your own hands, they would say. And rightfully so. Of course.

Instead, she picked up her cell, called the Manager and reported a strange car sitting on the premises. With that, she simply strode out to the barn, started up the old Wrangler, and drove out.

The consequences of that call alone would send the farm manager down the one-way farm lane, followed by a posse of his "old boys" - if not the sheriff himself: This was not an estate to trifle with. Trespassing was an offense.

The two hour drive passed quickly. And though she did return to her office for a quick hour, she picked up all the materials that Barbara had sent her, and went home. She got through the day, reunited with Gwynie, and a big thanks to Clara who was sent home for the weekend.

It was later that night that Amanda sat alone in her bedroom in Washington DC. The question that plagued her all day was this: *How did anyone know where she was that evening?*

She was definitely *not* imagining things. They had been followed. Or, if they knew where she was, then the real important issue was *Why*? She was pacing again. Yes, someone definitely had them as targets.

She went downstairs.

Attempting to get some work done was futile, even as she unpacked the materials she had asked for. She could hardly think.

Actually, she did think. One thing she had, sitting outside in the car that Clara had driven home, was a tape from a Web cam. That webcam would confirm the tag numbers, and give the owner's name. Clara had been asked to get a copy from the Police Office while she and Sandra talked together on campus.

Meanwhile, she had to concentrate on the business at hand.

Her cell phone rang. It was the Farm Manager. There was nobody there when they got there, he assured her.

She thanked him for checking.

They spoke, and he enquired after Trevor. It was only then that she realized how his absence was felt by others. Yes, the community did miss him. In fact, she had a creeping realization of something, and barely kept from uttering it on the phone to the Farm Manager.

If Trevor did not surface, she would sell the farm, she decided. Too much was coursing through her brain when he uttered something that jolted her "But, honestly, from my years of deer trackin' and huntin' I'd say they was fresh tracks down there from a heavy duty vehicle of some sort. I am certain of it. And the boys too..."

She thanked him again for his diligence and follow-up.

Sell the farm? My God. Had things come to this?

She was pacing again. Trevor. Trevor. Trevor? What was happening? To the corporation? If she was a target, then *she* was *he*...?

She walked to her bed and sat down heavily. Then a thought struck her.

She ran downstairs, picked up her belongings and ran back up. She emptied her bag. Lipstick. Make up. Note Book. Cleansing agents, jewelry, wallet, scarf, keys, toiletries, perfume...

She sat, staring at the items strewn on the bed. Like so many parts of machinery. From a life than ran smoothly, now all broken down. Something. Something. Something....*What* was holding back?

She lay back, staring at a dark ceiling, her thoughts a whirl, the night closing in on her.

What if *he* had been a target since...since...well since...just...?

She must have dozed off. It was two in the morning, she heard Gwynie tossing about.

She switched on the lights and calmly returned to her desk of paperwork. She had it.

The list. She wanted to see the list of stockholders present at the Annual General Meeting that she had attended for Trevor in Toronto.

Then she saw it. The name of the girl that she had aided, the one who had thrown up all over her clothing in her hotel room where she left her to rest...

Amanda suddenly put down the paper and looked up the stairs: No. Impossible.

She rose calmly, and walked up to the bedroom. She searched for something that would have been left in the bedroom at the time ...One by one, item by item, everything passed through her fingers. And then one last item remained. It lay there, too well trusted to have been a suspect...

Je T'aime lay there. The perfume that Trevor had given her - a perfume so exotic that its golden top was made of gold leaf. She had taken it to Toronto. She opened the lid and inspected it carefully. It never left her bag. She used it infrequently, but it was *always* there.

Inside was a hairline crack. She tugged at it. Then it broke open: A tiny transmitter popped out. Small, circular, the circuited device had its stem wound around the threads of the bottle lid.

By itself, she felt appalled. She had been used. But the greater question that lurked frightened her even more.

Why? Was she the intended *target*? If so, surely harm would have by now been done? No. She was a conduit. To whom?

The answer demystified as dawn appeared.

Trevor?

Calm and softly as ever, a feeling surfaced from deep within her thinking. A suspicion vaporous and undefined. What if Trevor were not alive?

* *

She and Gwynie spent a calm and uneventful weekend together. Simple things, like walks and TV shows; a jigsaw puzzle, then some gardening and reading. They made a puppet from satin bows and buttons left over from the school project, something to dangle from her window. Gwynie loved it, and took it to bed that night, exhausted.

The Saturday morning local market stroll, the outdoor café at the Baker's, some fresh shrimp from the seafood store...and back to the house. Gwynie would be rested and ready for School Monday. She napped and Amanda worked quietly at her computer.

She had to pull herself together, she decided. There was much work to be done. Much to *analyze*. Much to think through. *You are a Researcher.*

By Sunday evening, she had made a call to Argueta. His Report was completed, she said. She'd like to deliver it herself, if he had time. Say lunch?...

The report, she knew, petitioned for mining rights to offshore drilling lease-beds that her husband's company was involved with.

Argueta, she felt certain, would understand. She hesitated. They had discussed the incident at the college, and he had traced the tag number of the car to a local resident. He was, after all, the man to consult, if needed. This, Trevor had admonished in his letter.

But should she now tell him that she suspected the same man to be following them? Or that had a tracer device planted on her in Toronto. Even as a friend of the family, she felt such questions inappropriate for a Researcher.

Besides, Rebecca told her not to panic. Industrial espionage was a common occurrence in the general order of things up there. One should assume that competitors were watching, and listening – always.

But more than anything, Amanda wanted to ask Argueta if he had heard from Trevor. Was everything alright? Was he alright?

She said nothing.

* *

Dr. Stewart Ridell had just returned from the International Symposium on the A-Train Satellite Constellation. Oddly, nobody was talking.

He went over the data again sent from the MODIS tracking systems, then re-examined all the literature from the Conference. Ample material was published about aerosols, clouds, hydrological cycles and radiation.

Earthquakes were travelling along the Atlantic fault lines. In places, as they shifted along the transform fault line, he knew, energy stored at tectonic plates was being released through fissures and vents.

But increasingly, with tectonic plates pressing, the fault line moved further north, and the damage spreading.

The sea floor was opening up and spreading wider apart in unpredictable places. Contrary to subvention, the plates were bulging and opening up in places at the sea bottom. Whereas longitude and latitudinal lines could pinpoint survey lines established, what was changing was the accretion of surface area as tectonic plates spread apart; lava hardening and forming new mass of dense surface.

So. Why was there nothing on this? He picked up the data again. Then he held up an image, something sent to him by an air pilot on a small craft flying off the Nova Scotia coastline.

A dark stain sitting on the surface of the water looked remarkably like an oil spill. Must have been one hell of an oil tanker spilling that kind of oil.

Back to the literature. He read the abstracts of authors Rearhard, Jones, Tydor and Mitchell, knowing full well what their findings were. He hoped to find a clue that might have been overlooked somewhere.

"Natural oil seepage is the release of crude oil into the ocean from fissures in the seabed. Oil seepage is a major contributor to the total amount of oil entering the world's oceans. According to a study by the National Academy of Science, 47 percent of oil entering the world's oceans is from natural seeps, and 53 percent is from human sources – such as extraction, transportation, and consumption. Oil seeps cause smooth oil slicks to form on the water's surface. Oil seeps can indicate the location of stores of fossil fuel beneath the ocean floor."

He knew the effect of oil seepage on marine life and marine eco-systems. He had seen enough of *that*, thank you.

But this research... off the Artic coast, utilizing sun glint MODIS imagery to locate oil slicks, an area that had not previously been surveyed for natural oil seeps using remote sensing, was somewhat unusual.

Since 1982, the Atlantic Ocean had been closed to oil and gas drilling. Recently, however, the US Minerals Management Services cited the need to identify seepage sites in the Atlantic Ocean.

"Well I'll be damned." he muttered. So, there it was, in black and white, an official declaration of potential seeps in the Atlantic.

Still, what remained nebulous was the amount of the oil seep; the location or the explanation for the amounts spotted in the Northern Atlantic region. It was the site of a lawsuit directed against a British insurance company by a Canadian drilling interest, no less.

What he saw, though, bothered him even further. The divergent fault lines has been subject to recent changes and lay directly along the official territorial lines of the United States Boundary. In fact, it had just shifted to within inches outside that boundary line.

Silence on the subject truly could be explained by review processes at work. Or simply not being aware...

Regardless, he would have to report to Argueta. That was his responsibility to do.

"Someone is trying very hard to stitch the continental plates back together again...for legal reasons, perhaps. I don't get it. But the data has been suppressed" he said on the phone.

"Or re-define the boundary line" replied Argueta. "We've had some complications with our military boundary patrols caused by seismic and magnetic anomalies... Anyway, thanks Stew. I'll talk to the Administration about it."

What Dr. Stewart Ridell wanted to know was whether the various East Coast Nuclear Reactors had been barred from receiving this latest seismic activity information – something for which their regulation and requirements mandated.

He hoped to God they were. And for good reason. Seismic activity was a Nuclear Reactor's worst nightmare. This, Japan had discovered. Especially if older nuclear rods were left standing in pools for the lack of re-cycling.

He went home for the day.

* *

Argueta was totally distracted.

"Thanks Sergeant." he said, stepping out of the dark suburban that delivered him back to the Pentagon from the Whitehouse. He made it all the way to this office with a calm face and happy smile.

The notion that the White House was fully informed and withholding information was abhorrent to an old military man. That's what he could not reconcile.

"Come in. Come in." had said the Whitehouse Chief of Staff Bill Baxter. "The Front Office is full of Russians at the present time...I'm afraid we'll have to put everything on hold for a couple of days. I'm sorry. But I'm sure you understand Argueta?"

"Of course I do."

"Good. Now sit down. How's Sonia?"

"Oh, she's busy as ever with her teaching, writing, lecturing and novel writing..."

Baxter howled with laughter. "I saw her fielding questions about her latest at the National Press Club last week. Wow. What a gal..."

"Thank you Sir." said Argueta.

It was a good twenty minutes of chatting before anything substantial was said. Finally it was Argueta who was invited to make his case.

"As you know, my concern is biological and ecological conditions that affect the Navy. That, and coastal reconnaissance, related. So I want you to see something. We last received a disturbing report from one of our allies' submarines off Bermuda. It seems that they were witnessing greater effects of Magma magnetic anomalies than every known or fully understood. They sustained a loss actually, so off-the-compass they were. You see, it's a deep undersea cliff down there, and they were surveying the drop, or rather, the subsea conditions when they ran into some trouble..."

"that sounds scary as hell..."

"Yes. A lesser commander might have done real damage to an expensive piece of machinery. Actually, it was a Royal Navy sub working tandem with us. So, anyway. They believe it's an anomaly that is travelling up and down the Atlantic fault line, which as you know...is a large rift in the tectonic plates"

Baxter nodded, his eyes occasionally flickering to the phone on his desk where calls were clearly being held.

Argueta decided to make it short.

"She needs to come in for some repairs at Norfolk. Then I'd like her to pursue her surveys up the Fault line as safely as possible. You see, some of our continental boundary lines are ...."

Baxter interrupted him with a call when his secretary popped her head in. "He's just finishing up now..." she said, referring to the President.

Baxter had to go.

" May I have permission to run up those Fault lines to survey any subterranean damage?"

"Any extraordinary information, and we need to be the first to know...?"

"Absolutely."

"Fine. I'll send some commissioning orders over to the Pentagon. That should give the mission all the clearances it needs. Thank you."

Argueta rose., and he left the building.

Of course he'd been deflected. He knew that. What he failed to say to them was that such toying with the scientific data could seriously put military combatants in harm's way.

Back at his desk Argueta made notes and wrote a Memo to his staff for fresh directives. There would be work to do, he know.

The Arctic melt was opening opportunities that the Administration wanted to capitalize on. Period.

Anyone, or any corporation that had competing interests or threatened that agenda was at risk. To the Canadians would go the spoils, since they had bargained with a great deal of cash for toxic assets sitting in the Treasury: Never mind the plundering of a shoreline that could cause havoc. Nor even a sovereign boundary that was now spreading across longitudinal lines...

The worse, he knew, was yet to come. If he was worth his salt he would protest. And he would lose his post, of course, as environmental adviser for Naval affairs.

He had been warned off. The White House was buying time. Somehow they should find a way to collect political capital from this opportunity.

Or else...Or else what?

This was dangerous game playing.

Argueta would have liked to warn Amanda. He wanted to... *If everything weren't so darned rooted in politics.*

There was another phone call waiting for Argueta. It was Mel from JAG in Washington DC.

"Coming over for lunch?" asked Mel Taliaferro.

"Yes. Do I need to?"

"You bet you do" replied Mel.

There was little else that could be discussed over the phones.

Argueta got the Pentagon Shuttle over to the Navy Yard and met with Mel Taliaferro in his office before going down to lunch. The place was secure and Argueta received both a clearance and salute from the sentry at the Intelligence Office Desk.

The image went up on the screen.

"Roger Mustafa Badide LaMaas..." said Mel. "I'm surprised we didn't pick up on it before, he was Turkish. He is actually a highly qualified engineer. Has a degree in biophysics. Went to UCLA, and married an American in Santa Monica."

"Go on" said Argueta, suddenly more interested.

"He served in the US Navy, and travelled extensively.. He deployed to the USS Arkansas, then was attached to Pax River Naval Air Base for two years before retiring. He evidently liked the area, bought a house, and there applied for a job as an Inspector at Calvert Cliffs in Maryland. .."

He was South African born, of Dutch descent. Spoke Afrikaner, in fact. Had family assets taken from him when the black Africa Nationalized. Then affiliated with a foreign group trading in import and exports out of Africa to Turkey. He applied for US Citizenship in 1989."

"Where does his *heart* lie?"

"California, apparently. He loves to surf. Looks like that's where he met his wife" said Mel, popping up an eyeful of a woman on the beach wearing little.

"Wow." laughed Argueta.

"Her name is Una. She attends many of his corporate business accounts and identifies potential targets for trouble ahead..."

"Uhuh" nodded Argueta.

"But this guy is all business with associates in less than honorable places. Many involved in Extortion. Diamonds. ``Trafficking. Ivory. Gold. Nothing that could be directly linked to him. But then this..."

He put up an image. It showed him in talks with others

"*The Sowaldi Group*. Not exactly your typical fundamentalist group, but a nasty little cell of anti-establishment devotees that embraced the fundamentalism of a new socio-economic world order. They train in the desert of Africa."

"You're kidding. They showed up on a list of miscreants about offshore drilling in the Artic."

"That doesn't surprise me. They have access to deep money accounts and third-party banking. Not very visible these days, but historically known for a few well placed assassinations and Arms trading in the past."

Argueta narrowed his eyes. Its leader was a man whose name he didn't know. But here he was in consultation with Theodore LaMaas, of Afrikaner and Turkish descent, retired, US Navy.

"Are you sure about this?"

"Yes. This is the man you had us check up on. Is there something else we should know about Argueta?"

Argueta felt a little uncomfortable. While he lauded recruits into the Armed services, foreign nationals always puzzled him. Nobody knew, for example, what kind of upbringing and experiences that might have impressed them. Human nature being what it is, statistics showed a proclivity for activism amongst foreign-born military recruits.

Argueta was Latin-born himself. Grateful for a career in the US Military, if a little marginalized. But there were rising stars, and there were hidden agendas. How did this fit into things, he wondered. He looked down at his hands momentarily.

"Does he have a record of any kind?"

"Yes. A few unexplained gaps, here and there. But nothing too out of the ordinary. Except for one thing. Something of a domestic dispute brought him some attention while staying in Bangkok of all places. He was vacationing with his wife. She went missing. He has a daughter. They keep a sailboat."

"Is there anything here to be concerned about?" asked Argueta

"No. Except that he knows Nuclear Power plants. After all, the USS Arkansas is a nuclear powered Navy Cruiser. No ITAR violations on him. No criminal activities. But we found some lesser security violations at his present job: Apparently, he walked off with material in his computer that should have stayed on the premises at Calvert Cliffs. Nothing sensitive. And nothing the others don't know about. Just construction engineering plans. And some regulation compliance drawings"

"Can you send me that material? Perhaps it's an oversight. Perhaps something of interest." He said, rising. "Thanks for the info."

Argueta paused, pondering. "Maybe he was taking work home to complete at night?"

"Maybe. It's his job to maintain Compliance standards, after all. Probably nothing but plumbing-runs. God knows, Calvert Cliffs has enough of them at that cost of construction."

Mel Taliaferro looked at Argueta "And here, by the way, is a picture of his boss. Keep it. I have copies. He is known as Codename Coyote. So. Err... Lunch then?"

"Let's go."

Argueta enjoyed his lunch on 8th Street on Capitol Hill. By the end of it, he had made a decision.

He would call Amanda and warn her to keep an eye out. Her research report was more accurate than she realized. Any assailants might move with purpose if they found out that she was outlining the dangers pending a contract decision by the government.

He had some reading to do.

To damage the mid-Atlantic region of the United States with a failed nuclear reactor surprised even him. But it was a brilliant move. If an incident occurred that might propel the Mid Atlantic coast into a catastrophic failure...

Good work from that Firm of Amanda's. Good warning...

He got up. He had work to do.

Back at his office he was collecting a full package of information, including electronic discs and files that needed to be reviewed. He had them teetering on a pile on his desk when his secretary came in.

She looked at him, as if asking. He smiled at her, the printer spewing out more documents.

"For Amanda." he said "She is our Research specialist looking at anomalies in biosystems off our coastal waters..."

She nodded. As long as this "Amanda" was on his Cardex list, then she could handle it.

"Sure" she said.

A week later, it was time to clear his desk. She mailed the entire package to its intended recipient: Amanda Wells, address found in the Cardex.

Finished business was finished business.

It was five o'clock.

The next day he called NavSea Systems Command about the Research vessel operations deployments.

* *

"Any word from Trevor?" asked Argueta.

"No." Amanda sighed.

"I'm only my way down to the Royal Navy Special Projects office this afternoon. Perhaps I can ask them?"

She smiled. Of course she would like that. But she knew very well this was beyond discovery, even for Argueta.

"Thank you for asking..." she said, pausing thoughtfully. "So, how can I help?"

"Amanda, I am gravely concerned. I reviewed your analysis. There is cause for concern there: If our nuclear reactor were to be damaged, we'd be in big trouble. Not just because of the power it produces, but because of the location and density of the population around it. It would be catastrophic. Let alone hit the nerve center of the Nation and all its working parts. Like the Japanese, we can't be caught off guard. So, I'm taking the bull by the horns and initiating some precautionary measures"

Amanda was listening intently on her end of the line "Would you like me to come and meet you for security reasons?"

"Yes. Tomorrow. Ten o'clock, please."

"I'll bring two of my staff too."

"That's fine. Send me their names and I'll arrange Entry passes at the Gate."

They arrived early. Argueta liked the two men picked to assist her on the project. Both had security clearances and were familiar with Department of

Defense work. They came ready to take notes for the next research assignment.

Argueta gave them a briefing. He was not a man to waste words. But neither was he an alarmist. And words came to him easily, even if with the intonations of a Latin background. He had served honorably for all his career in the US Military. But now he was worried. There was too much going on, and he had to take action.

He came around his desk, and sat on the corner of it, leaning forward, as if talking to friends. The Nation's Capital may be in danger, he told them.

Amanda took notes. She needed to know the exact research requirements: He had identified a particular threat to the nation along the coast line. That was his job. He needed details to draw up a Response Team at the Pentagon. Her work should be done covertly.

"There was only thing that could avert such a disaster, and even *that* would take weeks if not months to achieve. That would be to shut it down and let it go cold. But again, that would take weeks, and two months of prep. Period."

Amanda thought a second. "So, it this a matter of politics?"

"Look" he said "the seismic activities of the Virginia tremor have already shot the safety margins off the Nuclear Reactor. That we know. But to shut it down?" He opened a second file and offered some images. "Your man worked there." he said to Amanda.

"I've already initiated the exercise under Compliance Mandates for special security reasons. However, I wish to alert nobody, other than routine operating drills. Two weeks?"

"Are you expecting such an attack on the facility?"

Argueta returned to his desk and produce another photo of the Coyote image "Have you ever seen this man?"

"No"

"Good" continued Argueta "Then you are not in his sights. But he's bad news. And he's been spotted lurking around the facility in the last two months on a steady basis. I don't like what all this adds up to. Worse, I know who he is hiring. But that's not my problem just yet..."

She nodded, her heart pounding. She should remain as professional about recognition of this man. Even if he was the one watching them.

"I know you've seen LaMaas. So far, he checks out as a retired military man. Are you ok with this research? ..."

She nodded.

"And don't worry. Your research was spot on. You identified all the necessary items to be addressed. So, know this: Shipments of fossil fuels and oil have been already been diverted to Baltimore."

Amanda was wanting to ask who the perpetrators might be behind such a threat. Or, that is, if the man was connected even. Clearly, that was beyond her security clearance level to know.

Argueta turned to her. "Here's a list of items I need for you to examine also. Can you go over it all, and let me know what you find? I'm groping in the dark at this point, since there is no actual clear and present threat. But outside my sphere, there is nothing that says I can't commission some private examination. And I know you're already trying to defend environmental issues for your husband's company."

"Right" said Amanda. "Is that a conflict of interest?"

"When it comes to national security, nothing is a conflict of interest to know. By the way. I have some limited information for you..."

Later that afternoon, Argueta received a call from Navsea Systems.

"Your man was UK attached, deployed to join a USRN at Norfolk on a vessel that slipped in for some repairs. His disposition is unknown. The vessel of his last command was on mission with a joint venture in the Arctic. Thought it would help you sleep a little easier"

"Thanks." said Argueta.

Amanda went home that night sobered at the thought that internal attacks on vital national resources were a real threat.

She drove home and considered all that Argueta told her. How it might avert damage if she were able to provide more data on the environmental factors at risk in the Arctic drilling venture. Not that the EPA wasn't doing enough to find ways to stop everything, but their task was an empirical analysis of data points. She turned off Massachusetts and onto the Wisconsin Avenue.

 On the other hand... the case for the defense attorneys that she was also working on would take a commercial evaluation. This had been to be a neutral position of finding motive behind a corporate takeover of massive consequence to the nation's policy? A policy that could undermine the country's national security and lay bare the new realities of an Arctic melting along the northern border of the United States?

How to reconcile the two positions, the one of national security; the other of commercial enterprise allowed by rights of free market capitalism?

Was Argueta articulating something here that combined both the commercial interests of a competitor and ...or...something else? If so, what?

If so...What? Her hands flew to her face. This was absolutely altogether *beyond* her. She felt overwhelmed.

That night she found little rest. There was something even deeply more sinister that stirred within her.

At 3 AM she awoke. Thirsty. Gwynie was fast asleep, the dogs calm.

She wandered around the house and went through her notes in a fruitless search for something. She could not put her finger on it, and finally decided to return to bed, frustrated. She was almost at the top of the stairs when it struck her. And the realization reverberated through her like a shocking bolt.

Yes. Definitely.

She had seen the man that Argueta showed her in the picture. And yes, it bothered her that the same man who she thought was there watching her, was at the center of a project she was now working on for Argueta.

But there was more.

There was a connection. She recognized him from *before...* She was almost certain of it. *He knew her.* Absolutely. LaMaas. *How could she have been so stupid*?

She had seen his picture already.

* *

The accommodations were new, but the concept old. The British had a special facility attached to their Embassy staff offices. Arguetta had an appointment.

It was a long day. There had been multiple meetings and discussions. Finally, later that day Argueta was led into a secure room at the Special Projects Office of the Royal Navy in Washington DC.

He was glad he had talked to Amanda. Because what he discovered now was more than he would have liked to know at the time of his conversation with her.

Trevor MacDonnel was indeed onboard the US/UK exercise.

He was informed, further, about what the Nuclear Attack Submarine was carrying onboard.

He closed his eyes.

* *

The week passed too quickly. Amand got through the early morning chores then got dressed. Her cell was ringing, three messages remained outstanding and her inbox was a dark list of unanswered mail.

This was no good. She arrived at work, engaged with the matters of hand and checked her watch.

"I'm sorry Janice" she said, "I'll have to get to that later. Could you take the lead on some of those questions, let me know what you decide? Oh...and ask Barbara to get back to me on the matter in New York?"

Janice beamed. "No worries."

It was how they worked - most of them able to take the initiative anyway, a place of courtesy and respect with deferential loyalty.

She would leave at Noon. Selfishness and high-minded principles had a price. Could she afford it?

That night, she knew, she would be wondering at the world that she and Trevor had built.

"Stay the course" he had said. Easy for him. He was not there. He was at sea.

Life and success held no guarantee for anyone, he would say. Pick you battles, and find your moral high ground.

What then? The responsibility of a firm's employment took precedence over your own sensitivities?

And what of tomorrow...she wondered. What then? How to reconcile things in a city built on negotiations, give-and-take; relationships?...

How?

* *

"Mom, are you alright?" asked Sandra when she called.

Amanda was well on her way. "Yes. I am alright. Thanks for asking…So how's your school work coming along?"

More than anything else, she wanted Sandra to know that her father was a man of the highest integrity, regardless what lay ahead. There was something innately satisfying to a young adult who saw love in the eyes of their parents. Such things had a lasting impact.

Amanda thought about it. Emotional security should lodge deep within a young heart. To know that two people once fell in love; took a chance and then proceeded through life working out their differences was important. It was a gift that parents could give. Even if the nucleus of their world had reshaped. Yes, she decided, it was important to find sincerity embedded in family commitments.

Even if she herself would fall victim. ..

"Mom…You sound, like… I don't know. What's up? I'm coming home."

"No."

* *

She and Jeff met for lunch. They talked like old friends, perhaps it was because of Jeff's early perceptions. This situation was his reality.

"Forgive me for taking liberties here, Jeff. But I want to be frank...I want to talk to you face to face..."

"Yes. Amanda. It is me that has taken liberties. Forgive me. What was I thinking? You and Trevor...My God I'm making such a fool of myself." he paused and looked down.

She reached over and touched his hand for consolation. "No you're not. You're just being honest about your feelings" she said.

He looked up. "Amanda....You just bowled me off my feet. You stood there, the minute I laid eyes on you..." He leaned forward "You, with your beautiful face; your evening dress and all your staff around you having such fun...You can't imagine how that stirred me ...I'm a victim of my own voracity."

"Jeff. I belong to Trevor MacDonald. I'm in love with my husband, and we are his family. I cannot forget that, even if I have to blow what chances I have for advancing my Firm. "

The waiter came. Jeff was ebullient in his ordering.

Amanda continued. "You know we need the work. *We all do...* But I cannot compromise my principles."

He waited, looking at her fiercely.

Then she said "Jeff, it's not that I'm significant, but we all need truth and meaning in life. Without it, we are lost."

"I understand." he said.

"Please do not steer the Congressman wrongly. He may choose whomever he wishes as his financial broker...But I cannot give you what *you* need...I am not negotiable."

There, she said it.

If she was a fool, she was about to find out. It could have gone either way. She was uncertain. But that's the way it came out...

She waited.

He was looking down. "Yes. I'm sorry. It was foolish of me to hope...But with Trevor gone on a mission of 'impossible-return,' I thought I could creep into your life..."

Amanda swallowed her concerns. Trevor, the man she loved, might never return to her, she knew. But hearing it from someone else rooted her with isolation.

Still, entertaining this man any further was something she could not do. She would not have an affair.

She looked him squarely. "You need never apologize Jeff Watson. You have great work ahead of you. And the front door of our home will be open to you. Enter it with nobility, and you shall be welcome."

"My God Amanda. I'm so in love with you."

"Jeff. The matter is closed. If you wish to sink the project, then so be it. I will take what comes. Please know this."

The lunch ended if not abruptly, with an air of finality.

Amanda almost ran. She hailed a cab.

She found herself repeating words she heard long ago.

If the heart is pure...the world will find you again.

* *

Sandra called back.

"Hia sweetie, How's everything…?" said Amanda.

Sandra gave her a stream of conversation that lasted a full five minutes.

"Done any sailing recently?" asked Amanda, changing the subject from toxic topics.

"No"

"Oh?"

"I dunno. It's just that…."

"Not that mishap with Gwynie, that's not stopping you is it? That was *not* your fault, and I should have not have burdened you with taking care of your sister while …."

"No. Mom. It's not that. Gwynie was fine. We all got wet. That's all. "

"So, what's up?"

"Nothing really. It's just this guy who keeps showing up by the boathouse. He's so creepy. It's like, he's… watching me."

Amanda's breath stopped. Was this an assailant called LaMaas? She waited.

Then again, at college-age, *everybody* was always watching them. It was that stage of life when all poets seeking to change the world should find a specter at every turn.

"*Oh No.*" mocked Amanda.

They laughed, Sandra relieved.

Then she said calmly "He doesn't have a green pick-up vehicle, does he?"

The answer was clear, even if met with silence. Sandra was not going to re-visit the incident with Gwynie.

"Mom, I gotta go. Talk to you soon. Loveya."

* *

Not often did Amanda deposit work at home, and her needs were few. However, on the premises they did keep secure cabinets and a safe. Locked, and in the library where Trevor used to work, she now opened the combination.

In these files, amongst necessary family business, were his papers. Trevor's corporate interest were marked, including the Annual Stockholders Meeting for which she had gone to Toronto.

She pulled out the photos. Images she had neglected to examine, really, in the rush of it all: The complete file that Barbara had made up came before her.

She looked at the photos again. There, at the Banquet Awards Dinner, seated at the same round table as Lauren Papenpodulus was a man with hair that was smoothly combed in the flash light of the camera, barely looking up between two others seated at the table.

Victor LaMaas.

How could she have been so stupid as to *not* make a connection? Of course.

If there was an issue with Trevor's company, he might be interested. Perhaps even knowing that Trevor had family in Southern Maryland where he lived...

But was he the man watching at the waterfront? She could not be absolutely certain.

Was he there on that night of the boating incident? Certainly, it was a waterside accident, but still, was he there just as an innocent bystander, or did he have recognition of who he was looking at?

Was Sandra known to him as Trevor's daughter? Was Gwynie? What of Amanda's arrangements on on campus as faculty even...

Perhaps not. Then again, why was his car seemingly recognized on their farm?

Perhaps there too she was mistaken.

Amanda was beginning to doubt her own suspicions when it occurred to her that he was also in the industry of nuclear power: He worked at Calvert Cliffs, as Argueta said. That would put him in direct conflict with the corporate interests of energy producers in Toronto who by definition, used fossil fuels as opposition to nuclear fuel.

Worse. If she were right, and he was in involved with corporate affairs and observing Trevor's family for reasons of possible non-competitive concessions - then they had been targeted by an angry industrial competitor, and that left them vulnerable. After all, Trevor was away...

 His intentions would be ...*what?*

She spent the night up thinking.

What if Trevor needed to be coerced into making non-competitive concessions?

Think.

First things first: The legal case being mounted against Trevor's company suddenly was citing the environment as being altered somehow. They has asked for an Environmental Impact Statement. She would need to talk with Barbara. *Jacob was examining evidence that would show damage to the environment?*

The Bird. *The bird?* What did it mean? Extinct? Not extinct? Historically known...for *what?*

The books he kept. What was he implying? That the bird was extinct?

Not extinct. Of course. If he could prove that the bird had existed for a long time in that natural habitat, nesting since the beginning of time at that location, then there was therefore no evidence of environmental disturbance. *No disturbance imposed by offshore drilling.*

Such a conclusion would surely strengthen the position of Trevor's company to receive the contract award for drilling.

As for this man, LaMaas. What was he doing on the arm of Lauren... then taking images of the family of Trevor MacDonald, her main competitor?

Amanda thought about it. Perhaps she was over reacting. Maybe her fears were ungrounded. If LaMaas were not there as a commercial competitor, he was no threat at all.

What if this man's intentions were *not* aimed at Trevor's company as competitor, but at the client, source of the contract, the government? A ploy to damage and limit energy production in one sphere might make the client favor another...

He was in the Navy, and had worked at Calvert Cliffs Nuclear Reactor.

Sabotage. That would make him a serious threat of the worst kind. Former employee as miscreant.

Don't be so stupid.

She went over her Notes. She read her instructions for the work to be done.

Amanda, I am gravely concerned. If our nuclear reactor were to be damaged, we'd be in big trouble. Not just because of the power it produces, but because of the location and density of the population around it. It would be catastrophic. Let alone hit the nerve center of the nation and all its working parts. Like the Japanese, we can't be caught off guard. So, I'm taking the bull by the horns and initiating some precautionary measures

Argueta was concerned about the security of the Nuclear facility.

Then it struck her. No. Wait. The reason Argueta was involved was because of a security *breach*. That could only mean one thing. Forget commercial competitiveness. This was terrorism.

Here was a threat to civil defense. An assault, on US soil would imply terrorism.

A Nuclear Reactor damaged sufficiently to render its plume of radioactivity into surrounding populations would most certainly include Washington DC.

Oh My God. Surly this man was not going to...Oh My God.

She turned to the package mailed her by Argueta's office.

* *

Chapter Eleven

Suffolk, England

When the Space and Planetary Sciences department saw the date off the MODIS imagery, they hardly stirred.

Only Dr. Stewart Ridell demurred. Something still puzzled him. It was the positioning of the latest data point along the fault line. "Are you sure about this?"

"Well...:"

"OK. I'll check it out." said his assistant.

Ridell looked carefully at the global latitudinal and longitudinal lines and couldn't believe his eyes. Ludicrous really, if only a novelty of the plant's strange stirrings. The divergent fault line has been subject to recent changes and lay directly along the official territorial lines of the United States Boundary. In fact, it had just shifted to within inches outside that boundary line.

Never mind that it lay under the sea along the Northeastern boundaries of the Arctic Ridge.

He was a geologist by training. And Great Britain was not without its interests in the Atlantic. Especially if natural resources were in question.

Here then was one of those anomalies that only politicians should solve.

The seabed fault line had not flattened into a small basin. That condition was ideal for an oil production platform since it concentrated upon entry spot which was clearly seeping oil naturally. The entire underground deposit of mineral was accessible at that one spot.

He had been called upon for UK oil drilling interests of the North Atlantic. Especially regarding geological features safe to mine. Usually, it was surface weather that was topmost on his mind.

However, this was unusual. In question was the incident of an oil rig had been recently exploded, albeit without anchored feet to the seabed.

Further, it was the site of a disputed mining permit and contract offering by the government.

"Jim" he said at last on his phone "Isn't Trevor's group under scrutiny by the Americans for his permits to drill off the Arctic?"

"Yes" came the reply in London. "He has his claim. But so do the Canadians, evidently. They've applied to the Americans for the permit to drill there, citing Trevor's company as non-compliant with environmental standards of proof that no damages shall be made to extant species..."

"Sounds like the proverbial bird of flight from Noah's Arc if you ask me"

"Right. The rig wasn't even in play, let alone drilling. It was in transport."

"Well. I have something interesting to tell you. They won't be issuing any permits to anyone. The site for penetration at the seafloor is United States Territory no more."

"What?"

"The plane basin is *not territorial* bottom any more. It was on the borderline. It has geologically moved: It shifted in a recent fault-line accretion that leaves the US Territorial boundary on a lava mountain at the apparent entry point for drilling."

"No way. The Mineral Mining Department in the United States Department of Interior is considering a permit to drill there."

"Not anymore. It is now in International waters."

* *

"As I understand it" said Rebecca, calling from Toronto, "the dispute that is being claimed by the prosecution is that the lease bottom is not within US territory. Rather, it is in international waters and therefore warrants international disputation resolution."

"But at that global position, the common border is with the Soviet Union is it not?" asked Amanda.

"It is. But so is a lot of the region open to sea..."

Amanda was appalled at the way the case had taken. Not only was the burden upon them to prove that no environmental harm had been done by the oil rig approaching the leased-bottom, but that the leased bottom and its rights were now in question. How could that be?

In the first instance, what the Canadians claimed was the exposure to risk along their coast *if* the drilling went wrong.

What Lauren wanted to claim was that her company would limit those risks...*if they were awarded the contract.*

"You know...if Lauren wins this case, that will leave the entire region off limits for *any* drilling at all, by anyone" said Amanda.

"If she can't get the contract, she wants nobody else to get it. For sure." said Rebecca. "She's not your garden variety snake in the grass. She's THE snake who visited Eve..."

Amanda laughed.

"What puzzles me about your Administration" continue Rebecca "is the lack of motivation to defend their territorial rights under the present circumstances? The rights for leasing don't seem to matter?"

Amanda sighed.

"Look. I'm coming down to Washington DC. I need to talk to a few policy makers. The first one I need to meet is Mr. Argueta. Can we arrange something?"

"Sure. We'll make a cultural event. I have an idea."

"OK."

"I'll send you the details. Maybe a dinner evening together at the Kennedy Center on Friday. How's that?"

"Really? I'd love it." said Rebecca. She paused thoughtfully "Arctic melting or no Arctic. What worries me even more is what Lauren might do next. She is not above foul play, you know. So...err... be careful, will you? I'll talk to you later...."

Amanda poured herself more coffee and made some ticket arrangements. She left a message for Argueta to call her back, and then sat down in the Library. It was Wednesday. Tomorrow she had a final class at the College.

Thank God. End of the semester was as much welcomed by faculty as by students.

She was taking Gwynie down, yes, because Sandra wanted to go to the Eastern Shore for the weekend and take Gwynie to the farm with her: There was a parade for kids on the 'Shore, and they could have dinner at the Club. Sandra was then going sailing with some friends. So it was all arranged.

That left Amanda with the entire weekend to entertain Rebecca in Washington. She looked at her desk and decided to catch up with a little research before assembling her materials for tomorrow's class.

She settled in, wishing like hell that some breakthrough had come in on the ecological analysis Jacob was working on before he died.

She had given the team time, Barbara had been in close touch with the boy's family. What she needed was affirmation, preferably coming from his valuable contribution, that there was evidence of little environmental impact along that shore.

"As long as it was done within regulatory compliance" said Barbara. "If the bird was found alive somewhere, then the case against bird extinction id moot. And if *one* could be disproven, then the *other* also..."

Barbara and Amanda knew one thing. The boy Jacob should not be forgotten. His effort was proving invaluable. Especially with regards to his observations about extinction of a bird species and their nesting grounds. Clearly, he had an interest in bird watching. This was clear from his attentiveness to an exquisite rendition of a bird richly ornamented in the colors of a species once indigenous. And more recently affirmed by his grandmother.

"Get some rest" admonished Barbara. "You look beat...I'll take it from here."

Amanda was relieved. In fact, she knew that their work on this project was almost done. All that remained was a written final report.

Later that evening Amanda looked at her watch. Outstanding was the matter of her business for Trevor's corporate interests. The case was building for Rebecca in Toronto. She had written a report and compiled the data to support it. She felt satisfied that she had done a good job of it.

"I'll see what I can find.." Amanda had promised.

"Send me what you can. I'll leave your findings with the Attorneys in the morning" said Rebecca. "Then I'll be coming down."

"Great." said Amanda. "I'll see you then."

* *

It was almost midnight when the phone buzzed by her bed. She was actually dozing, papers strewn out in preparation for the next day's class.

"Hello my darling" he said, ever so softly.

"Trevor." she said, incredulous. "Oh what a wonderful surprise..." The phone line was static

"Yes..." the signal was intermittent.

"Oh it's so good to hear your voice. I can't tell you how we miss you..."

She couldn't tell how close or how far he was, or if he was able to respond. Static dissolved into lapses, then recurred.

"I can't say where I am ....Love..."

 "Trevor. *Hello?* Trevor, can you hear me?.."

"Are you alright?...Trevor? *Hello*?"

* *

The last night of class had arrived. It was the Final Exam.

She handed out the exam sheets, wrote some key reminders on the board, and answered multiple questions. Including funny questions.

Everyone was a game changer, she once told her fellow Faculty members when preparing for the semester's program. That is not to say that Amanda was easily manipulated by a class. She was entirely managing every precious minute of lecture time. Tuition was expensive. It should pay off for everybody. This she knew.

They looked up, nodding from fatigued pale faces, all them attentive but clearly weary from the rigors of study. Some had to attend college for five years to complete the full four year curriculum for a University Degree. Others did not survive the pace at all, and dropped out altogether without a degree conferred.

"Two essays only. Pick from the selection before you. This, added to your research papers, will constitute your grade and be posted to your course at the Registrar's office. Everyone ok?"

They nodded.

" Ms Peckering will collect the blue book essays at the end of class. Thank you."

 Amanda wondered how they did it, many of them on tight budgets and no breaks. Sandra explained.

"It's all heart" she said of her student to fellow members of the faculty.

"The thing is, the students feel safe in your class. You're terrific." they told her.

That meant a lot to Amanda. It was the kind of feeling that gave her the satisfaction of having been a successful parent. Or successful instructor. Cheating was the last thing to worry about. Each student had two essays to write, and they would right it in full...Supervision was not an issue, here.

Still, she was glad it was all over. She had a lot on her mind. Chief in her thoughts were the call she got from Trevor. She would talk to Argueta tomorrow...

Tonight, especially, she was glad to be handing Gwynie over to Sandra's care. Not that Gwynie needed any encouragement. As far as she was concerned, sitting in the rear of Sandra's college CJ7 Jeep was her idea of heaven. Even if still with school clothes on, and a pink Patagonia backpack tossed somewhere in the rear.

"Be careful" admonished Amanda to Sandra with a bug hug. Sandra looked at her mother's face, and gave her an extra pat of assurance.

Finally, the sun set. And as the class all bowed their heads to attend to the worksheets before them, she passed by the window, fully expecting the car to be gone by now.

It was still there.

She could she see the translucent pond surface through its rear windows behind the parking lot. The car was vacant. But not far away from the vehicle was a figure actually sitting on the visitors bench, head down.

As if asleep. Or waiting...Who?

The picture of a man sitting on a park bench less than 200 feet away irked her. It was LaMaas. What was he waiting for, just sitting there?

Bloody Hell.

Anger gripped her. This was the same man who observed Gwynie get swamped though binoculars.

This was the man sitting beside Lauren at the Head Table of the Annual Gala Banquet in Toronto.

This was the man whose presence influenced decisions made in board rooms, court rooms and other points of financial strategic importance....

Even at the Pentagon, Argueta had informed her, he was subject of interest in sensitive medium, like Nuclear Power Plants...Who did he think he was, sitting there?

Right there. As if he didn't know that *she* could see *him*?

 Her eyes shot about wildly. Then she made a sudden decision.

"Is everyone happy with the assignment?" she asked again, as if someone outside her body. "Anyone have any further questions...Do you have what you need?"

It was dark when she left the building, a full hour before scheduled. With the exam papers collected by Ms Peckering, they would be mailed to her in a sealed envelop. This completed her task.

She walked to the Student Center, ordered a coffee and trailed across the lawn to the Visitor's Center where she needed to deliver some papers for a student who was already taking another exam for another course: Amanda's exam test was handed to the supervisor of that class room who would keep it sealed until that student could take the test later.

 With the street lights on, the campus was a veritable wonderland in shadow and contrasts. Where window lighting fell, shrubs and red colored leaves shone brightly as if waiting for a hallowing party. It appeared particularly inviting and warm in the Visitor's Center for another hour or so.

She saw him look up.

Yes. It was the same man. *What was he doing here...*

 Sure. Argueta had told her...

Could it be a normal coincidence that he should have been in Toronto? If so, you'd think he'd be smart enough to establish a rapport with fellow stockholders...or *something sociably polite.*

Why sit there like a ...voyeur?

Innocent as daylight, she trotted past his green pick-up and with the windows still open, and she casually reached in for a handful of rolled drawings that lay on the back seat of the vehicle.

She proceeded back across the lawns to the Student Center. She moved to her own car, started the engine, and calmly drove off.

Her eyes never left the road for an hour. Up route 5, across 301 to Waldorf, through Route 228 up the Potomac and all the way to her office off Massachusetts Avenue.

By the time she switched off her motor, it was as if the world were buzzing in the air, but without actual direct sound. Nothing. Total silence. The city was unusually quiet. No sirens. No lights. No traffic.

Wow. She had made it all the way home, and hardly breathing... She could barely believe what she had just done.

She opened the car door, the entrance to her office building now securely locked. She advanced to the front door, a baroque wrought iron gate over cut glass panels, and she looked up at the sconce beside it portal.

A brightly polished Fireman's brass plate designating her Firm's name shone. She stood up, pulled the key and entered the building. She closed the door, disarmed the intruder alert and moved quickly up to her office where only a few wall lights remained illumined for police patrols to observe as amber warmth from outside.

She opened the vault of the offices and inserted the drawings. She sealed it tightly, exited the building with the same systemic stealth as she had entered, and started to breath, it seemed, for the first time since she helped herself to them from the green vehicle.

Whatever the bastard had in his vehicle was now firmly locked up in her office vault.

It never occurred to her that she had just stolen something. Hell, it never even occurred to her that she didn't even know what was on the documents, or if they worth stealing in the first place. It was an act of vengeance against a man who could clearly do damage. That was satisfaction enough.

She made her way up Wisconsin Avenue to go home for the night.

Actually, she *had* fingered a couple of them while driving at sixty miles per hour back to Washington: They were drawings alright. Blueprints. She saw just enough on the Legend key annotation of one drawing to see the designation of the Calvert Cliffs Nuclear Power Plant.

The man was walking about with plans for a secure facility. God knows what his intentions were, she decided.

Still she was determined. She looked in the rear view mirror before turning into her street. Nobody was following.

Argueta would see these plans. Tomorrow. She was meeting with him and his wife at the Kennedy Center for the season ticket's performance of *The Magic Flute*...Rebecca too. She was flying into Regan around lunchtime, staying at the Watergate.   They had reservations for a lovely dinner altogether downtown.

 So, go to work tomorrow in the morning, as normal, she decided.

Later in the day, she would take the content out of the office vault and hand them over to Argueta. That was the plan.

 She would not even go home. With Gwynie gone, she was free for the weekend. She would take a change of clothes to the office...

All she had to do, was get through the day.

Maybe call Argueta.

* *

Her world had been jolted from one extreme to the other. First her sudden abandonment when Trevor was called away; then his affairs in Toronto - coupled with the pressure of her work. This had been a stressful time, if marked by a few victories, she had to admit. Like the one enjoyed at the Kennedy Center with her staff in celebration, and she did smile.

But that was before things got complicated. Trevor's call came as a shock. It evoked such unexpected surprise as to leave her puzzled, if not alarmed. Truth was, his call was unexplained and left Amanda with more questions than answers.

Where was he? Why the silence? Was he in any danger? Did his words, such as they were, sound like an expression of assurance or an *appeal*? What was the meaning of the few tender but fragmented words they shared?

Then the *stranger*, was it LaMaas? What was he doing down there?

For sure it had been a busy week: She had to bring the class to a close with the final examination.

Rushed, she almost flew down the road, it was a time most stressful for students and faculty alike. Examinations were tantamount to contract-completions as far as faculty were concerned. Every consideration had to be given to fairness and equal opportunity for each student to perform well. After all, they were graded on their studies, and that grade was lodged on their record, each one working on their program to graduate with a University degree.

But then to find him again on campus was too unsettling. He was sitting there as if on a park at a public facility. What was he doing there?

Unless he was a staff, a patron or an official who served a function there, this man was on the premises of a college without authority.

Most unfathomable was her own behavior: What was she thinking stealing from the man's vehicle?

She had hardly slept at all, dawn arrived not a moment too soon. She was up early and had the house to herself, leaving plenty of time to get ready for the day. She had coffee and a bite. Her thoughts were racing.

Getting those documents - actually drawings to Argueta was important, and if that meant hauling them across town to do so, then so be it. But hardly justifying her actions, nonetheless.

Why was she feeling so threatened?

What if those drawings held critical information for Argueta to see? What if they were highly classified documents, she thought. You don't just hop the Metro with an armful of rolled up drawings. That was not, well, the way you did things in this city, she decided. She felt torn. She felt ridiculous.

The first thing that Amanda wanted to do was image the documents in her vault. Firstly, she needed to see what they contained. Then she needed to reduce them in size for concealment...

She went into the office early –even before Janice unlocked the building.

Amanda disarmed the burglar sirens. The Cleaners would be arriving early. They were regulars, Amanda had insisted on top grade janitorial service for the building: They would be coming in soon to wash out the bathrooms, clean the base-floor kitchenette, empty the trash outside, dispose of the shredded and generally spent the early hours of the morning dusting railings, polishing, waxing floors, fixtures, desks, windowsills etc.

The cleaning crew knew the staff. Amanda had made a management decision about it. She wanted cleaning crews to work with personnel on the premises during day hours rather than at night. Twice a week, Fridays and Wednesdays. That usually made for a clean building scheduled for conferences with clients. Or allowed for Friday evening events, such as office gatherings, off-hours meetings; rendezvous for special outings; civic and museum gatherings and parties. Also for seasonal affairs like catered Christmas parties...

Amanda unfurled the drawings and laid them out on her desk. It took her ten minutes to calibrate her eye to what she was looking at.

"Of course." she said, taking aim with her digital camera. She set it at high resolution. She would image the lot, she decided. Then she would reduce them to digital files.

The first drawing, labeled "Generation II" consisted of a maze of loops and pipe drawings. She was looking at a pressurized water reactor. These were saturated steam plants.

Click. Click.

*Page One. Page Two...*She talked her way through them as she labelled them on the laptop profile platform.

Plan upon plan itemized details of exhaust, one of the single high pressure main turbine in superheated states; others of two-stage reheater drawings; delivery systems of superheated steam in parallel, three low pressure turbines...

Next came Generator drawings, main turbine designs, one a General Electric, another a Westinghouse design.

Thermo nuclear reactors with coolant piping details, bends, lines, electrical engineering, heat sink looping and returns for the plant runs of more pipes...

Drawings of reactor vessel closure heads.

"My God" she muttered. She typed

> *"Legend contains items the Nuclear Regulatory Commission Advisory Board needs on all drawings for compliance issues and recognizing...recognizing exposure levels for...for...err... inhalation of airborne radioactive contamination"*

Amanda felt her heart pounding at a million a minute. *This makes Fukoshima look like child's play.*

With her forehead beginning to bead, she continued to image the drawings. Finally, she felt satisfied that she had captured them all. She looked up. "Bob." she blurted with alarm, her face pale and her camera in hand.

"Hi" he said" Err...Did I err...catch you at a wrong time?" he asked

"No." she said, perhaps a little too quickly. "No. Not at all. I have some plans that I needed to image before the creep of the day's clock..." she laughed. "You know how it gets around here."

"I do" he said, playful again "I come in early myself to catch up before the chaos begins. Look. I have a gift for Gwynie from Alexandra my daughter. Said she wanted to give her a book she made at school for her friend..."

Amanda softened.

It looked like First-grader project made into a book of pages stapled together *"The Things I like about Gwynie..."* it said in crayon.

"Thank you. Tell Alexandria it's beautiful."

Amanda moved to the desk and casually rolled up two drawings that had been flattened out for imaging.

"But there is something else..." said Bob. "Entirely selfish: Susan and I would like to take a couple weeks off this summer. We'd like to visit the family up in Maine. Would you mind? With all projects finished by then, I'll have an empty slate. And I can telecommute if needed."

Amanda smiled.

" See Janice about coordinating with everyone else. The answer is *Yes.* You've worked very hard this year Bob. I'm happy to give you the time..."

"Sure?"

"Absolutely." she said, a lot calmer now.

He left, and she was glad she had started early. It was all done. She proceeded to roll up the rest of the drawings, some of which were pushed off the desk and onto the floor. One batch of three she bundled and was about to roll when she stopped. Something caught her eye.

It wasn't much. After all, what did she know? She certainly wasn't a trained engineer. But it had a faint red line around it. It was labeled "device"

On the next drawing was a similar duplicated pattern labeled *"Leads to device within plaster molding"*

The same sequence occurred on the second Reactor. But in mirror fashion. The third schematic left no room for question. *"Timing device, external control to electromagnetic signal"* She imaged them.

On the legend at the bottom of the blue lines was a Post-it tag description that looked like a manufacturers warning.

----"Plaster Embedded Detonation Receptacles Explosive. Warning. HAZMAT----"

What was that?

Her hand went to her mouth. No. Surely not. No. No way. No way was this man planning to *blow up* a...nuclear power plant. She stepped back.

If she had any doubts, this perished them: If she thought he might damage the facility or shut it down she was mistaken. This was far worse than even she had anticipated.

Argueta said...Argueta's words...

The thought of a nuclear power plant being rigged for an explosion was almost debilitating. The path of fall-out and destruction would definitely encompass Washington DC. Anyone wanting to be blow up a thermonuclear reactor and render the nation's capital - nerve center of the western world...was definitively a radical.

Oh my God.

No. Wait. She paced her office, her head spinning. Surely not. This was not a man just off duty caught with work in his truck.

Manager of Compliance my ass. This was a Terrorist.

Think. How would Trevor would want you to handle this, calmly? Oh My God. *A terrorist*?

Breath. Calm down: She would call Argueta immediately. She left a message, her fingers shaking.

"Following our last conversation…" she said "I have managed to…err…'get my hands on?'" She paused. The message rolling.

How should she say it " stole…?" No.

"acquired critical information. You may want to re-organize your time at the Kennedy Center tonight. Please call me back…It is important. Thanks. Have a great day." *Bleep.*

The office downstairs was populating, she could hear.

With all images secured on her computer, she made a copy onto a stick hard drive. This she would hand to Argueta tonight.

The size of a lipstick compact, it was easy enough to drop into her clutch. With systemic clarity, she placed in her bag. She was ready to go. She gathered the drawings and carried them like an armful of blossoms and called up Sonia, head of the Office Janitor Team still in the building.

"Hello Sonia" she said, handing her the waste basket full of drawings. "Could you please take this down to the ground floor and have them run through the shredder for me?"

"Si Signora." said Sonia grinning. Related to Clara the housekeeper, Sonia viewed Amanda as someone who could do no wrong. And Amanda knew that whatever she asked, it would be done. Twenty minutes later she went downstairs to confirm that Sonia had disposed of the drawings as instructed.

"Si Signora. Here…the piles in the bag for the trash when he come to collect trash, later today."

Amanda recognized the fragments and saw the blue ink on some that clearly showed the drawings shredding to bits. Satisfied, she returned to her office.

Amanda muddled through the day as if numb.

She talked twice with Rebecca who was flying in from Toronto. She promised to pick her up from the Marriott Hotel. Amanda told her that she had arranged for an evening at the Kennedy Center. Pick up at 5.00 pm from the Hotel.

 Rebecca had landed at Reagan early in the day. She had taken the Metro to the Marriott and was meeting for lunch with certain key clients of the Bank: They were US Defense Contractors with offices not far from Navy Yard in Washington DC. A few hours of rest at a beautiful Hotel suited her just fine.

"Do you like Mozart? Amanda asked.

"He's my favorite."

"Good. We're going to see *The Magic Flute*."

* *

If checking repeatedly for a call back from Argueta, Amanda managed to address the rest of the day's agenda by taking one calm step at a time. Her schedule was advancing nicely.

She would change into her evening clothes here at the office, then go pick up Rebecca.

Argueta and his wife would join them at the Kennedy Center by 6pm. So far so good.

Ordinarily, a visit to the Kennedy Center with Trevor at her side, and she would be flowing in a pretty black tulle dress and diamante jewels...*Oh how she missed him.* But for herself alone today, she had picked an ordinary cocktail dress. Well, ordinary, by casual standard. Plus it was *The Magic Flute.* She picked a colorful striped shawl for frivolity, with pearls. Period.

For make-up, she opened her clutch and saw the electronic stick. On it were all the images. She had it with her.

Amanda looked at her wrist watch. It was approaching 2.35 PM. She had spent a good half hour getting ready. It was quiet. No interruptions. And still no call back from Argueta. Still, in this city, no news was good news...

 Her office suite was a place she liked to retreat to. That is, whenever she had the time, which was less and less frequent these days.

She took out a few items from her office briefcase, and sealed the pretty clutch with a click. Finally, in her hand were two earrings she was clipping on as she walked downstairs. On her way day down she bumped into Bob.

"Hey. Hey. Hey. Don't you look good."

She smiled at him.

"Amanda, I can't tell you how much Susie and I appreciate the break you're giving us…"

"Don't worry about it Bob. Tell Susie Hello from me. Alexandra too…" she called out, descending the stairs.

"Will do. Oh… Janice is trying to reach you. She says you have a visitor waiting for you down at the Reception Desk"

"OK. I'm on my way…" said Amanda, picking up her pace. She was getting excited.

Overall, she had slugged through a variety of decisions and meetings through the day, and in a way, it was a good day especially when Barbara called.

"You'll never guess what I found amongst the paper work that the kid was planning to submit…"

"What?"

"We'll. Let's just say evidence to silence the case against environmental damages…Here Let me read you bit…"

"Go ahead"

"You ever heard of Crypsis?" said Barbara in her New York inflection

"No. What is that?"

"Well it *ain't* something you eat." she chuckled "It's a condition whereby organisms make themselves difficult to detect. Like in nature…They come under something called cryptozoolology."

"Yes?" Amanda knew never to laugh at suggestive leads that sounded a little odd. In legal evidence, such leads could solve disputes. Especially if it related to a marginal case."

"An' I got more..." said Barbara crinkling papers close to the speakers.

Amanda waited, the brass rail at her hand melting down the steps of her descent. At the bottom, she paused. "What Barbara?" she said.

Barbara surprised her. "You'll never believe what I found amongst the boy's research conclusion. The very species being cited in the case for environmental damages caused by offshore drilling to the nesting area...he claims the rare birds is not extinct at all..."

"Wait. What are you saying? That he found proof of the existence of the rare bird?"

"Well yes. And no" she said, then added "See, that's what makes us - those of us of Russian descent, so smart."

"Barbara?"

"Ok. Ok. He found evidence in the scientific journals that the bird is not extinct. It has been cited by scholarly papers. And observed in the field. For all we know, the kid was out there searching for evidence of their nesting grounds." she finished.

"Can you email me that report?"

"Done. It's on your computer...So listen to this. "According to Myers and Greenberg, of the Ornithological Society, the Little Stint breeds on arctic tundra from northeastern Scandinavia eastward to the central Siberia. Only ONE published Nearctic record for this species is an individual photographed in Bermuda *June 1975*. ...Probably because of the remoteness of its nesting area, this species in the only Calidris sandpiper that has not been recorded from mainland North America. .."

"Well that makes sense with regards to its rarity...But wasn't it supposed to be extinct, or very unusual, like hard to identify?"

"Sure. And listen to this: *The richness of color and well defined pattern indicates that the bird can be in full nuptial plumage....*"

"That's what we got honey." said Barbara. "Cited by the Depart of Psychology and Museum of Vertebrate Zoology, U Cal, Berkley, 1978. Ha- hah...*I'm telling you...*" she chortled.

"Really?"

"Then. According to the US Fish and Wildlife Service and the Naval Arctic Research Lab, it is listed as observed in the field by University of California, Berkley for a project work funded by National Oceanic and Atmospheric Administration."

"Well done. But are you sure it's the right bird we're talking about?"

"Not only is it the right bird, but it's the bird painted years ago by an artist that became a jeweled ceramic. No wonder he cherished it"

"So, are you sure it the *right* bird?" persisted Amanda. As head of a research team, she was always the necessary skeptic.

"OK Listen to this then" continued Barbara "*The key features of Little Stint – calidris Minuta, of the Siberian Arctic, is like a Sparrow sized shorebird; fox-red upper parts extending to sides chest, otherwise white below; white stripe above eyes and across the wing span. Its upper parts are soft gray in winter. A juvenile has a distinctive white V on its back. ...*"

"that's it." shrilled Amanda, a softness to her eye for the boy's troubles. Her eyes glazed. The boy had been smitten with the beauty of identifying the jewel, exactly. And finding the right bird. How wonderful...

"It lives." she said. "Not extinct at all. Case made. Thank you Barbara."

"We can thank Jacob" she said solemnly "I'm going to tell his grandmother about this...He made a real contribution that kid did."

"Yes. Please do."

Amanda was elated.

With her hand again fingering the earring on her right ear Amanda rounded the corner to the front Reception and said to Janice "What's up?"

Janice looked up. She turned to the guest seated in the waiting area.

Nothing could have prepared Amanda for the shock that froze her as a man stood up. He looked her full in the face.

"Miss Wells?" he said, putting down his magazine, now six feet away from the Front Desk.

The dark leather jacket with a contrast color hood did nothing to belie the power in his presence, even if wearing casual dress pants over Bostonian leather shoes. He stood silent, aggressive, waiting, as if wanting something.

An expression was written all over his face. *You have something that belongs to me.*

How she chose to address him remained up to her. He didn't care.

Was this the same LaMaas that sat at the Head Table of the stockholder's Annual Meeting Dinner Banquet?

What of Lauren Papenpodulus? – Amanda's thought began to coalesce.

Actually. Come to think of it, what of Trevor MacDonnell, *her husband*...As in, the CEO of one the chief Banks in that stockholding group that deserved not to be ignored. Even *underwriting* large portions of its ventures?

No matter. Amanda understood one thing.

This man was not interested in negotiating. There was a smoldering anger to his expression. A steadfastness that did not waver. His senses were focused to the point of laser vision.

She took a step forward towards Janice. This was not a man. He was a man on a mission with singular and dedicated anger.

"Sit down, Please." she said. She circled to the far side of the desk.

He did not sit. He was not going to be disarmed. This she understood. So, how to proceed?

Janice introduced him as Mr. LaMaas.

* *

The phone rang on Janice.

"How can I help you Mr. LaMaas?" said Amanda, playing the ditz.

"You have the matter of my papers..." he began, glancing just briefly at Janice for appearances. His athleticism and Scandinavian features were worn and oblique, direct.

Janice, a young beauty in her thirties with a Master's Degree in statistical research needed no prompting about discretion. She left the room, as soon as she closed her phone conversation, glancing briefly at Amanda for any indication of distress.

Amanda showed none. This was a hand to be played by her alone.

"Mr. LaMaas..."she began. "I am concerned about the nature of your intentions. And I took action that was appropriate for a ...concerned citizen and for the public safety of our campus at St. Mary's..."

His eyes were cold and unmoving, his gaze fixed.

She continued "where you appear to spend much of your time..."

He looked upward, inhaling through nostrils like a bull sniffing the air. Or preparing to gore, she thought.

Then he smiled suddenly.

"I see that you have made arrangements to pick up a mutual colleague of ours...Ms Rebecca Counts of the Sterling Bank of Toronto? Perhaps to spend an evening together...Is that right?"

Amanda's eyes must have widened in surprise. If she was calculating the extent of his range, she need calculate no further. He knew everything. Including, probably what she had in her clutch on her little electronic drive, and into whose hands it was going to be placed before the evening was out.

He lifted his arm like a gentlemen showing her the way to the computer console at the Front Desk. "You doubtless have much on your computer that you wish to erase? Perhaps we proceed directly to that application in which you delete all?"

So yes. He had anticipated that his plans had been digitally imaged. Clearly, he guessed that she had made a copy of those imaged and put them on her computer for safekeeping.

What he had *not* calculated for, evidently, was that she had made a second copy. A copy to her stick, an electronic hard drive sitting within her fingers in her bag.

He seemed satisfied. For now. So. Play along. She would comply.

"Alright" she said, moving solemnly to the computer and calling up her files from her office. She punched in a few passwords, found the files, then hit DELETE. He hovered.

"Your back-up?"

She found other sister files. Hit them one by one, DELETE.

Finally, she stood up and stepped back, looking at him with a big sigh and said "There." as if she were talking to a child.

He was not moved.

Had she pulled it off? Would he believe her in full? Why not? She had behaved like a normal person with total reliability in their systems...never anticipating a confrontation or need for backup, exactly on the premises.

"You understand we are a Research Firm with top level security clearance. I am obligated as a government contractor to safeguard anything found lost; waylaid or unsecured properly, as you know..."

"Shall we?" he indicated the exit. "My car is..." she began

"Yes. In the rear garage, across from the Embassy of the Marshall Islands. I can wait for you to come out, and we shall together pick up Ms. Rebecca. That is, if you are prepared to lead the way through traffic in an orderly progression?"

There was no mistaking the threat in his voice. "You will drive your own car, and I will follow."

Amanda decided for one last showdown, if she was lacking in courage, at least she was thinking with clarity now "You seem to know your way around, Mr. LeMaas..."she said

"Let us just say that I know *Your* way around, Ms Wells. I have been following your routines for oh...err.. almost three months now. Yours. Your daughters. Your friends. Why, even your husband."

She looked at him suddenly.

"Yes. Even Trevor, who is presently serving on a Royal Navy Special Projects submarine recently docked into Norfolk, I believe?" His eyes were fairly gleaming.

She was seized suddenly by anger. *Who was this monster? What were his intentions?* How could he know Trevor's whereabouts...when even Argueta was unable to share such information without a breach of security?

He seemed to read her thoughts, nodding to the kitchen stairs where she would have to go to walk outside to her garage through the garden. He, evidently, would be waiting to pull out from the front of the building as soon as she emerged from the alley.

She considered her options. To alert everyone in the building? What could he do, but create damage in her place of work, and a showdown. No. She needed to steer this monster away from the others in the building. An innocent method of moving him out, sure. But this was now a horrible game, she realized.

At least she would remain in her own car. But what was he playing at? It was a clever tactic. A tactic designed to make her exit the building calmly, thinking that she still had agency over the situation by being in her own car.

Why not cry 'Wolf' exactly?

They walked out of the front waiting room just as Janice returned, holding a delivery of yellow roses. "Just arrived" she said "sent by Rebecca for the ladies of the night going to the Opera." she smiled.

"Thank you." said Amanda, and gathered them in her arms as if reaching for a lifesavers "I'll take them along...and we'll pin a rose to our gowns for the evening."

Because you must draw him away from the others, that's why you don't cry 'Wolfe'

In the car she tossed the yellow reasons on the seat beside her.

She decided to stall for time...

The timing that filled her with hope was the time-line between this moment and the moment when she would reach Argueta and hand off the electronic device in her clutch...

As she pulled out, she realized this was wishful thinking. This was not a dreadful game.

This was a killer's game.

* *

Chapter Twelve

Amanda backed out the alley behind her building. The gate in the alley of the Embassy of the Republic of the Marshall Islands was locked, and no guard was walking about. *Clever.* He had avoided the webcam on the gate by staying out front...

She turned into Massachusetts Avenue, and followed a bus that stopped at Sheridan Circle. Amanda looked in the rear view mirror. He was behind her - the city now swarming with tourists and pedestrians, progress slow.

She turned down 21st Street, straight down to Virginia Avenue where she waited for the light. Finally she turned Left and joined Constitution Avenue at the Washington DC Monument.

At the Ellipse of the White House, security was evident everywhere. He kept close, but dodged frequently, but bringing the bumper of his vehicle close enough to touch hers. She knew of his presence. The closer she drove towards the Capital the higher the number of police cars that dotted street observation positions.

The street numbers descended in order as she on the Smithsonian Mall, passing the monumental structures that marked the Nation's Capital.

At 14th Street, she was driving passed the Mellon Auditorium; at 12th the National History of Natural History. She slipped easily between cabs, tour buses and bicycle wagons toting tourists.

At 9th street the National Archives steps flooded with kids arriving in buses to view the Constitution Document.

At the National Gallery of Art West building Amanda made a decision. She picked up her cell.

"Rebecca: This is Amanda. I'm running late. If I don't get to the Marriott by 5 o'clock, please proceed directly to Restaurant downtown. I'll see you at the Kennedy Center... I'll see you there."

She tossed the phone to her seat and turned abruptly down 4th street to park on Madison Drive along the Smithsonian Museum Mall.

 With any luck, she could blend into the tourist mobs. She slipped in behind a car that had just loaded its young passengers and left.

She unbuckled, flew out of the car and started up the wide granite steps of the Art Museum amid a slow and thick procession of tourists. As she entered the building, she saw a green vehicle pass slowly down 4th, searching. She passed her bag through the security front desk, and smiled at the guard.

Evidently, LaMaas never spotted her swerve into Madison and park.

Amanda moved passed the exhibits and hallways. She took a big breath, and walked normally through the new exhibition of the Art Gallery.

"Citizens of the Republic" rang out all around her. Portraits from the Dutch Golden Age, featured as the main floor gallery exhibition showed Dutch citizens distinguished for their contributions to their Republics at every wall.

Appropriate for upcoming American elections, she walked through the exhibit. Rembrandt van Rijn; a grisaille portrait of Anna Maria van Schurman by Cornelis Jonson van Ceulen. Engravers, painters, sculptors, all displaying public life that prevailed in the 17th and 18th centuries. All of them entrepreneurs of a new young Europe emerging into domestic economies.

She moved on, barely aware of the famous drawings and watercolors; then the Still-life paintings that could take a man's breath away. One, she knew, and glanced at quickly. It was the elegant painting of William van Aelst.

Down through the sculptures; the tea giardin and beyond the long columns that support the elegant gallery spaces. Amanda remained focused, ignoring George Bellows, Barnett Newman, her breathing hard…

Down, down the stairs to the deeper levels of the Museum she paced, passed the John Cage exhibition of Rocks, Paper, Fire.

Finally, she reached the East Building's underground passageway - passing precisely under the street from which she had just turned off.

She walked beneath the hanging mobiles of Andy Goldsworthy and followed the electrified ground levels of Armand Hammar. She turned across the granite floors and steps, down passed the gift shop and moved steadily through the dark hallway to the eating area whose view was the under-girth of a glassed waterfall above on 4th street.

She stood there, almost panting, trying to calm down. She had succeeded in evading him, she concluded. Thank God.

Finally, as the pounding in her heart calmed, she approached the coffee-bar and ordered a cappuccino and a brownie.

She was chewing, with a coffee cup in her hand when she felt she could relax a little. Or at least breath normally. She had eluded her pursuer.

She took in the glass view from where she sat. At random, items tossed into the waterfall fountain above come gradually down the concrete washboard and into the pond. A pond surrounded by blossoms, pots and trees, like a magical land.

She sipped.

Evidently the waterfall at street level was not entirely sealed by glass: Who could resist tossing their treasured coins and dreams into a fountain for good luck? How strange.

At last, well, at least her nerves were beginning to thaw. . .

Then she froze. It was the second blossom that got her attention, blossoms falling down the waterfall at intervals, yellow. Another one. One rose. *Yellow.* As if someone had reached in to her car ...

She turned.

"Surely you did not think you could lose me?" he said, standing there with a smile across a square bony face, his blue eyes cold, fixed, and unsmiling. He was holding a coffee.

"No. Not at all...I came to..." she swallowed her mouthful "buy a gift for Rebecca from the Museum gift shop before picking her up..."

"I know" he said, lifted his cell to indicated that he had clearly tapped into her phone calls. Then he sat down and put his coffee down on the table.

It was all Amanda could do to squeeze the clutch handbag that contained the stick with his drawings on it. Surely it was only a matter of time before he would become suspicious...

"So. You think I'm a public threat do you?" he said casually. "Perhaps you have something to give to someone....Like my drawings?"

To say "what drawings?" was about as infantile as you could get. So get real.

"Yes. You left them in your open truck. I came to talk to you Mr. LaMaas. I had recognized you from Toronto...I was wrong to take them. But you've been watching me on campus for a while. I wanted to see what you were about."

"Why not just ask?"

"Who? Lauren Papenpodulus"

"Why not?"

"Because she's the source of a suit against my husband's corporation at the present time, as you know. Wrongfully directed... since she wants his interests in the drilling area of the balding Arctic region..."

He smiled.

"Clever. So, here I am out to sabotage ...err...your husband's interests?"

"Perhaps."

He laughed.

"Well. I'll be damned. We are a suspicious lot aren't we?" He sipped. "It must be all that Research work that you do. Maybe you take your work too seriously Umm?"

He was fishing. She knew it. "Not all my clients think so..."

"Oh! I see So, you find me a public threat because...why? I work at the Calvert Cliffs Nuclear Reactor Power Plant?"

She said nothing.

"And you think that I could do damage ...just to add pressure to Washington - in the case of a disaster there, to grant easier leasing rights for drilling for energy *elsewhere*?"

She looked at him calmly. "Yes. The thought had crossed my mind"

She wanted to run. To escape. She could have, in this high gloss environment, and be lost in a crowd. But what he said next tied her to him with no less gravity than a steel chains.

"That is stupid. Why would I want to damage the Nuclear Reactor's of Washington DC to achieve pressure? No my dear, that is wrong...But...err. You are right: I do plan to do damage to a well placed Nuclear Reactor. And I wish to employ Trevor, your husband."

He watched her reaction, as if a boy wanting some reward.

She lowered her eyes, hiding the horror of the thoughts that could have played across them. She picked up her coffee, her mind moving like lightening. Then in a sudden display of irritability, she shrugged in ennui and said "Look. I need to get that gift...I'll be right back.

I promise not to run off... You can watch me from here?"

He scrutinized her.

"Why not?" he said, a look of satisfaction on his face, knowing he had delivered the mortal blow.

Amanda moved to the Gift bookstore not far from the tables. She picked out a scarf, and moved quickly to the Register for payment. A mob surrounded the cashier. She had to think fast. The stakes were higher now. He would find her electronic drive in due course.

She dove into her bag, pulled out her wallet, the electronic stick *and* scarf together as she handed over three ten dollar bills, the scarf draping loosely and the crowd pushing, and the cashier was swamped ...

The Cashier opened up for change. Over the counter the hands went, back and forth came the receipts, the gifts, the paperwork and the change... And just as easily as the cashier took the money from Amanda's hand, Amanda let the electronic stick slide down the scarf and into the cash register drawer where it was promptly slammed shut for the next customer.

Amanda returned, her face flushed. "A gift she said" holding out the package. He had kept his eye on her.

"As you were saying...the Plans, now please?" he said.

"I had them shredded."

"I know" he dug into his pocket and pulled out a handful of shredded paper with the blue ink of drawing marks on them.

"I mean, the plans to be electronically delivered. How were you going to transmit them? Please?" he asked, pointing to her bag.

"What do you mean? I don't have anything like that. What are you saying. I was going to forward my files, tomorrow."

She gave her purse to him. He was discrete enough in public not to upend the contents on the table. He looked in it entirely, felt the soft lining, squeezed, checked the compacts; the money, the wallet, and then passed a small magnet over the entire bag."

The look of horror on her face prompted another remark from him. "Your car is clean. D*emagnetized...*" he grinned.

"What do you mean?" she said, her thoughts beginning to fuzz.

"No matter. Trevor will know." he said, and stood up to leave.

"Trevor?"

"Oh yes. You don't think that Lauren is so base as to damage the seat of the nation with a nuclear reactor disaster just to get herself a lease for drilling more oil, do you?"

Amanda's eyes were unseeing. He had uttered Trevor's name.

A man who watches a family and follows you for months, then uses Trevor's name, is a menace of the most dangerous kind. She felt fear seeping up through her nervous system.

Her thoughts were a muddle. Then she remembered Rebecca's sinister words. *If Lauren can't have what she wants, then nobody can...*

He was almost smiling "You see. Why would I do that when a nuclear reactor system failure on the site itself could leave the place unusable for decades to come due to nuclear contamination?"

"What?"

He paused "Anyway, you are too late."

He walked off. *He walked off.* Just like that? A warning. A...*what did that mean?*

Amanda raced out of the museum and fairly ran to the car. She gunned the engine and blew her way through traffic and within twenty minutes of traffic would be confronting Argueta and his wife at the Kennedy Center.

Trevor. *Trevor.* Where was Trevor? Why would you employ him...?

She recalled Arguetta's explanation: That Trevor had been deployed to a Royal Navy vessel in Norfolk...That Trevor was going on a Joint US/UK Mission. Royal Navy offices in Washington DC.

What did that mean?

She entered from the bank of the Potomac River at 2700 F St., squealed her tires all the way down to the parking garage.

There was no quick way through the pre-performance activities, and by the time she made her way up to the Eisenhower Theater level, she was almost running.

Along the Grand Foyer, she passed the Interactive Exhibit besides the bust of Kennedy and she was panting.

She turned the corner for the Concert Hall Box Office and walked into the elevator where she slammed head first into Ed Turner, Executive Chef of the Rooftop Restaurants.

"Amanda Wells." he said, he face alight with enthusiasm. She and Trevor had enjoyed many evenings at his Restaurant before a performance. He was frequently on their guest list when Trevor was in town. "How good to see you..."he began

"Oh Ed..." she cried, then composed herself. "I'm so sorry. Can we catch-up later?'"

"Of course" he said, and the elevator doors closed.

She raced up to the Restaurant and announced herself at the Maitre D'.

"Miss Wells? Yes" he said "I 'ave this note to give you Madam...Admiral Argueta sends his regrets. He is on call at the Pentagon. Please to excuse him."

She opened the note.

"I'm sorry Amanda. Trevor made this choice himself. He plans to disable any damage if he can. He deployed from Norfolk...This I can tell you. We are still searching for the details... Call me in a day or two."

Argueta.

Amanda froze. There was no need to spell things out. The only other system that housed nuclear reactors were Nuclear Powered Naval Vessels, Special Projects. Like submarines.

LeMaas had infiltrated the systems of the Reactors not on Calvert Cliffs, but in a submarine. Clearly, it was to detonate at the site of the lease bottom. Trevor was on a Commission to disarm, deter or contain the damage.

Whatever Lauren had planned would equal the Fukishima disaster in Japan, yet be done silently, away from public view. And without causing the political damage it could have done in Washington.

She called Arguetta on his direct line.

"Amanda!" called a voice.

Rebecca found her. Amanda explained everything.

The plans were on her stick. Details. Drawings. Precise infiltrated intelligence related to an impending explosion beneath the sea, a spot where the Arctic was opening up potential new leased oil drilling lands...

Rebecca walked her outdoors where they ordered a cognac.

Amanda downed her food and drink in a maze of whirling thoughts, fear, regrets...She could barely believe the words she was uttering. She was to wait for news from Argueta, she said.

Rebecca made it abundantly clear that they would drive down to the shore where they would all be resting for the weekend.

Amanda could wait for news while with the family.

The next day Argueta called.

"Good work." he said.

* *

End